STAGE FRIGHT

Kate Lloyd

UNION BAY
PUBLISHING

W0010959

Union Bay Publishing

Stage Fright
© 2020 by Kate Lloyd

ISBN 978-1-7352411-0-4
ISBN 978-1-7352411-1-1 (ebook)

Cover Design: Monica Haynes, The Thatchery
Interior design: Colleen Sheehan, Ampersand Book Interiors

Printed in the United States of America

To Roberta Kehle

CHAPTER 1

THE CASTING DIRECTOR opened the door to the auditorium and scanned the high school's hallway, then frowned at her clipboard. "Jessica Nash?"

My mouth went dry. "Um—" I cleared my throat. "Over here."

A dozen or so community theatre wannabes jabbering or leaning against trophy cases fell silent and looked me over—no doubt sizing up their competition.

Clutching my sheet music, I lifted my chin and followed the director through the door onto the stage. She descended a staircase, melded into the blackened seating area, and landed between a man and a woman.

Downstage right, above the empty orchestra pit, a middle-aged guy sat at a piano. Trying to appear poised, I passed him my music with a shaking hand.

Had I ever been more terrified? I hadn't stood on a stage for decades.

My shoes pinched my toes, and my throat felt scratchy, like I was coming down with a cold. Getting sick would knock me out of leaving on the church choir's performance tour of England in two days. A once-in-a-lifetime trip I'd looked forward to for months.

I turned to position myself at center stage but before I could reach my destination, the pianist started plunking the introduction to "I Dreamed a Dream" from *Les Misérables* at a walloping speed. With only one bar to go, my brain scrambled for the first words. I gulped a chest-full of air and parted my lips.

Nothing came out.

Get a grip, Jessie, I told myself. I looked to the pianist for help, but he'd dropped his hands into his lap and stared at the sheet music as if he'd forgotten I was there.

Feeling the backs of my knees weaken, I reminded myself this was only an audition for community theater. A frivolous Gilbert and Sullivan operetta. What was I doing here anyway?

Oh, yeah. The audition was my vocal coach Muriel Frank's idea, to help me conquer my paralyzing fear of singing in front of an audience. There was no reason to come unglued. Yet I'd be thrilled to snag the smallest role in the chorus just to prove I could sing.

Cottoned-mouthed and woozy-headed, I blinked against the harsh lights. My eyes struggled to focus on three faceless heads floating in the darkened auditorium. I forced a meager smile aimed in their direction.

"Could I start over?" I asked.

The pianist yawned, then pounded the keyboard at an even faster tempo. As I sang, my legs trembled too much under my black calf-length skirt for me to think about breath support or intonation, the exercises I'd studied for months with Muriel. What was wrong with me? In front of my darling third graders, I was easygoing and confident Ms. Nash—most of the time. And I tried my best to remember all the kids' names after the first week.

In a flash, my song was over.

"Thank you." The casting director scribbled on her clipboard. A tall man and a lady perched on either side of her spoke in her ear. The three conversed for several minutes, no doubt assessing my feeble voice and lack of stage presence. Then they chuckled. Couldn't they contain their laughter until I was offstage?

The casting director called out to me: "We'll let you know." I figured her polite way of saying "take a hike."

I wanted to say I typically sang better, but why lie? I only sounded good in Muriel's living room or my shower. In front of an audience, I was plug-your-nose material. Week-old tuna on stale rye.

As I found the exit, tangled thoughts flooded my mind. Producing a luminous vocal note, alive with color and mood, filled me with joy. But singing also exposed my core, displaying me under a microscope for the world to see. I wished I didn't care what others thought. I wished I could laugh off the audition, but I'd endured rejection too often.

Out in the hall, the air buzzed with chitchat.

Roxanne Miller, my friend from our church choir, breezed over to me cradling a songbook of show tunes for altos. Her longish tunic and loose pants draped her rotund figure, and her short, hennaed hair framed her round face.

"Hi, Roxie," I said.

"How did it go, girlfriend?" Her voice swelled with optimism.

"A disaster. I should be a standup comedian." I was still miffed at the man and the women who'd laughed at me.

"Jessie, I bet you sounded great." Before she could speak more words of encouragement, the casting director called out a name. A willowy beauty in a mini skirt strutted forward and disappeared through the stage door.

Roxanne hugged the book to her ample bosom. "I hate auditions, don't you?"

"I can't think of anything worse, except being pushed over a cliff by a gorilla. And that might be less painful." I folded my music and stuffed it into my purse. "I'm glad we don't have to audition to get into our church choir or I wouldn't have anywhere to sing."

"Don't be silly, Jessie. Old Hal would let you in."

"I'm not so sure." I remembered joining the choir nine months ago. Director Hal Sorensen had welcomed me by pointing to a vacant seat in the soprano section and hadn't spoken to me since. "Sometimes I wonder if he even knows I'm there."

"That's just Hal and his peripheral vision. He'll get to know you on our choir's trip to Great Britain and maybe offer you a solo when we get back."

"I doubt it." Thinking of the other sopranos who sang with me on Sunday mornings, I knew there wasn't much chance. And for good reason. Young and flashy Clare Van Arsdale could fill the sanctuary with dazzling sound without even warming up first. Marci had a lovely voice too.

"We should have been born tenors." Roxanne's gaze skated over to a young man leaning against a metal wall locker. "Then we'd be singing three hundred and sixty-five days a year."

I couldn't help smiling. "You're lucky to be an alto." I thought of Roxanne's grand, confident voice. Standing six inches taller than me, she possessed chutzpah, as Mom would say, capturing the audience's attention even when not in the spotlight.

"But all I get are old-lady parts." Her plump shoulders sagged as she expelled a breath. "Never the lovely young ingénue."

"Be glad you're not a soprano. At age thirty-seven it's hard reaching the high notes. I'm too old to compete with these young women."

Onstage, I thought, or anywhere.

CHAPTER 2

HALF AN HOUR later, I crept down the stairs into the windowless, low-ceilinged church basement, with its beige vinyl floors and closets containing our robes for Sunday mornings. My hunch was that Hal insisted we rehearse where no one could hear us floundering with new pieces. I tried to slip into the chair next to lead soprano Clare without disturbing the other choir members already practicing.

Hal raised his hand to stop our pianist, Bonnie Lin. The room fell silent. Perched on a stool, he stared down his beakish nose at me. "You're late."

"Sorry, it won't happen again." My ego deflated, I wouldn't use the audition as an excuse for fear he would ask how I did. I wanted to forget the traumatic event and was glad only Roxanne knew I'd bombed. I rummaged through my purse and found a pencil for taking notes.

Hal gave the downbeat and the others began singing again. Flipping open my score, I mouthed the words as Clare's voice glided up and down the octaves. If she'd been at the audition, they would have offered her the leading role. Except she sneered at Gilbert and Sullivan. "*I Love Lucy* set in Victorian times," she labeled their operettas. She was saving herself for "real" music— Puccini, Verdi, and Mozart.

After tonight's ordeal, I was ready to give up singing forever.

I scanned the nineteen other choir members. Except for Roxanne, who was meandering in and sitting with the other altos at the far end of my row, how many would I want to travel with for a whole week? They were a fun group—when Hal was out of earshot—but I should be spending spring break with my twelve-year-old son, Cooper. One reason I taught at a public school was to share his vacation schedule.

Yet since college I'd dreamed of seeing Great Britain, home of Daphne du Maurier and Jane Austen, my favorite authors. I was a single mom on a fixed income. How many other opportunities would swim my way? Though I loved my students, I might spend the rest of my life grading papers in Seattle.

"People, on page four, no breath before the word 'pardon.'" Hal's thinning hair sprawled across his domed scalp. "I don't want to hear any *r*'s. Pronounce it 'pa-ahdon.'"

My mother could do it right, I thought. She was born in Brooklyn and try as she might, she couldn't disguise her accent.

We sang the phrase again and he snorted. "What did I just say?"

I was relieved I wasn't singing with bravado—loud enough to be heard. Peeking at my wristwatch, I calculated I could tumble into bed in forty-five minutes. I envisioned Mom and Cooper sacked out on the couch watching TV when my son should be doing his missing homework assignments. Lately, he'd turned cheeky and acquired a lackadaisical attitude his teacher and I didn't appreciate. Mom continued calling her only grandchild *bubeleh,* her perfect angel, and spoiled him. But I should not complain. As a single woman, I often counted on her willingness to babysit.

A dark-haired man in a three-piece charcoal-gray suit strode into the room with an air of indifference, his lofty head barely clearing the doorway. He appeared in his early forties and was handsome. Fiercely handsome. But hard, his face like a steel door.

Hal jumped up to shake the man's hand. "There you are. This is such an honor." Hal tapped his fingertips together and scowled at the choir. "Dear, dear. I suppose you heard our little group just now. Not at our best tonight." He steepled his hands and bowed his head as if presenting royalty. "People, I told you I had a surprise." He'd announced last week that he'd lined up a tenor to accompany us on the tour. Welcome news, since the choir's three tenors strained to reach the high notes.

"It's my pleasure to introduce Martin Spear, a man I'm sure you've heard of."

Anyone interested in classical music would know of the famous tenor's successes at the Metropolitan Opera and La Scala. And he'd recorded two knock-your-socks-off Christmas CDs. I remembered reading a newspaper article several years ago predicting Martin Spear would be the next Placido Domingo. Then Martin had mysteriously disappeared from the opera scene.

Martin glanced at the choir. For a moment, his scrutiny rested on my face as if he recognized me. A bemused grin tugged the corner of his mouth. I was beyond grateful he hadn't been at the audition earlier. Had he? No, I was turning paranoid.

His gaze moved to Clare and finally came to rest on Hal.

"Good evening," he said to Hal with a crisp British accent.

"Would you have a look at these?" Hal furnished Martin with several sheets of music, which he leafed through, then returned.

"Thank you, I'm familiar with these pieces," Martin said.

"Of course, I should have known." Setting the music on his stool, Hal grasped Martin's hand and shook it again. "We're so fortunate you'll be coming with us. I'll bet a busy man like you has more important things to do than sing with a small church choir."

"Not at the moment. I was planning to be there anyway."

"How fortunate for us. Do your parents still live in England?"

"Yes." Martin glanced up at the wall clock.

"And you'll be seeing them?"

Martin's features sobered. "No."

I detected a quiver of anxiety in Martin's voice. Why would a man travel halfway around the world and not visit his parents? Not that I ever saw my deadbeat dad, who only lived across town.

"What a shame. Is there anything I can do?" Hal asked.

"That's kind of you, but it's not possible." Martin ran his fingers under his shirt collar and backed toward the door. "If you'll please excuse me, I need to be on my way. A prior commitment." He held up a hand and gave Hal a vague wave, then made a speedy exit.

"How did you land Martin Spear?" asked bass singer Drew Riley, a midthirties man built like a linebacker, his red hair in a buzz cut.

"We met through a friend a couple of weeks ago," Hal said, puffing his chest. "When I mentioned our shortage of tenors, Mr. Spear seemed interested, so I joked we'd be delighted to take him with us. I practically fainted when he agreed. Imagine a man of his caliber allowing me to direct him."

Hal's explanation didn't quell my curiosity. Why would a renowned tenor join our group of amateurs from a congregation of two hundred? It wasn't as if the choir had been invited to sing in Great Britain. We'd booked the tour through a travel agency and, with assistance from church donations, paid our way.

Hal began collecting his music. "Let's call it a night, people. See you at the airport." He wagged his index finger in my direction. "Don't forget your passports and don't be late."

As I reached for my purse, long-legged Clare stood up. She wriggled her hands into the sleeves of her mohair coat, its hem flicking my cheek. Then she tossed her frosted hair over her shoulder and tramped on my foot. I suppressed a yelp, my little toe throbbing. It was nothing personal, I told myself, watching her sidle up to Hal. She ignored all the women in the choir, saving her pleasantries for the men.

I looked across the room and noticed Roxanne slumped in her chair, reminding me of a wilted hydrangea. I moseyed over and placed a hand on her shoulder, startling her. "Are you okay?" I asked.

She blinked. "Yup." She grabbed her water bottle and took a lengthy swig. "Guess it's been a long day."

I eased into the chair next to her and scanned her pale face, noting a haggard expression. "You need a ride home?" I knew she was single and lived alone.

"No, I'll be fine. Just tired." She stood and wrestled her arms into her jacket—one size too snug to cover her broad hips. "A week's vacation is exactly what I need."

I followed her into the hall and up the stairs. Steadying herself with the handrail, she scaled each step as if it were two feet tall. At ground level, she dawdled for a moment to catch her labored breath. Then her face came alive and she looked her usual self again.

"I've got a vital question for you." Her voice turned upbeat. "What clothes are you bringing?"

This afternoon I'd sorted through my bureau drawers and closet deciding what to pack. "Nothing fancy.

Except my black knit dress for performances, just casual
stuff and comfortable walking shoes."

"Don't think you'll be sipping tea with the queen?"
She curtsied and lifted her pinky finger.

Her good humor was infectious My mouth broad-
ened into a grin. "She sent me the sweetest invitation,"
I said, "but I RSVP'd I'll be too busy sightseeing with
you."

She tilted her head. Her dangly earrings danced in
circles below her copper-tinted curls. "What if a prince
cruises up in a Rolls-Royce?"

"Sounds tempting, but unlikely. The last guy I dated
drove a thirty-year-old Volkswagen bus with a dent on
the passenger side."

"You never know maybe we'll both get lucky."

I shouldered open the door and we headed out into
the parking lot. The asphalt, wet from a recent downpour, glittered under the church's floodlights. The
atmosphere, charged with electricity, felt ten degrees
warmer than the night before. And the north wind
had shifted to the southwest, delivering a new season
of possibilities.

CHAPTER 3

A T SEA-TAC AIRPORT, I gazed out the window of the giant aircraft and imagined landing at Heathrow in eleven hours.

A man's acerbic voice echoing down the aisle shattered my thoughts of cathedrals and castles. I turned my head and saw Martin Spear arguing with a flight attendant. A moment later, his angular frame advanced toward me. Decked out in a navy-blue suit and striped tie, he looked like he was heading to a stuffy business meeting rather than relaxing on holiday. When he reached my row, he doubled-checked his ticket, then stared at the empty seat next to me with what seemed to be disbelief.

Ugh, I was stuck sitting next to him? I had no doubt if he'd seen my pitiful audition, he'd tell Hal I was a loser with no business singing in the choir.

"Hello, Mr. Spear." I put on my unruffled teacher facade. "I'm Jessica Nash. I remember you from choir practice the other night."

He flung his leather carry-on in the overhead bin, then lowered himself onto the seat beside me. "I'll be upgraded in a minute," he muttered, rigid as ice. His eyes were glued to the flight attendant chatting with new arrivals.

Good. Apparently, he didn't recall my insignificant face. Still, it irked me that I'd grown invisible. And I assumed he'd ask me to call him by his first name.

I scanned the other seats. Most of the choir members were onboard, but I couldn't locate Roxanne. Then I heard her exuberant laughter as she hustled down the aisle lugging a leopardprint tote bag.

"I made it." She heaved a weary sigh and patted her chest with her free hand, then squeezed into the seat behind me, next to Drew. My seat jiggled as she wedged her bag under it.

"Can we both fit in here?" she said and let out a girlish giggle.

"You bet." Drew's bass voice rumbled. "Sitting with you will be a treat. We never get a chance to talk at rehearsal."

The flight attendant approached Martin and gave him a simpering smile. He began to rise, but she placed her hand on his broad shoulder to stop him. "Sorry, Mr. Spear, business and first class checked in full." She bent forward to let another attendant pass. "I'm sure we can make your trip a pleasant one. I'll keep a good eye on you." She winked in a way that said she was single and available. "By the way, I loved you on TV a few years ago in the *Christmas at the Met* special."

As soon as she left, Martin said, "I can't believe it." He looked around as if he'd found himself on an alien spacecraft.

I slid my elbow off the armrest to give him more room, and to gain space from him. His sour mood was oozing over onto me.

"I'm Jessica Nash, a soprano," I said.

Martin said a brisk hello without really looking at me, then massaged the back of his neck. "Our lead soprano?"

The absurdity of that notion made me chortle. Or was he making fun of me? "No, that would be Clare," I said. "I'd give anything to sing like her." And she was twenty-four, the perfect age to start a vocal career. I craned my neck to find Clare's beautiful blonde head on the other side of the jet. By a window, she sat next to a swarthy man sporting a mustache who was staring at me. I didn't know him, but I smiled. His eyes widened, then he buried his face in his newspaper.

Martin followed my gaze. "I say, do you know that fellow?"

"No, never seen him before."

"Was he watching me?"

Wasn't it possible the stranger found me attractive? "I suppose," I said. "He could have recognized your face from a CD cover."

His jaw set, Martin scrutinized the man, his face now angled down as he perused his paper. I was surprised Martin wasn't used to fans intruding on his privacy. I thought celebrities ignored unwanted attention.

He finally sank into his seat and loosened his tie. After a minute or so, he cleared his throat, sounding like my aged professor from the English Department at the University of Washington, who'd be retired by now. "You say you're a singer?" Martin said, more an accusation than a question.

"Mostly a mom and a schoolteacher. I've only taken voice lessons for two years. But I've always wanted to perform onstage. Or at least sing 'Happy Birthday' in tune."

Disregarding my levity, he pulled out a magazine printed by the airline and skimmed through the pages. "Some people get by without decades of study."

I tilted my head toward Roxanne. "Like Roxie Miller, behind us. She performs with the Seattle Opera Chorus and does community theatre. She lands almost every role she auditions for. I'm lucky to be able to sing at church." I leaned closer to him. My auburn hair brushed his shoulder. "I turn into a jellyfish and forget my own name when I do solos."

He almost cracked a smile, then straightened his mouth again. "Frankly, a professional singer's life is highly overrated."

"Maybe, but I'd love to find out the hard way."

The hatch thudded shut. I checked my safety belt to make sure it was secure. "I'm nervous about flying," I said, crossing my ankles, then uncrossing them. "I've never been out of the country before, except Canada. I suppose you travel a lot?"

Martin shoved the magazine back into the seat pocket without answering.

The jet shuddered, then rolled away from the ter-
minal building. Raindrops pelted through the clouds
and bounced off the tarmac. The interior lights flick-
ered. A female spoke over the sound system with a slice
of urgency, explaining the safety features of the Boeing
767, noting the exits and stating what to do in the event
of an emergency water landing. Another flight attendant stood demonstrating an oxygen mask. She jerked
down hard on the plastic tube and placed it over her
face.

Dampness gathered under my armpits. "I'm worried
about leaving my son all week," I said when the air
quieted, anxiety making me chatter. "I've never been
away from him for more than a couple of days."

The roar of the engines drowned out my words. I
cinched my seat belt tighter. My thoughts rambled like
an atonal melody, hitting discordant notes, planking
the sharps and flats. Would I get to and from England
in one piece? Would I remain a widow, no prospects
on the horizon, living paycheck to paycheck, chipping
away at Jeff's credit card debt? What was up with my
son, Cooper? Why had he turned obstinate?

The jet clambered into the turbulent sky, heading
northeast. Ten minutes later, a voice came over the
speaker system, reminding passengers the seatbelt sign
was still on. I glanced at Martin and noticed his long
legs cramped against the seat in front of him. He was
staring toward the nose of the plane. Was he pouting
over how much more comfortable he'd be lounging on a
cushy leather recliner in first class, sipping champagne
while the flight attendants gushed over his magnifi-

cent voice? For a moment I felt sorry for him. Being trapped in economy with a nobody like me wasn't a close second. But when I considered a dozen other options— like traveling by steamship or bicycle—my sympathy evaporated. Self-important Martin needed to make the best of the situation.

To get a civil conversation rolling, I said, "When was the last time you were in Great Britain?"

His face turned stony, his eyes blackening like a crow's. "It's been over a year. I haven't been back since my ex threw me over, not that it's anyone's business."

"I'm sorry." I was surprised by his candor and imagined how low he must feel. Being jilted would be devastating, as well as embarrassing. I thought of my departed Jeff, the only man I'd ever loved. It seemed as though he'd deserted me, the way he never came home.

"People in the States don't seem to make lasting commitments," Martin said, his words punctuated with scorn. "I should never have married an American woman."

Was this wry British humor? I said, "Are you serious?"

"Quite."

My empathy took a U-turn. "Come now, Mr. Spear. Don't tell me only Americans have relationship and marital problems. How about the royal family?"

"I suppose you're right. Perhaps women are the same everywhere."

Heat surged up my neck. "What about men?" I said through clenched teeth.

"They can make fools of themselves—when they trust women."

Was this turkey for real? I didn't care if he was a hotshot opera star. I could think of several choice insults to fling at him but reminded myself I was traveling with a church choir, not facing off an opponent in a boxing ring. And if I argued with him, he'd use my words as further evidence women were to blame for the world's woes. He might even complain about me to Hal, who would boot me out of the choir. There was no way to win.

I riveted my glare on Martin until he looked away. Then I dove into my purse to find the Junior Mints I'd planned to nibble on after dinner. As I pitched a chocolate-covered disc into my mouth and flattened it with my tongue, I imagined what Martin's former wife had endured.

When the jet reached cruising altitude and the seatbelt sign flicked off, Martin got to his feet and moved up the aisle.

Roxanne spoke over the seatback. "Wow, girl, you're sitting next to Martin Spear. What's he like?"

I loosened my belt and rotated in my seat. Drew seemed absorbed in a Tom Clancy novel, so I spoke my mind. "He's a pompous windbag."

"Really? Hal thinks highly of him." She sent me a suspicious grin. "Come on, he can't be all that bad."

"Want to trade seats and find out for yourself?" I noticed Drew's demeanor stiffening. He didn't want to sit next to me either? Or maybe he preferred Roxanne.

"No, thanks," she said. "I love men with British accents, but I'm happy where I am. Tenors and altos don't mix."

"I've never heard that one before." Curving the corners of my mouth down, I tried to appear a miserable waif. "Come on and switch, pretty please." I offered her several mints. She snatched them out of my hand and gave one to Drew.

"Aren't you the woman who tolerates squirmy kids all day?" she said, then lobbed a candy into her mouth. "Next to managing a classroom, one man can't be that much trouble."

"But I'm on vacation. I'm supposed to be having fun."

"Oops, here he comes." Roxanne shrank back as Martin returned with several magazines. She said between the seats, "Why don't you turn on the charm and melt him into submission?"

"What for? I have no intention of wasting time befriending him." Once we disembarked, I would avoid Martin the rest of the trip.

BRIGHT SUNLIGHT FLOODING in through a window of the airplane woke me. Was it the next day already? Yawning, I inhaled the nutty aroma of freshly brewed coffee laced with a delicious whiff of aftershave—a spicy fragrance. I pushed back my bangs, cracked an eye open, and saw a female flight attendant handing out beverages to passengers sitting six rows ahead of me.

I tried to stretch but felt a strange weight pinning my shoulder down. I turned to see Martin's face only inches from mine. He was slumped against me, sound asleep, his black hair tousled. I shrugged, thinking he'd roll his head away, but instead he nestled closer.

Sleeping, Martin looked like the prince in my childhood fairytale book, not the ogre I'd tried to ignore while drifting into slumber six hours ago.

"Excuse me, Mr. Spear," I said, but he only released a long breath. "Martin?" I said, louder.

He remained motionless.

I wanted to call for Roxanne's assistance, but all was quiet behind me. She and Drew must be snoozing.

As the flight attendant's clinking cart approached, Martin's arm twitched, then his eyes popped open. After an initial look of astonishment, a curtain fell across his face. He snapped his head back, straightened his spine.

"I say! Why didn't you wake me up?"

"I tried."

He smoothed his collar, then straightened his tie. "Well, you should have tried harder."

Did he think I enjoyed serving as his headrest?

"For your information." I saw movement and noticed Hal trudging our way from the rear of the aircraft. His bloodshot eyes were rimmed with purple, and his hair spiked out on the sides.

"Martin, I'm sorry about the mix-up," he said, kneeling in the aisle and slowing the flight attendant's progress. "We'll get you in business class on the way home. I promise."

"I'm fine, quite comfortable," Martin said, although I didn't buy it.

Hal rested his small chin on his knuckles. "We're so fortunate to have you along. It's such an honor. I want everything to go perfectly." He shifted his gaze to me and narrowed his eyes. "Are you keeping our star entertained?"

I fabricated a pleasant face but was too exhausted to actually smile. "He's been entertaining me," I said. "Martin Spear is an unusual man."

"Indeed, he is. Without his voice in the tenor section, we'd be sunk." Hal stood as the cart prodded him out of the way. "I guarantee the rest of the trip will go like clockwork."

CHAPTER 4

A FTER A TURN of the knob, I entered my hotel room. Rubbing my eyes, I felt like I was sleep-schlepping, as Mom might say. It was midday in London. I needed to ignore Seattle's time—an eight-hour difference—but I couldn't stop yawning. I dragged off my jacket and collapsed onto one of the two twin beds, its springs comforting my stiff back. I listened to the whoosh of traffic on the street below and started sinking, floating through a cloud.

Someone in the hall jimmied a key into the lock and wrestled with the knob. Expecting to see Roxanne, I turned onto my side. The door blew open and Clare strutted in. My breath caught in my throat. Roxanne and I had requested to room together. I'd assumed we'd be sharing this darling room, with its laced curtains adorning the window and the pint-sized balcony with wrought-iron railing, right out of a British novel.

"Good grief, this is tiny," Clare said, her hands clasping her Barbie doll hips. Noticing the mirror above the bureau, she stepped toward it and sang the first bar to Roy Orbison's oldie, "Pretty Woman."

I had to agree with her narcissistic assessment. A svelte five ten, she could have stepped out of a fashion magazine. Her hot-pink silk blouse and black clingy miniskirt weren't even wrinkled.

She unzipped her carryon, extracted her makeup bag, and dumped the contents on top of the doily-covered dresser. Then she applied blue shadow to match her eyes—the sky-colored irises I'd always wanted. Instead, I saw the world through hazel-green eyes, the exact color of my dad's, the last person I wanted to think of. Growing up, and even today, when gazing at my reflected image, I remembered my father, respected oncologist Dr. Theodore Rosenthal, the bum who hadn't sent me a birthday card since I was eight. If only there were a way to erase him from my mind.

I had to ask, "Are you sure this is your room?"

"Yeah, Hal did a switch. First, he had me in with that little mouse Bonnie. But I said, 'No way.'" She grabbed a comb and straightened her part with precision. "Then he tried pairing me with Roxanne Miller. Good grief, I couldn't put up with her yacking. And have you ever noticed she never has a boyfriend?"

Clare's words sounded like pebbles banging in a tin can, making me want to plug my ears. Or should I jump up and give her a piece of my mind? No, I wouldn't dignify her mean-spirited comments with a reaction.

I closed my heavy lids and bathed my eyes in darkness. In the past, during rehearsals, I'd heard Clare complain about Roxanne and Bonnie, our sweetheart pianist and organist, but was surprised she'd choose to room with me over them. The entire time I'd known Clare she'd artfully turned her head so I didn't enter her field of vision. It occurred to me she and Martin had much in common. Maybe by the end of the week they'd be crooning love songs to each other.

"The group's meeting downstairs in fifteen minutes for the optional tour," Clare said. "But I have a date. No one you know, so don't even ask."

"Okay." In a moment I dozed off.

She poked my shoulder with her acrylic fingernail, catapulting me back to consciousness. "Don't fall asleep," she said. "You'll be up all night and keep me awake."

"I guess you're right." Although by tonight I hoped to have Roxanne or anyone else for a roommate. I pushed myself to a sitting position, leaned against the wall, and watched her unpack. She commandeered three of the four bureau drawers and draped her clothes on most of the hangers. Then she splashed her throat with a heady perfume and gave herself one more satisfied inspection in the mirror.

"Lookin' good," she said and waltzed out the door atop three-inch heels.

The phone by the bed jingled. I reached for the receiver. "Hello?"

"Jessie, get your act together and meet me in the lobby," Roxanne said, rekindling my energy.

Leaving my suitcase where it lay—to make switching rooms easier—I fluffed my hair with my fingers, grabbed my jacket, then headed out the door. Downstairs in the lobby everyone from the choir looked beat. Opposite the front desk, several sat on overstuffed chairs facing a stone fireplace or on couches lining the walls. Others stood chatting, their voices subdued.

When I saw Roxanne, I gave her a hug. "I want to room with you." I heard a whine in my voice, reminding me of Cooper when he stayed up past his bedtime.

"Me too, girlfriend." She leaned my way, speaking into my ear. "Clare threw a hissyfit and Hal caved in without a fight. When did he turn into a wimp?"

I couldn't picture inflexible Hal submitting to anyone's demands—until I'd seen him fawning over Martin. "I'm going to insist Hal puts us in the same room," I said.

"I already tried. And you know I can be persuasive. But he won't budge. We're stuck, at least for tonight."

"Maybe once we're on the road?"

"I hope so. We could have a pajama party."

"Sounds fun. I've never been to one. Growing up, I wasn't a member of the popular crowd." If I hadn't been self-conscious about not having a dad, I might have taken the initiative to invite the other ostracized girls over. We could have stuck together and formed our own club. As it was, I spent my free time outside of school with Mom or in solitude.

I noticed a slim man in his early forties sauntering across the carpet, carrying with him the impression of confidence. He was a head-turner—thick hair the color of espresso, symmetrical features, full lips, and wearing a well-cut gabardine jacket over slacks. He greeted Hal, and I heard him say he was the representative from the tour company.

He increased his volume. "Good day, everyone. My name is Nick Toscano." His flowing English was woven with Italian vowels. With casual sophistication, he began handing out brochures and city maps, but stopped when he reached me. "The motor coach should be here any moment to drive you through this magnificent city. Tomorrow you're free to explore by yourselves. Then it's off for five days of singing and, who knows, perhaps adventure."

Moving closer, he aimed his intense chocolate-brown eyes at me like we were old friends. "Will the *signorina* be coming to see the sights?" he asked.

"Absolutely. I wouldn't pass up a chance to see London. Although I can barely keep my eyes open." My head felt like a lead weight.

"You'll get over your jet lag in a few days. It's best to jump into this time zone right away, no?" His smile widened, showing straight white teeth. "I tell you what, I'll come along to make sure you do. I have nothing scheduled for this afternoon." He handed Roxanne and me brochures and maps, then continued strolling through the lobby distributing the rest.

Roxanne's elbow jabbed me in the ribs. "Like my trout-loving father says when he hooks a big one, 'Fish on.' You've only been here an hour and already landed a keeper. He's as cute as they come. An Italian accent is even sexier than a British one."

I shook my head. "Don't be ridiculous." But when I watched this engaging man, I saw nothing not to like.

He introduced himself to the others with decorum and poise, then chatted with Hal.

Martin strode through the foyer toward us, wearing twenty-four hours of stubble and a trench coat, its belt dangling loose like a snake.

"There you are," Hal said, standing in his path, blocking his progress. "I hope your room is satisfactory. I told the hotel manager nothing but the best."

"It's very nice. Thank you," Martin said in staccato. His gaze swept the lobby, coming to rest on me, without a show of recognition. I was transparent again? I'd had enough of Martin's erratic behavior to last me a lifetime. He'd ignored me the remainder of the flight, but inside busy Heathrow Airport, he plucked my suitcase off the luggage carousel and set it before me. Then he hurried away before I could show my appreciation.

He broke eye contact and turned back to Hal. "If you don't mind, I shall be going out," Martin said.

"Of course, anything you like."

Nick attempted to give Martin a map. "Aren't you coming with us to see the fair city?" About the same height as Hal, Nick also had to elevate his chin to speak to Martin.

"No. Thank you." Martin jammed his hands in his coat pockets. Sidestepping Hal and Nick, he barged out the hotel's front door, forcing the porter to move aside.

Nick raised a hand to gain our attention. "Ladies and gentlemen, we're ready to leave. Please, *andiamo*. Come this way."

We all followed him outside where a Greyhound-type bus idled at the curb. Mom would be pleased I'd dressed

warmly—the overcast sky hung low, and the temperature hovered around sixty.

Nick rapped on the bus's glass door. A burly man
in a worn tweed jacket slouched behind the steering
wheel. Nick rattled the door until the codger got to his
feet and opened it without greeting us. Nick assisted
several choir members onto the bus, taking my hand
as I boarded, followed by Roxanne. Before I could get
settled, Nick climbed in, then removed papers from
the two seats behind the driver.

"I saved you a place," he told me, gesturing to the
vacant seats. He was feeding me a line—after all, we'd
just met. But when was the last time a gentleman fussed
over me in Seattle?

"Thanks," I said and slid in by the window.

Roxanne plopped down next to me. "It pays to hang
out with you, girlfriend," she said, unbuttoning her
jacket. "Best seats in the house."

Nick switched on the microphone. "Welcome aboard.
It's fortunate I'm coming today. It seems our driver is
losing his voice." He gave us a playful grin. "Too bad,
because Dave has a delightful sense of humor."

Dave opened his side window and snarled at a motorist in our way. Moments later, the bus nosed out into
traffic—on the wrong side of the road.

I spotted Martin lingering at the corner, glancing up
and down the street. He must be worried about fans
hounding him for autographs, but so far no one had
bothered him. British good manners kept them at bay?
Or had his popularity faded? Back in Seattle, Barnes

and Noble still carried his CDs, and recently I'd heard his voice on the sound system at my local grocery store.

A silver Jaguar sedan cruised to a halt in front of Martin. He stepped in on the passenger side. I couldn't see the driver.

My seat lurched as our bus nosed out, then labored through heavy traffic. Nick announced we were approaching Hyde Park. "The land was acquired by Henry VIII in 1536 and was the site of the Great Exposition in 1851, as well as a venue for many rock concerts."

Feeling like a kid on a field trip in Disney World, I pressed close to the window to see gnarled trees bursting with spring's chartreuse and expansive manicured lawns. In the distance, horseback riders cantered across an open space. I wondered which kings, queens, generals, and famous statesmen had ridden through the four-hundred-year-old park.

While Dave steered the bus down narrow streets, blasting his horn every so often, Nick embellished his descriptions with humor and history. Something intriguing appeared around every corner. I stretched my neck to see the top of Saint Paul's mighty dome and drank in crowded Trafalgar Square with its four bigger-than-life bronze lions and a statue of Lord Nelson standing atop a towering column. I could hear Hal and the others chattering behind me, their voices bubbling with excitement, using words like *awesome* and *incredible*.

"Now I understand why people love London," I said to Roxanne.

"Me, too, girlfriend. And to think I almost didn't come."

"Really? I thought you asked your boss for time off six months ago."

"Something came up—unexpectedly." Her voice seemed stressed, tentative. "But I decided it could wait."

"I'm glad. This trip wouldn't be half as much fun without you." I recognized our hotel at the end of the block.

As the bus coasted to a stop, Nick switched off the microphone and spoke directly to me. "What do you think of London?" he asked.

"It's more wonderful than I imagined. My Fodor's guidebook didn't do it justice. Roxie and I are going sightseeing tomorrow, but we don't know where to start."

"*Perfetto.* Tomorrow's my day off. I'll come pick you up and give you a personal tour. Would ten o'clock be convenient?"

I looked up at his striking features and felt a buzz of attraction. "I couldn't impose."

"It would be my pleasure. I've done all the talking today. Tomorrow's your turn."

"Just the two of us?"

"Would your choir director not approve?" He angled his head toward Roxanne. "We'll include your lovely friend too," he said. "I wouldn't expect a young lady to go off with a stranger unescorted."

Roxanne gave me one of those amused looks sisters probably shared. I had no siblings for comparison. "Okay with you, Roxie?" I asked her.

"You bet. I don't mind being the third wheel."

"In that case," I told Nick, "we'd be delighted."

CHAPTER 5

B ACK IN MY room before dinner, I headed for the telephone on the bedtable and dialed my home number. My cell phone was worthless over here. It was low on juice and my plugin didn't fit the socket. I chided myself for not being better prepared. Well, I had no choice but to use the hotel's phone.

After several rings, I heard my mother's exuberant voice. "Having fun, dear?" Her words were clear, like she was only across town.

"Yes, things couldn't be better." Did my being happy when away from Cooper qualify me as a bad mother? "How's my boy?"

"Fine. I was just fixing him matzo brei." Mom's specialty, something her mother used to make—a cross between French toast and scrambled eggs.

Her voice became muffled as she called, "Your mother's on the phone."

I heard Cooper yell that he was in the middle of a *Fortnite* game. If he stopped now, he'd die. I would never let Cooper play video games before breakfast. Mom was indulging him again.

"How's it going?" I asked.

"Piece of cake once I took his rat to the pound. And I've only had to lock Cooper in his room once to get him to stop lighting matches." Mom snickered. "Just kidding, darling. Really, neither has been a problem. Cooper taught me how to play *Fortnite*. And you know how I hate rodents, but Pepper's growing on me. I didn't realize pet rats were so friendly."

The fact that the home front was running smoothly should have been good news. I'd tried to raise my son to be independent and self-assured. Not an easy feat without a dad steering our ship. But it hurt to think Cooper barely noticed my absence. And did I trust my mother's evaluation of his behavior? What about his missing homework that needed to be made up?

He finally came to the phone. "Hi, Mom."

Hearing his small voice, I felt my heart being tugged through the telephone line. "Darling, I miss you," I said, wishing I could enfold him in my arms.

Yet part of me longed to stretch my wings and experience a new freedom.

FOLLOWING THE TROOP into the hotel dining room, I spied two empty chairs at a round table set for eight. I scooted in next to Roxanne, who sat chatting with Drew. From what I'd seen, Drew didn't have a girlfriend. I thought he and Roxanne would make a cute couple. But I knew better than to meddle, no matter that Mom had declared that a *shadchen* or matchmaker—not a *yenta*, which means busybody—would have done a better job picking a spouse than she had. And I supposed that was true for me as well. I still didn't trust my judgment when it came to men.

Roxanne leaned against my arm. "I'm almost too tired to eat," she said. "That's never happened before."

"I know what you mean," Drew said, running a hand across his short bristly hair. "I shouldn't have taken that nap. Now I can't wake up."

To the left of my dinner plate sat a linen napkin folded into the shape of a lily. As I pulled open the cloth and dropped it in my lap, I still found it difficult to believe I was here, having my supper in paradise. The room was elegant, its ceiling two stories high and its walls adorned with carved molding. I breathed deeply to inhale the thick aromas of stewing meats and gravy wafting from the kitchen. I'd heard British cooking was blah, but whatever the chef was preparing smelled scrumptious.

Someone yanked the chair next to me out. I looked up to see Martin, who made a slight bow to the table at large and sat down without acknowledging me.

"Who wants to lead us in prayer?" take-charge Roxanne said. When Drew shook his head, she turned to Martin.

"All right." He bowed his head. "We thank you for a safe journey and this meal." His voice faltered as he added, "Lord, please help us remember that no challenge is too great for you." He sounded on the verge of tears, which puzzled me. I assumed he was the kind of man who'd rather die than show his emotions. Was he playacting a pious role, like he did onstage?

A quiet moment followed as heads rose and all eyes gravitated to Martin. He snapped open his napkin, folded it neatly in half, and placed it across his lap.

Drew finally broke the silence. "Martin, we missed you on the tour. But you probably know the city well enough to give us one yourself."

"Yes, I grew up just outside London."

"I heard you mention your parents still live here," Roxanne said. "But you won't be seeing them?"

"No, it's highly improbable."

"Why not?" I asked. "I'd hate living far away from my mother." She seemed like my only parent after my father split.

His mouth grew stern and he threw me a sideways glare. "That's personal, Ms. Nash, if you don't mind."

Hey, I was an adult. A teacher. But I felt like a child being dispatched to the hall for a time-out. I grabbed a roll from the breadbasket and tore it open, allowing a burst of steam to escape its center, then smeared it with butter.

"What brought you to the States?" Roxanne asked Martin, then she reached for a roll.

"Career and bad planning."

"Oh, yeah." Roxanne nudged three pats of butter onto her plate. "You were married to Dorothea Platt from Dallas, weren't you?"

Martin nodded once.

"Rumor has it she's got a nasty temper," she said.

I knew of Dorothea Platt, the feisty diva who had received standing ovations at the finest opera houses. She looked like a Greek goddess with waist-length hair.

"She has a fabulous voice," I said, wishing I possessed half her beauty and talent. "I heard her sing *Norma* at the Seattle Opera."

Martin's face blanched. "Must you speak about her?"

"Sorry." I shifted in my seat. "I only meant—"

"Gals, give the man a break," Drew said.

"Yes," said Martin. "Let's not mention her again."

Drew lifted his water glass. "I propose a toast to a trip filled with good music, new friendships, and old skeletons left behind."

Roxanne clinked her glass against mine. "Here, here," she said.

"If only it were that easy." Martin left his water glass untouched. "I've got a closet full waiting for me here."

CHAPTER 6

CLARE GROPED BACK into the room after midnight. On the way to the bathroom, she tripped
over a chair.

"My toe!" she squawked, then stumbled into the side
of her bed. "This stupid little room."

Once awake, I listened to her snore for most of the
night. The air hung heavy with stale booze and cigarette
smoke. During choir rehearsal last month, Clare had
voiced her distaste of smoking and claimed she didn't
drink. And she'd mentioned she was an only child, like
me, what Mom called a *bas-yekhide*, who lived with her
parents through college and still did. Was Clare experiencing her first taste of freedom?

Finally, as the sky began to lighten, I plunged into
a deep fog. In a dream—the same nightmare plaguing
me for a year—Seattle Opera's massive curtains swing
apart to expose me frozen at center stage. My heart
flip-flops, and my legs wobble like Silly Putty. I choke

for air but can't inflate my lungs. In the clutches of stage fright, I forget the words to my aria. The audience hisses and booes.

Struggling to wake up, I heard Clare speaking into her iPhone. "All right, I'll meet you there," she said, cupping her mouth. Noticing I was watching, she quieted her voice and said goodbye.

When I emerged from my shower five minutes later, Clare was gone, leaving her bed a shamble and her dirty clothes heaped on the floor. I slipped into my brown pants suit, the same hue as my hair. A fashion statement or a blunder? I wasn't sure.

Breakfast was included in the tour, so I headed for the dining room. Along the sparsely lit hallway to the elevator, I heard men's voices arguing, sounding like two pit bull terriers. I slowed my pace as I neared a man bellowing into a partially open door. He wasn't much taller than I, his shoulders wide like a wrestler's. The guy sitting by Clare on the jet?

Inside the room stood Martin, wearing an unbuttoned shirt, slacks, and stocking feet. "I'll call security if you don't get out of here!" he shouted, his face white with rage.

"But I'm giving you a chance to come clean, pal. Walk away without a hitch." The man spoke with an accent somewhat similar to Mom's. Was he from the Bronx or New Jersey? "Look at it as my gift to you," he said, not noticing my arrival.

Martin tried to close the door, but the man jammed his foot in it.

"Why you little—" Martin's eyes grew wild. He shoved the door open and lunged out into the hall.

The man's arms flailing, he whirled around and plowed into me, almost knocking me off my feet.

I steadied my balance, feeling like a bowling pin. "Hey, be careful." I made note of his mustached face and short-cropped hair. Unless I was suffering from an overactive imagination, he was the guy who'd sat next to Clare on the plane. What was he doing here?

The man exploded into action, pushing past me, dashing down the corridor, and ducking through a fire exit.

"Good riddance!" Martin said, smoothing a hand over his damp hair.

"What was that all about?" I was more unnerved than angry. Still, I didn't appreciate being run over.

He fixed his stare down the hall, then glanced my way. "None of your concern," he said, like I was the source of his problem, when in fact I was an innocent bystander. Then he lumbered back in his room and slammed the door.

My mind struggled to make sense of things. Who was the man and what did he want with Martin? I balled my hand into a fist to rap on his door, but I stopped myself, deciding I couldn't face his condescending scowl again.

I rode the elevator downstairs. Crossing the lobby past a family with small children just arriving at the hotel, I followed the yummy aroma of sausage and toast. Ahead lay a buffet table of eggs, kippers, meats and pastries. Roxanne, her plate almost empty, was sitting with Bonnie at a table in the center of the room.

"You wouldn't believe what I just saw." I closed in on their table and settled next to Bonnie, across from Roxanne. "The guy from the plane, who was sitting by Clare—he and Martin Spear were verbally duking it out." I wouldn't tell them how nicely Martin's shoulders filled his collared shirt or describe his well-defined pecs. Apparently, he worked out with weights.

"Maybe the man's a reporter," Bonnie said in her whispering voice. Her small face looked freshly scrubbed and her shiny black hair was pulled into a ponytail.

"Martin's pretty famous over here," Roxanne agreed, her elbows on the table. "And I've heard the paparazzi are ruthless."

"It's possible." I poured myself coffee from a silver urn. "But he didn't look like a reporter." Not that I'd had experience with the media. Who would want to interview me? The only time my name had ever been mentioned in the papers was in the obituaries after Jeff's death.

"I wonder if Clare plans to get together with him," Bonnie said.

"They were acting chummy on the plane." Roxanne nibbled on a strip of bacon. "And I saw them talking at luggage pickup and customs, too."

"I thought there was something strange about him." I scanned the room and spotted Clare sitting with two baritones. She was picking at her breakfast like a dainty princess, not the woman who'd tossed her clothes on the floor. "It seemed like he was watching Martin and me out of the corner of his eye," I said.

"You must be used to men looking at you, you're so pretty," Roxanne said.

I coughed a laugh. "Then how come I haven't had a date in six months?" My last attempt was a blind date who ordered a martini, expensive wine, a fillet mignon, and later dessert, then suggested we split the bill. In hindsight, I should have refused to pay. I was never going to see him again, anyway.

I sipped my java, then covered my mouth to yawn.

"You look beat, girlfriend," Roxanne said.

"My roommate kept me up." I watched Clare freshen her lipstick. Then she stood and left the room.

"Why don't you let me bunk with Clare?" Roxanne poured herself more coffee and emptied a packet of artificial sweetener into the syrupy liquid. "I can sleep through anything. I grew up in a tiny house with three sisters all wanting the bathroom at once. We drove my folks nuts. They'd scream at us to shut up." Her face grew somber. "When we kids moved out, my parents kept screaming. They never got divorced, but they threatened to a hundred times."

"There's no perfect marriage," I said, noticing a couple wearing bored expressions mosey to the far end of the room. Memories of Jeff's and my unhappy eight-year union sprang into focus. Fun-loving, hard-drinking Jeff had pushed life to the limits: scuba diving, hang gliding, and plunging down mountainsides on his snowboard as if he were indestructible. But he couldn't survive the head-on collision. If only he'd come straight home from skiing instead of stopping for a beer on the way into town. There'd been a woman in the car with him who'd escaped with minor injuries, someone his buddies said they'd met on the slopes. No big deal, they'd assured me. She didn't come to the memorial service.

"My mother says it's better for kids to grow up in a house where parents aren't arguing," I said. "But I'd do anything to have Cooper's daddy back, no matter how we were getting along, for my son's sake."

Martin came into the room and sat at a nearby table facing the door. As the waiter poured him coffee, Martin glanced around, inspecting everyone, even the waitress replenishing the eggs. For a moment his eyes rested on me, then he reached for a newspaper sitting on the table next to him and opened it with such force one corner ripped.

"Looks like our tenor's still in a bad mood," I said. "I wonder if he ever gets up on the right side of the bed."

"He doesn't seem like a happy person, does he?" Roxanne said. "But he sure is cute."

"I have one of his CDs at home." Bonnie's cheeks brightened. Her wire-rim glasses enlarged her almond-shaped eyes. "I've listened to his amazing voice and looked at his face on the cover many times, but I never thought I'd get to meet him in person."

I tried to view him as a stranger. "He is good looking." Extremely. "But best kept at a distance." The further from me the better.

Her gaze dallying on Martin, Bonnie stood and pushed in her chair. "Several of us are going to the British Museum. I'd better get ready." A moment later, her small silhouette disappeared from the room.

I stretched to my feet and headed for the buffet line. As I spooned a poached egg onto my plate, I saw a bellboy approaching Martin's table with an envelope. After tipping the young man, Martin tore the envelope open, yanked out a piece of paper, and read it at arm's length. Then he crumpled the note into a ball and stashed it in his jacket pocket.

I returned to the table with my plate piled high. "I got some of everything. Even the baked beans and grilled tomatoes." I broke a muffin in two and offered half to Roxanne.

Her hand shot out to take it. "I shouldn't eat this." She lathered butter across its surface. "My doctor told me to consume less and exercise more."

"That regimen wouldn't hurt me, either." I munched on a sausage link, savoring the salty sweetness.

"You're so skinny you don't need to worry. What are you, a six-petite?"

"Vanity sizing," I said. No need to tell her I could fit into a four.

Roxanne set the remaining muffin on her plate, then patted her tummy. "I need to lose forty pounds. The day before we left, I found out I may have Type 2 diabetes. Adult-onset." She nibbled at the muffin but had difficulty swallowing. She gulped a mouthful of coffee. "I should have been taking better care of myself. My mother has diabetes, which puts me at higher risk. She taught me to clean my plate, but I can't blame my bad eating habits on her."

"How do you feel?"

"Just tired." Her lips pulled in. "Last time I had it checked, my blood pressure was high, but I thought it was stress-related. All work and no play."

"And it's okay for you to be here?"

"Yeah. My doc encouraged me to take the trip. She'll start me on medication when I get home." Her voice grew faint. She fidgeted with a button on her blouse. "To complicate things, I have crummy health insurance with a high deductible."

"Let me know if there's anything I can do." Not that I had a bundle in my savings account. Without health insurance, Cooper and I would be sunk.

Roxanne's mouth shaped into a lopsided smile. "I don't want to get hysterical and spoil everyone's fun. Let's forget about it until we get home, okay?"

"Sure." I reached across the table and found her hand. "We'll be having too much fun this week to worry about anything."

Martin's cell phone began tootling "Rule Britannia." He snatched it from his pocket and checked the caller ID. Glancing at Roxanne and me as if we were spying on him—I guess we were—he pressed it to his ear, and said, "Martin, here."

After a moment, his face broke into an uncharacteristic grin.

CHAPTER 7

STANDING IN THE darkened room, I had no doubt Roxanne, Nick and I were being evaluated by hidden cameras and armed security guards. I stared into the illuminated case at a scepter encrusted with diamonds and rubies and emeralds so humungous they looked fake. Nick had told Roxanne and me the Crown Jewels were the most valuable royal collection in existence, worth billions but priceless because their true value rested in their symbolism and historical significance. People had coveted them, fought for them, died for them. And now I had a glimpse of why this could happen; their tantalizing power pulled at me through the glass.

"The only thing more beautiful than a rare jewel is the woman who wears it," Nick said over my shoulder.

His declaration caused a smile to fan across my face. Waiting for his arrival earlier, I'd wondered if he'd show up. It was his day off, after all. Not that I didn't get attention from men at home, occasionally. But suave, sophisticated Nick knew I was traveling with a church choir, not the typical femme fatale for a one-night fling. But he had zoomed to the front of the hotel at ten o'clock sharp in his silver Alfa Romeo sedan, its leather interior free from the papers and debris that accumulated in my car back home. And he employed impeccable manners.

"I need a diamond tiara like that," Roxanne said. "One reason I love being onstage. It's the only time I can wear custom-made evening gowns and glitzy costume jewelry." She placed a hand behind her head à la Marilyn Monroe. "A girl likes getting all dolled up."

Nick's eyes flashed with amusement. "And so she should."

I admired the tiara, each tiny facet sparkling like a rainbow under the bright lights, and imagined it on my own head. I remembered myself as a child adorned with my mother's silk slip, scarves, and costume jewelry, spending hours singing to my reflection in the full-length mirror in Mom's bedroom.

"I guess we girls never outgrow loving to play dress-up," I said. "Although you wouldn't know it looking through my humdrum wardrobe." Over the years of New Year's Eves spent at home, I'd turned boring. *Nudne,* Mom would call it.

"Our dreams stay young," Roxanne said. "Too bad the rest of us has to age."

"You're both young," Nick said. "Not more than twenty-five or thirty?"

"Keep on talking," Roxanne said, "even though I don't believe a word you say."

"Tell me something." Nick leaned against the rail, his back to the case. "You seem like intelligent women. How is it that you're traveling with a thief?"

My jaw dropped open like a small-town girl. "What do you mean? No one in the choir fits that description."

At that moment, an older couple wearing berets atop heads of wavy hair wandered past us. Speaking a Slavic language, their exclamations filled my ears. Roxanne waited for the couple to move further down the walkway before she addressed Nick.

"If you're talking about Martin Spear," she said, her voice colored with annoyance, "he was never formally charged. He claimed the necklace was legally his. His parents', anyway."

"But his former wife, *la Signora* Platt, said he'd given it to her." Nick spoke with conviction. "Once you give something away, it's no longer yours. No?"

"It was in Martin's family for centuries," Roxanne explained to me. "A cross made of rare saffron yellow diamonds, my favorite color."

"Yes." Nick inched toward the exit as a group of two dozen French children mobbed the room, flooding our ears with high-pitched squeals and laughter. "The Canary Cross is as valuable as the ones in that case. I'd love to get a glimpse of it."

Roxanne and I followed close behind him. "How come I've never heard anything about this?" I asked.

"Because you don't read the tabloids, girlfriend," she said. "You know, on the way to the checkout stand?

That's where all the juicy gossip lives. I only saw one little article about it in a real newspaper. The reporter stated someone lifted the necklace from Dorothea Platt's hotel room in London. Nothing about Martin."

"There was no forced entry." Nick shrugged. "The thief must have had a key."

"I don't believe it," I said. "Martin Spear might be full of himself, but he doesn't strike me as a man who'd commit a crime, if only to avoid bad press."

"Can we ever know another man's motives?" Nick opened the door, allowing a block of daylight to fill the hallway. "Owning such priceless stones could change a man's destiny. Given the right circumstances, could anyone resist taking it?"

I could withstand temptation, I thought. Yet I had to wonder about myself. As a teen I'd shoplifted, blaming the fact that Mom and I were strapped for money, and she wouldn't demand child support from my father. Once I became proficient, I'd relished the adrenalin high accompanying my forays as much as my stolen booty.

But I had grown past such despicable behavior. Hadn't I?

PERCHED ON THE front passenger seat of Nick's sporty car, I watched London whiz past us—a kaleidoscope of vistas. Every block or so, Nick pointed out a church, landmark, or historical building. Roxanne and I stretched our necks for better views.

I glanced at Nick, his voice and arms relaxed as he drove confidently through the frenzied traffic. Taxis blew past him and tinny horns blared, but he paid little attention, calmly maneuvering his car to Knightsbridge.

"You two must go to Harrods." He took a left onto a side street. "If nothing more than to see how the wealthy buy their food." He jockeyed his car into a tight spot, then led Roxanne and me down the bustling sidewalk to the giant department store.

The doorman, clad in olive green, tipped his hat and swept the door open. As we crossed the threshold, we were met by a sea of shoppers and lights reflecting off polished counters. After a stroll past designer purses, scarves, and diamond-faced watches—nothing I could afford—Nick guided us to the food hall. Elaborate chandeliers cast light across the tiled walls, and decorative pillars supported the high ceiling. With Nick at my side, I gawked at the expansive cases crammed with meats, cheeses, and baked goods, all displayed with meticulous care—edible works of art. The air smelled rich and doughy, like my mom's kitchen when she'd just pulled a loaf of *challah* from the oven.

I selected a tin of Scottish shortbread for her and a box of handmade chocolates for Cooper. Standing at the counter, I brought out my wallet and handed a twenty-pound note to the cashier. I glanced down at Cooper's photograph, across from my driver's license. Taken last summer, he wore his favorite Mariners T-shirt and a toothy grin, which made me smile in return. His treasured baseball cap sat atop his mop of blond hair—his father's hair. Looking closer, I marveled at how much he resembled Jeff.

When we met, Jeff looked like a young Robert Redford. I didn't feel in his league and was ecstatic when he pursued me with roses and love notes, even though he drank too much and drove his car like a hellion. After we married, I got pregnant right away. Jeff went ballistic, insinuating I'd forgotten my birth control pill on purpose. His amorous kisses faded into bland pecks on the cheek, followed by snide remarks about how I was inflating into a blimp. Even after Cooper's arrival, when I practically starved myself to regain my waistline, Jeff avoided gazing at my body when I exited the shower. "Turn off the lights," he'd say on the rare occasions he embraced me in the bedroom. He must have found solace elsewhere. Another woman or something connected to his late-night hours spent on the internet.

"Miss?" said the cashier, yanking me back to the present. I put out my hand to receive my change and receipt.

Roxanne came over, carrying a bag of snacks to eat in her room later. "If we had a week in London, I'd come here every day."

"That would be fun. And there are one hundred other places I'd like to visit too."

Nick picked up my shopping bag—a gentleman. "Perhaps you'll come back some day." His gaze discreetly moved across my figure. "I'd like to see you again."

Minutes later, he ushered us toward the exit. "What brought you to London?" I asked as we slowed to make way for an elderly woman carrying a Norfolk terrier.

"Can you hear an accent?" he said, seeming disappointed.

"Only a little."

"And you throw in darling Italian words every once in a while." Roxanne's statement made him smile.

"My parents moved here for my father's work when I was a teenager. Italy remains my first love, but it's difficult to find good work there." His voice swelled with enthusiasm, making his inflections more pronounced. "Tuscany is the most beautiful place in the world. My grandparents still live in Sienna."

Roxanne peeked into her bag, then back at him. "Are all the men there as good looking as you?"

"Now you are teasing me." He raised a hand in protest but seemed used to the flattery.

We reached the store's front door. "It's time for lunch," he said. "Are you hungry? I'll take you to my favorite restaurant. Italian, of course."

"You two go ahead without me," Roxanne said. "Drop me off at the hotel. I'm ready for a nap."

"Will you be okay by yourself?" I asked.

"Sure." She patted my shoulder. "And I think we can trust Nick to bring you back safely."

"Absolutely." Nick wrote his cell phone number on the back of his business card and gave it to Roxanne. "I'll have Jessica back to the hotel in two hours. That is, if she'd care to join me."

"I would," I said. Why not? What could possibly be wrong with having lunch with Nick? Yet, I hoped we wouldn't run into anyone from the choir. Especially Hal. Or Martin.

"PLEASE, YOU MUST forgive me." Nick's dark amber eyes gazed into mine. "Again, I talk too much. A hazard of my job. It's your turn. Tell me all about yourself."

Suddenly the small restaurant seemed stifling. "My story's pretty dull." I unbuttoned my jacket.

Nick reached across the red-and-white checkered tablecloth, took hold of my left hand, and examined my ring finger.

I pulled my hand away, placing it in my lap. "No, I'm not married." The white groove where my wedding band once resided had faded years ago. "I do have a twelve-year-old son, Cooper."

"I'm sure he's wonderful."

"Yes, he is." But I was glad he wasn't dining with us. He never liked the men I dated. Not that this was a date.

"And you are a professional singer, no?"

"Hardly." Noticing his puzzled expression, I confided, "I'm a rank amateur."

"I'd love to hear you."

My jaw tightened as I imagined giving him a private concert. An accordion rendition of "'O Sole Mio" was playing in the background. Did he expect me to break into song?

I decided to give him the straight scoop. "I'm not soloist material and doubt I'll ever be. I earn my living as a schoolteacher." I sipped my water, finding a sliver of ice to munch on.

"I think you're charming—*simpatica*. And I'm sure more gifted than you know. I can hear it in your speaking voice. We Italians have an ear for such things. Your words resonate music."

I'd heard about Latin-lover types, their tongues as smooth as glass. "Since your company specializes in vocal tours," I said, "I'm sure you've heard voices far better than mine. We're just a small church choir."

"The size of the choir means nothing."

A waiter brought us menus, but Nick set his aside.

"You're being too humble," he said. "I'll come hear you and be the judge."

I opened my menu and skimmed the list of appetizers without recognizing any of the Italian words. Should I point to something and hope for the best?

Glancing up, I said, "We're not booked to perform in London."

"Then I'm sorry to miss that—and you." His gaze penetrated mine until I looked down and scanned the menu again. This was just a silly flirtation. There was no reason to feel nervous.

"Please." He took the menu from me. "May I order for you?"

"Okay, I'm in your hands," I said, and he grinned.

Later, when Nick dropped me off at the hotel, he brought my fingertips to his lips. "I hope we meet again someday."

As I entered the hotel, part of me wished the tour wasn't leaving in the morning. I'd never see Nick again. Although we'd agreed to communicate by email, our correspondence would probably fizzle out after a few weeks. He'd discover another touring American and forget all about me.

CHAPTER 8

STUCK ALONE WITH Martin Spear? I glanced around the windowless room, with its five rows of chairs facing a stout podium, confirming he and I were the first to arrive at the mandatory meeting before dinner.

Clad in a tweed sports jacket, Martin was planted in the back row. Finding a seat in the second row, I recalled his tussle with the scuzzball from the plane. During the fracas, Martin had looked like a wild bull—the opposite of the composed mannequin sitting behind me now. Which was the real man? Nick insinuated Martin was a thief and a fraud. I knew a good portion of newspaper reporting was sensational fluff, but I also knew men were capable of lying and cheating, turning their backs on their loved ones and family. My father had proven that.

Bonnie wandered in and sat next to me. She'd changed into comfy clothes and her pencil-straight hair was in its usual ponytail. "The British Museum was incredible," she said when I asked about her day. "They have one of the best collections of mummies and sarcophagi in the world."

I pictured Bonnie working her job at the northeast branch of the Seattle Public Library, helping kids find books and information for term papers.

"Sounds interesting," I said. "Cooper's fascinated with Egyptian history. He'd love to see a real mummy."

At least he used to be interested in history and science. Now I wasn't so sure.

"And we saw the Rosetta Stone," she said. "Amazing."

Hal arrived, and the room filled with the other choir members. Roxanne, carrying a water bottle, dropped into the chair on the other side of me.

"How're you doing?" I said, noticing pillow lines across her cheek.

She chugged down water, a drop leaking out the corner of her mouth and landing on the arm of her flowery blouse. "My nap left me groggy, but I'll perk up."

Hal positioned himself next to the podium. "We should be holding rehearsal tonight, but the hotel's only piano is located in the bar."

The group broke into tittering, making me chuckle.

"No hint of impropriety," Hal had instructed us last week. "As representatives of our church, we must be on our best behavior at all times."

He clapped his hands to harness our attention. "Listen up, people. I want everyone down at the bus on time tomorrow morning. We need to be on our way at seven thirty AM sharp. Please, save your late evenings for the last two nights of the tour when your vocal cords won't be needed. We want to sound our best tomorrow evening."

Scrutinizing each face, he lowered his eyebrows. "Where's Clare?" The room went silent. "I know I told her to be here." He spied me. "Clare's your roommate, isn't she?"

I felt myself squirm. "Yes." As far as I knew, she hadn't been back to our room since this morning.

"Tell her she'd better not pull this stunt again," he said.

I didn't want to become their go-between but nodded to get the subject behind us.

After the meeting adjourned, Roxanne swiveled in her seat to face me. "Tell me all, you lucky dog. How was lunch with Nick? You seeing him tonight?"

"No, he has a previous engagement." He'd assured me he'd rather take me out.

I stood, feeling achy legs and tired feet. "Anyway, what's the point of getting to know each other better?"

"Guess you're right." Roxanne stood and tugged her blouse down over her hips. "I've heard of long-distance dating, but Seattle to London is too far."

We made our way to the elevator, but as the doors opened Roxanne stopped short. "I need to run to the front desk. Meet me in the restaurant in thirty minutes, okay?"

"Sure." I padded into the lift and pushed the button to the third floor. Before the doors could slide shut, Martin slipped in and jabbed the same button. I inched

to the far corner, leaning against it. As we floated slug-
gishly to our floor, I watched his distorted image in
the metal door and decided he looked like Ichabod
Crane, the gangly and unappealing schoolteacher from
The Legend of Sleepy Hollow. Martin had alluded to old skeletons. Was he worried about meeting up with his own
version of the Headless Horseman?

The elevator lurched to a stop and paused for several
seconds. I imagined us trapped in this cramped cubicle
for the rest of the evening, causing me to shudder.
Martin and I were two north poles, repelling each
other.

The doors finally parted, and Martin cleared his
throat. "Ms. Nash, I assume you weren't hurt by that
brute this morning?"

"Nope, just startled." We stepped out into the hallway.
I asked, "Who was he?"

"I'm not sure, but I hope never to see him again." He
took off down the hall, his long shadow trailing him.

I trotted to catch up. "Did he give you his name?"
I said.

He spun around and peered down at me. "You certainly are inquisitive, aren't you?"

"Maybe I am, thank you." I encouraged curiosity in
my students. "Don't I have the right to know who almost
mowed me over?"

He lowered his chin and squinted like I was a speck
of mud on his shoe. "If you hadn't been listening in
on a private conversation, it wouldn't have happened."

I stood tall, my hands on my waist—my stance for
silencing my classroom when unruly. "Are you accusing

me of eavesdropping? I was simply walking down the hall on the way to breakfast, minding my own business."

"Then I shall ask you to continue to mind your own business." He stalked away, his arms swinging stiffly. When he reached his door, he checked his pants pockets then his jacket then his pants again.

Locked out? The spiteful side of me enjoyed his predicament. I came closer and cocked my head. "A problem?"

"I must have left my key in the room. I've never done that before."

"No, I'm sure you haven't." Until this moment he was perfect?

He rattled the doorknob. "I'll need to use your phone to call the front desk and have them run a key up."

I was tempted to pretend I hadn't heard him but smiled into his stern face as only a veteran teacher could do. "Is that a request or an order?"

"I suppose I could go down myself if it's too much trouble."

This man didn't have a humorous bone in his body.

"Just kidding," I said. "Come on, my room's only a couple of doors away." I opened my room and motioned for him to enter, and left the door ajar. Not that I had any fear he'd make a pass at me. At worst, he'd bore me to death.

Once inside my room, Martin called the reception desk. "Ten minutes?" He pressed the receiver to his ear "I could come down there and be back myself faster than that. Please, make it snappy."

He clunked the receiver back onto its cradle and turned to leave. "I appreciate your help."

"No problem."

"Well, then, goodnight." As he proceeded into the hallway, he almost bumped into Hal.

"Martin, hello," Hal said. When he spied me, he added, "Dear, dear. What have we here?"

A hint of impropriety? I didn't want Hal getting the wrong idea. "I was helping him. He can't find his key."

"I hope you don't believe that," a man said. Moving into the hallway, I found Nick standing next to Hal.

"Are you suggesting I forced myself into the lady's room?" Martin said, blustering at Nick like a sergeant reprimanding a private.

Nick moved closer. "Ah, Mr. Spear, I meant no offense."

"He was calling the front desk." My words tumbled out, making me sound guilty. Of what, I wasn't sure. "Martin came in for two minutes and was just leaving." Trying to regain my composure, I said to Nick, "What brings you back to the hotel?"

"Senior Hal interrupted my evening. Dinner with my parents—"

"I asked him to come." Hal waved a map and some documents. "We need to go over the itinerary."

"I assured your director there's nothing to worry about," Nick said. "All is arranged."

Hal pulled the map partway open. "There's no such thing as being too thorough."

"Exactly," Martin said. "I should like a look at the schedule, too."

Nick quieted his voice, his gaze almost devouring me. "Since I have the pleasure of running into you, I can tell you how much I enjoyed our day."

"Me, too," I said. "I had fun. Thank you."

Martin cleared his throat. "Shall we?"

Ignoring him, Nick sighed. At just above a whisper, he said, "You are a beautiful woman. And it is such a pity—"

"Are you coming?" Martin asked with a twang of impatience, and Nick fell in behind the other two.

Our final farewell, I thought, watching Nick depart and feeling my chest sink.

CHAPTER 9

THE NEXT MORNING, I wheeled my suitcase out of the hotel and across the sidewalk to the waiting tour bus. In the street, taxicabs, mini cars the size of washing machines, and double-decker busses swished past, ferrying people to work.

As I attempted to stow my suitcase in the luggage compartment at the side of the bus, Nick jogged out.

"Good morning," he said with a ring in his voice. He took the suitcase from me and shoved it in next to half a dozen others.

"Coming to see us off?" I asked. He looked like a movie star in his black bomber-style jacket.

"There's been a change in plans" He sent me a grin. "Our driver, Dave, is sick in bed, has laryngitis, so I offered to fill in. I could use a break from sitting at my desk."

Was he kidding? I stared into his face but saw no hint of insincerity.

"Don't worry." He lifted his right hand. "I promise, I know what I'm doing. I started out as a driver and when there's an emergency I still lend a hand."

The rest of the week with Nick behind the wheel? Whoopee, this tour was improving by the minute. Not that I wanted to play the gullible female tourist indulging in a trivial love-affair. No, the world was too dangerous for such frivolities.

"You already proved yourself to be a good driver," I said. "I'm surprised, that's all."

"And, I hope, pleased?"

I was delighted but played it cool. "Yes, Dave seemed grumpy." While Nick radiated charisma and good humor.

Martin shuffled over, looking like he'd just stumbled out of bed—mussed hair, his collar unbuttoned, and his tie crooked. Why had he bothered to wear one? He positioned his leather suitcase beside mine without acknowledging Nick or me, then headed to the bus's open door.

"Come sit behind me," Nick said as soon as Martin was gone. "Keep me company." I turned to board the bus and saw Clare, who stood half a foot taller than I.

She deposited her luggage at Nick's feet. "Don't you dare let anything happen to my suitcase."

"I'll guard it with my life," Nick said, and for the first time since I'd met Clare, she seemed at a loss for words.

He watched her long legs climb onto the bus. "I've never seen her before."

"Meet my roommate, Clare Van Arsdale."

His eyebrows rose. "Ah."

Great, Clare had already beguiled him? If he liked willowy blondes—and what man didn't?—I couldn't compete.

Hal rushed over, his thinning hair poofing with each step. "Let's go. We must keep on schedule."

"We're still missing a few people," Nick said. "Don't worry, this country is much smaller than yours. We'll make it to Norwich in plenty of time."

"I want to get there early. I've never kept an audience waiting and I intend to keep it that way."

"Yes, sir." Nick gave him a mock salute.

Hal's hands flew up to cover his cheeks, and his mouth shaped into Edvard Munch's silent scream. "Oh, no, I forgot my travel clock in my room." He spun around and ran back into the hotel.

"It seems I will have the pleasure of hearing you sing after all," Nick said to me.

The thought of him watching my lips move and hearing my bloopers whacked into me like a tidal wave, making my legs go stringy. But I was determined not to let stage fright ruin this day. Our performance was in ten hours, I reasoned with myself. Anything could happen between then and now. The bus could break down. We might not even make it to our destination. And I stood in the second row behind twenty-something Marci, with her raisin-black spiky hair. If I slumped, no one would be able to see me.

When I got on the bus, I noticed Clare taking up the front row by the window. Behind her, Martin sat reading a newspaper. I scanned the length of the bus. Most of the choir members were already seated.

Next to Clare lay a caramel-colored jacket that matched her slacks and her fringed shoulder bag.

"Is this seat taken?" I asked. She frowned as she laboriously removed her belongings.

I smiled as if she were the most gracious person on Earth. "Thanks," I said in a cheery voice, and sat beside her. I normally got along with women. Mom taught me we were part of a sisterhood and needed to stick together. But Clare acted like I had halitosis.

Nick strode aboard, slid into the driver's seat, and started up the engine. Then Roxanne scurried on and sank in behind me, next to Martin.

She leaned into the aisle and tapped my shoulder. "Ooh, la-la. I like our driver," she said. "How terribly convenient."

I tried not to giggle like a schoolgirl. What was happening to me? I felt younger than I had in years. Giddy.

Roxanne wriggled out of her jacket. "Marty, you look like the cat just dragged you in."

Martin lowered his paper and sniffed. "I can't say I feel much better than I look. I'll sleep well once we're out of London."

"Here, let me fix your collar. I used to help my father on the rare occasions he wore a tie. Funerals and weddings."

"Not the formal sort?"

"No. T-shirts and Budweiser in a can. With four daughters, you could say I was the son he never had. He even took me trout and steelhead fishing. I still have my waders and can tie a mean fly."

"Very impressive."

"But I can't mash potatoes or make gravy. My older sisters shooed me out of the kitchen and left me the grunt work, like cleaning up their mess and taking out the garbage."

A moment later, Hal jumped on and did a final head check. "We're all here," he told Nick.

"Yes, I counted already."

"Still, it never hurts to double-check."

"Of course, but I've never left anyone behind." Nick's gaze found mine in the mirror. "I'll keep an extra-good eye on this group."

"I'm responsible for these people" Hal rubbed his palms together. "We must not have any problems while I'm in charge."

"Yes, sir." Nick closed the door, eased the bus into first gear, and rolled away from the curb as Hal found his seat.

Nick flicked on the loudspeaker. "Ladies and gentlemen, we have an exciting day ahead of us. First, we're off to the university city, Cambridge, then we'll head through East Anglia to Norwich to sing and spend the night."

As Nick inched the bus through London's snarled streets, I tried to take in every detail, hoping to see and remember everything. The bus passed a formal garden dotted with bronze statues of famous statesmen. Nick, his voice confident, slowed down and identified each man. Petals from blossoming trees twirled to the ground in the breeze, and rows of yellow daffodils stood brilliantly against the green lawns.

"Not too much in bloom yet," Nick said. "April's too early to see our gardens in their prime. You will all have to come back in the summer."

"I like it when it's cold out," Roxanne said. "It means I don't have to expose my legs."

"You don't have anything to worry about," Drew said from across the aisle. "You look great."

Roxanne shook with laughter. "Maybe I do like American men the best."

"Does she have to talk so loud?" Clare said to me.

I felt my shoulders lifting. "If you're referring to Roxie, there are few people in the world I admire more."

Clare gave a huff and rotated her torso to face the window, blocking half of my view. Thankfully, I could see out the front windows.

The bus crept along until we were in the outskirts of London.

"Dave sticks to the main highways, but I prefer the back roads." Nick slapped the turn signal. "So much more interesting. Don't worry, Hal, we'll be in Norwich on time."

Nick drove us through Epping Forest. Out the window, I saw mammoth oak and beech trees sprinkled with lime-green leaves, tall against the pastel blue sky. We passed a grassy meadow. Mist rose as sunlight warmed the ground. The earth looked thick and supple. I imagined a knight galloping across the clearing, his steed's hooves kicking up clumps of sod.

"Queen Elizabeth I used to hunt here, as did her father, Henry VIII," Nick said through the microphone.

"Henry wasn't great marriage material," Roxanne said, and Drew chuckled.

"You're right," Martin said. "Off with her head and all that."

Roxanne patted me on the shoulder. "Remember the Tower of London? I wouldn't want to spend my last days there."

"No room service or central heating," I said, turning to speak over the back of my seat. "Maybe marrying a king isn't the way to go. But how about a prince?"

"Depends," she said. "Do I have to kiss a toad first?"

"You never know who your prince might be," Martin said. "Don't judge a book by its cover."

Was he referring to himself? That behind his stuffy exterior lived a fuzzy-wuzzy pussycat? Or was he suggesting that despite his fame and reputation, he was indeed capable of committing theft?

We drove past ploughed obsidian-black fields dotted with new growth. Nick announced we were nearing the thousand-year-old village of Thaxted and suggested we stop. "We can stretch our legs and sample the pastries."

"Are you sure there's time?" Hal called out.

"I need to use the powder room," Roxanne said, and several others agreed.

Five minutes later, he parked in front of a white building with *The Cake Shop* proudly written over the door and lace curtains hanging across the front windows.

I followed Nick off the bus. He turned and took my hand as I descended the steps. I could get used to all this gallantry.

Once inside, I sat at the table nearest the door and Bonnie settled across from me. Roxanne dashed to the ladies' room, then joined Martin and Drew at the table next to us. The three other altos—Gloria, Leticia, and Florence, compatible women who never griped and could sight-read with proficiency—clustered together. And Clare made sure she was surrounded by men. Soon our talkative group occupied almost every chair. The air smelled like vanilla icing, teasing my appetite.

Nick sauntered in and pulled up a chair next to Bonnie and me, as I'd hoped he would.

A curvaceous thirty-something waitress sashayed out of the kitchen and set a cup of coffee lightened with cream in front of Nick. "Hi, Nicky," she said, her voice cooing.

"Hello, Kim." He rubbed the back of his neck.

"I haven't seen you in ages." She brought out a pencil and pad from her apron pocket. "Where have you been?"

"I got a promotion. I don't drive much anymore."

She took Bonnie's and my orders, then circulated to the other tables, and returned to the kitchen. As she disappeared, Nick's glance followed her swaying hips. I guessed I couldn't blame him for watching her—most men would. But I had to wonder how well the two knew each other. A girl in every port?

"You come here often?" I asked him.

"I used to, several times a year." He sipped his coffee. "It's a convenient location, and our passengers like it. "Moments later, he pulled out his cell phone to check his text messages, then excused himself. "I need to make a call."

Kim brought Bonnie and me freshly baked scones and a pot of tea. Not seeming to hear Bonnie's request for jam, she scanned Nick's empty chair, then the room at large, and finally moved to the front window, searching for him, no doubt.

As I poured the pecan-colored brew into our cups, I could hear Martin and Roxanne conversing at the next table. "Our driver probably gets a kickback for bringing customers in," Martin said, all snooty.

"Maybe," Roxanne said, but this place is cute."

"In any case," he said, "there's something unpleasant about that fellow."

I squeezed a lemon wedge over my cup. A droplet of juice spurted into my eye. As I blinked away the stinging, I wondered how Martin, an accused thief and a pain in the you-know-what, dared put Nick down. I hated Martin's snobbish mentality. I imagined he considered Nick and me lower class—beneath him.

"Maybe he's just trying to impress one of our passengers," Roxanne said. Out of the corner of my eye, I could see her tilting her head in my direction.

"Whoever it is should be careful." Martin upped his volume. "No point getting mixed up with a gigolo who might take advantage."

"Yes, Father," said Roxanne. "I'll keep that in mind."

"I didn't mean you. You look like you can take care of yourself."

"I'll try not to be insulted by your remark. But you're right. I don't fall for malarkey, not that a smooth-talker has fed me any recently. Maybe because I'm bigger than most of them."

I wanted to point out that husky Drew outweighed her by fifty pounds and Martin stood a head taller.

"I like women with meat on their bones," Martin said. "Not scrawny little imps."

Was he referring to me? I was no beanpole, mind you. But at one hundred and twenty-five pounds, Martin might think I was. Leave it to him to find yet another characteristic to dislike about me. Not that I cared what he thought. Not in the least.

I sipped my tea and found it too acidic. Why had I added lemon juice instead of my usual tablespoon of milk? I took hold of the creamer and dribbled in a splash. As it combined with the tea, it curdled, ruining my drink. I looked around for our waitress to ask her for a fresh cup, but she was nowhere to be seen. Had she followed Nick outside?

Hal got to his feet and said, "Time to go, people. We need to get moving."

The choir finished their snacks and straggled back to the bus, where Nick stood speaking on his cell phone. No waitress hanging on his arm, after all.

"Are we ready?" He quickly folded his phone and opened the coach's door.

"No thanks to you," Martin muttered.

"Play nice." Roxanne bumped him jokingly. I wondered how many people dared speak to Martin as an equal. But that was audacious Roxanne for you—afraid of no one. I could use a dose of her gumption.

As we drove on, my gaze swept from left to right to catch sights of quaint farms, thatched roofs, and distant church spires. Never had I been more entertained. So why did I have this itchy feeling like something bad was looming in the distance? Maybe I was picking up on Hal's apprehensions about making it to our hotel and performance on time. Or was I experiencing a case of nerves before singing? No, my heart wasn't pounding or my pulse racing. Instead, a heavy feeling dominated my stomach, like I was watching a scary movie and waiting for the hammer to drop. Which was silly. Why was I wasting gray matter inventing problems? Everything was peachy, what my mother would call *vunderlekh* on the occasions she spoke Yiddish—tidbits left over from her German-born parents, who moved to the States in the 1930s.

Once in Cambridge, Nick pulled to a stop in a gravel lot crowded with cars and other tour busses.

"Don't be late." Hal tapped the face of his watch.

Off the bus, the choir scattered in gaggles. Four of the men tagged after Clare like she was Scarlet O'Hara. The altos, save Roxanne, and our three second sopranos strode off purposely. Bonnie walked with Marci and our other soprano, Shirley, in her early sixties, the receptionist at church. Under Nick's supervision, Roxanne, Drew, and I crossed a footbridge spanning the River Cam, moving toward the center of town. Ahead of us marched Martin, his gait stiff, reminding me of the Tin Man from *The Wizard of Oz*. Didn't he need a heart?

"I think Martin mentioned he attended Trinity College," Roxanne said as we watched him disappear into the street teaming with tourists, college students, and shoppers. "He said something about finding an old professor."

"Trinity is Isaac Newton's alma mater," Nick said. "Would you like to see it?"

"Let's go somewhere else." I wanted to avoid running into Martin.

"Certainly, I'll take you to see a very important example of late medieval architecture where the famous choir sings. You might have heard them. Their Christmas service is broadcast on radio and television."

He steered us along cobbled streets to the chapel at King's College, a splendid stone structure ten times as large and ten times more beautiful than our church at home. Entering, I breathed in air alive with color and light. Soaring stained-glass windows holding dazzling magentas, turquoise, and golds spread across two-thirds of the walls. The vaulted ceiling looked like it was made of lace.

Nick stood at my side. "The fan ceiling is supported by twenty-two buttresses," he said. "It was completed in 1515."

I glanced over at him and admired his strong profile. "We're lucky to have you with us."

"Yes, aren't we?" Roxanne stood on my other side.

"It is I who am fortunate," Nick said, "to be traveling with such lovely companions."

"You've got that right." Drew glanced at Roxanne. "If I were at home, I'd be staring at my computer screen."

"I thought you loved working at Microsoft." Roxanne turned to him.

"I'm not with them anymore. I set up my own software business. But I'd still rather be here with you."

"Sir, are you flirting with me?"

"Uh, no." Drew's freckled face reddened. "I meant I like being here with the choir."

"Phooey," Roxanne said, her blushing cheeks matching his. "I thought someone was finally coming on to me."

Leaving Roxanne and Drew, I wandered over to examine an intricately carved wooden screen surrounding the huge baroque organ. I marveled at how every detail had been executed with precision and grace. It was hard to believe mere human hands had crafted something so exquisite. My mind couldn't grasp how natural selection prevailed when it came to the arts. Why were some people oozing with talent and others bone dry? Mom claimed God gifted every person with the potential to be creative, that musicians, artists, and craftsmen—even gardeners and chefs—were God's instruments here on Earth.

When I was nine, after my father went AWOL, Mom stopped attending synagogue and became a Bible-toter, much to her parents' distress. They threatened to cut her out of their will. Not that I blamed my grandparents. Mom dropped most of their traditions, what seemed like her heritage. She insisted I go to Sunday school and I continued to attend church as an adult, but never completely digested the New Testament's rigmarole. It all fit together too precisely, like a fairytale. I knew from experience, life wasn't a birthday present tied neatly with fancy ribbon. Why, if I hadn't taken charge of my life, I would have drowned in my sorrow years ago.

Nick approached me, interrupting my thoughts. He slipped his hand under my elbow, a gesture seeming too familiar, yet not offensive. "Are you hungry?" he asked.

"Ravenous." I stepped away, gaining several feet between us. "I'm used to snacking all day, one reason I bring crackers and fruit to school for my students to munch on."

"Lucky children to have you for their teacher. Let's have lunch."

We found a restaurant two blocks away, brimming with tourists and students. After a short wait, we squeezed into seats at a window table and spent the rest of our allotted two hours in conversation. My soup broth tasted of fresh basil and stewed vegetables. The rustic bread and creamy unsalted butter melted in my mouth. Every flavor seemed tastier than anything at home. Was I turning into an Anglophile or was my enthusiasm stemming from attentive Nick, his chair fitting snugly against mine?

Across the table, Roxanne and Drew were discussing their miserable high school years. "I went to a school where kids drove BMWs and Mercedes," Roxanne said. "I was the poorest kid there."

"No one rich at my school," Drew said, between bites of his steak and kidney pie. "And there were eight hundred in my graduating class."

"Wow, that's bigger than my entire student body. Lots of cute girls?"

"A few, but I was too shy to ask them out." He stared at his plate. "I didn't even make it to the prom."

"Me neither. I sewed myself a dress, but didn't have a date."

"Too bad we didn't know each other back then." He snuck a peek at her. "I would have taken you."

"That's sweet to say, but it's too late now." Her eyes turned glassy, making me wonder if she still harbored sadness from missing that horribly inflated evening. I remembered, right before my prom, I'd started dating foul-mouthed Bart Peterson, who was later arrested for grand theft auto. I hadn't wanted to go out with him, but with the prom nearing I simply had to say yes. Better I was on the arm of a hood headed for prison than home alone. And I'll give him this—he brought me a corsage, which I guessed one of his parents had purchased. I paid for the photos, but by the time they arrived, Bart had transferred to an alternative school— or was it a detention home for juvenile delinquents?

"How do you like the tour so far?" Nick said to me.

"It couldn't be better." Except for my disagreeable roommate. "I've always wanted to see where the characters in my British novels lived."

"You teach English?"

"No, elementary school. Thirty squirrelly third graders I adore." As the waitress refilled my glass, I thought about the turns my life had taken. Although I liked my job, I'd dreamt of being a stay-at-home mom with a minivan full of children.

"I got my teaching degree out of necessity," I told him. "To pay the bills."

"What about your son's father? Does he refuse to take care of his own child?"

"My husband died in an automobile accident." I wouldn't mention that Jeff had left me responsible for numerous debts.

Nick's fingers covered his lips for a moment. "Forgive me, please. I had no business asking personal questions."

"That's okay. It doesn't bother me anymore." If I said it enough times, it might be true.

"We should return to the bus." He waved to the waitress for the check.

I glanced out the window and spotted Martin walking with a bald man in his mid-seventies, who spoke rapidly, his hands illustrating his words. Martin's gaze sifted through the crowd. What was up with him?

Nick noticed Martin. "I wonder what those two are talking about," he said under his breath.

"I was thinking the same thing."

CHAPTER 10

THE BUS JOGGLED over the uneven cobbled roads of Norwich's oldest section and rolled up in front of our hotel, a stone building one block from a spectacular church Nick told us was Norwich Cathedral.

Once off the bus, I stared up at the cathedral's towering spire, jutting up against a fading sky.

As Hal disembarked, Clare asked him, "Is that where we're singing tonight?"

Hal paused a moment to gaze at the steeple. "Sorry, no. We'll be in a smaller church, but I'm sure it will be more than adequate."

He led the way into the hotel's wood-paneled lobby. "You'll be in with Clare again," he notified me as the clerk at the front desk handed out keys.

A surge of frustration dragged the corners of my mouth down. "Now just a minute. Roxanne and I signed up to be roommates over a month ago."

"Think of it this way. Choirs are like baseball teams."
His glance floated to the ceiling, then back to me.
"Team members are asked to play different positions
from time to time." Was he making up the lame analogy
as he went along?

"Since when has Marco Gonzales played outfield?"
I folded my arms to keep myself from collapsing.

"Well, I don't know, but I'm sure he would if his
coach asked him."

"If I can't room with Roxanne, how about Bonnie
or Marci or Shirley?"

"We don't have time to squabble about roommates.
You should be getting yourself ready for our first performance. Why, I'd think you'd be thrilled to share a
room with Clare on this auspicious occasion."

I could hear Mom telling me to pick my battles.
"Okay, Hal," I said. "One more night." After all, when
we got home he might decide he had too many sopranos and cut me from the team—I mean, choir.

Riding the lift to the second floor, I reminded
myself I was supposed to love my neighbor. But Clare
reminded me of the stuck-up girls from high school
who only dated football players and who snubbed girls
like me. That kind of narrow-mindedness shouldn't
bother me anymore, but it did. Even in my students
I could spot the future queen bees and the girls who,
through no fault of their own, would be excluded.

I lugged my suitcase down the hall, found room two
twenty-nine, and opened the door.

Clare stood in front of the mirror affixed to an
armoire fiddling with her hair. "You again?"

"Clare, if you'd prefer someone else, please make your wishes known to Hal."

"I did. In fact, I asked for a private room. My mother warned me ahead of time hotel rooms in Europe are smaller than in America. This one's barely big enough for one person."

She was right. The space was cramped, and the two twin beds sat only feet from each other. Clare had already laid her purse and jacket on the one nearest the window. I placed my suitcase on the luggage stand crouching at the other bed's foot and unzipped the suitcase's lid.

Raking a comb through her hair, Clare let out a theatrical sigh, then tossed the comb on her bed. With her shoulders hunched, she seemed smaller, almost vulnerable.

"What's up?" I said.

Her nostrils flared like I'd offered her roasted garbage. "Nothing." Then she sneezed three times rapid-fire.

I found a box of Kleenex and handed her a tissue. I noticed her wistful expression and thought she might be homesick. "Want to call your folks?"

"No way!" She must have heard the harshness in her voice, because she added in monotone, "That's not a good idea. What time is it back home? They might still be sleeping—or already at work."

I changed into my black knit dress—midi length and flattering, but plain enough to wear to funerals. I thought about my years of experience salving Cooper's hurt feelings and nursing his ailments, not to mention coming to the rescue of the kids in my class. But with Clare, I felt helpless.

I forced a yawn to open my throat. "We have vocal warm-ups in twenty minutes. Do you feel good enough to sing?"

"Of course." She blew her nose, then coughed. "I'm allergic to dust mites. This hotel is crawling with them." She threw her wadded tissue at the wastepaper basket in the corner, missing it. "They probably haven't swapped pillows or mattresses in thirty years."

I didn't buy her explanation. I had a dust mite allergy and sneezed when vacuuming but wasn't experiencing symptoms. If Clare were one of my students, I'd predict she would stay home sick the next day with a cold.

The choir met in the lobby, then we followed Hal for several blocks. "Nick should be here leading us." He glanced at the directions to the church printed on a sheet of paper. "What if we got lost and never found the place?"

Bonnie took hold of the paper and turned it right side up. "It should be around the next corner."

Ahead of me, Clare shimmied in her black narrow-hemmed skirt and scoop-necked top, revealing a crease of cleavage, even though Hal had asked the women to dress modestly.

Clare's spiked heels battled the uneven pavement. As Drew passed her, she latched onto his arm for support. "Would a gentleman help a lady in distress?" she said with a faky southern drawl, and he slowed his pace to assist her. "If I'd known how far away the church was,

I would have worn hiking boots," she told him, then giggled.

I'd seen Clare's wardrobe and I knew her most practical footwear was a pair of flimsy sandals. Hal had warned us to be prepared to walk, which is why I wore my one-inch Naturalizer pumps, when in fact I could use extra height. Except for diminutive Bonnie, who never stood with the choir, I was the shortest member.

At the corner, Clare said, "This is it?" and discarded Drew's arm like he was a mugger after her purse.

I rounded the bend and watched Hal make a beeline for the small gray structure and couldn't help but compare it to the cathedral we'd admired earlier. But who cared? I figured the smaller the church, the fewer people would hear me if I goofed up. And Nick had mentioned that this church was constructed three hundred years ago, when America was still colonies. I was awestruck by the age of the buildings we'd seen. All this time I'd thought my 1947 home in Seattle was old.

After dragging open the front door, Hal stepped inside. His gaze shot around the plain interior. His face sagged with disappointment. "Let's get ourselves warmed up, people." He located an empty room with a piano and the choir members positioned themselves.

Bonnie plunked the piano keys and found it out of tune. "Sounds like my Siamese cat," she said.

"I'm sure the organ will be in better shape," Hal told her. "But you'd better give it a test."

"Good idea." Bonnie sprang to her feet and scurried out the door. Minutes later, the organ began pumping out Bach's "Toccata and Fugue in D Minor"—great

Dracula music. Humble and unassuming Bonnie was a master.

Clare plodded to the end of the soprano section next to me. "Is this Hal's idea of more than adequate?" she muttered.

Martin arrived and stood on the other side of Clare.

"Hello, there," she said, dipping her chin and sending him a pretty smile. If I wasn't mistaken, she was batting her eyelashes.

He nodded. "How are you this evening?"

"Fine, now that you're here," she said. He gave her a doubtful look, and she added, "I can't wait to hear your solo," and fluttered her lashes again. Maybe those two were a match made in heaven. Or Hades, depending how you viewed it.

Insisting the voice needed to connect with the breath before a sound was attempted, Hal started our usual stretches and breathing warm-ups. Then he sat at the piano and we sang the scales—at first quietly, then with gusto.

"All right," he said, once Bonnie had returned and taken her place. "You sound in fine voice. No need to go over every piece since we're short on time. Let's skip the Handel and the Vivaldi. You know those two well enough. But there are several tricky spots in the others. I'd like to go over them with Mr. Spear."

Hal rifled through his music, then made a small bow in Martin's direction. "Let's hear Martin's solo first." He gave Bonnie the downbeat and her hands moved across the keyboard.

"If with all your heart you truly seek me." Martin's voice shimmered, clear and bright on top, round and robust at the bottom.

I imagined a breeze floating among summer leaves, a brook babbling down a hillside, birds singing to the sky. Listening to such beauty, I stood spellbound. Sure, Martin was snooty and obnoxious, but I couldn't remember hearing a finer voice.

When Martin finished, Hal said, "Ah, how I love Mendelssohn." He flattened his hands together, bringing his fingertips to his chin. "Particularly when it's sung like that."

Martin nodded, but seemed uncertain, no satisfaction shining in his face. If I could sing that well, my mouth wouldn't stop grinning. What was wrong with him? Could he find contentment in nothing?

A few minutes later, Drew went out to check on the audience. "They're beginning to show up," he said on his return. "Two vans just pulled in from a retirement home. About forty people so far."

Clare's lip curled. "A bunch of old fogies on their way to play bingo?"

Fine with me, I thought. Older listeners might be more appreciative and forgiving.

Hal narrowed his eyes at her. "Every audience deserves our best."

Minutes before we were scheduled to sing, he asked us to bow our heads. A circle formed naturally, and we held hands, as was our custom. I somehow ended up between Roxanne and Martin, not a touchy-feely kind of guy. His palms were clammy and his grip lifeless.

Clare stood on his other side. Maybe he was grasping her hand ardently.

As Hal prayed aloud, my skin tightened and my heart rate mushroomed, gathering too much blood in the bottom of my esophagus—my old enemy pre-performance jitters. I drew a cleansing breath, but my thoughts began spinning. What if during the concert I sang out of turn? In my mind, I could hear my voice blaring across the silence like a razor ripping through cloth. And what if I sang the wrong words? I'd done it before—manufactured words that made no sense—but so far Hal hadn't noticed. As I tried to swallow down the growing lump in my throat, I reassured myself I'd have the music in hand. Keep your eyes on the music, I told myself. And Hal—don't forget to watch him.

"It's time, people," Hal said solemnly, as he always did before we made our entrance.

As we formed a prearranged line, my nervousness ratcheted up another notch. I followed Clare into the choir loft at the front of the sanctuary. Trying not to look at the audience, I stared at Hal until he lifted his baton to start the first anthem. Notes began flying out of the organ pipes. It felt like a locomotive was barreling down on me, but I jumped on at the right moment and began to sing. The vaulted ceilings sucked up our voices and reverberated them back, amplifying our volume— one being with many parts, expanding with each crescendo. The acoustics couldn't be better.

In the third piece, Martin's solo lines rang with passion. Surprised he could express feelings other than anger or indifference, I glanced over at him. His features had softened and he wore an uncharacteristic look of humility. A façade he'd learned to wear onstage?

It was time for Clare's solo by Gounod. "The king of love my shepherd is." Rather than flowing through the music with her usual ease, her voice sounded like a taut rubber band. Her final high notes were strained, almost sharp. After, she cleared her throat to contain a cough.

Hal pursed his lips in her direction, then signaled Bonnie to start the introduction to the next piece. Time seemed to dissolve and soon we were singing the last anthem by Rutter.

"The Lord is my shepherd..." I longed to lie down in a lush green pasture, I thought, beside still water. I was tired, parched. Not just physically, but emotionally.

"Yea, though I walk through the valley of the shadow of death..." Death was a dark hole, my Jeff's candle forever snuffed.

"I will fear no evil..." Roxanne had diabetes. How could she not be afraid?

"And I will dwell in the house of the Lord forever."

Hal was staring at me, his eyes discharging electrical currents, zapping me out of my musings. How long had I been singing on automatic pilot? I refocused my eyes until his features sharpened again.

"And ever," I sang, watching Hal mouth the words.

He had an uncanny way of knowing when a singer's mind was adrift. His gaze darted down to the bass section. He winced. I figured he'd heard a pitch, vowel, or dynamic that was less than perfect.

At last, he lowered his baton for the final time and smiled at us with raised eyebrows—his signal for well done—then turned to the audience.

Phew, I'd made it through the performance.

I finally let my gaze rest on the faces of the almost one hundred people in the pews, and was shocked to spot the man who'd argued with Martin this morning sitting in the tenth row.

CHAPTER 11

OUTSIDE THE CHURCH in the cool evening air, Roxanne swooped over to me. "Did you see that guy in the audience, about a dozen rows back?" Her mouth was pinched.

"The one who was sitting next to Clare on the jet?" I said, and she nodded.

I didn't want to admit I was too scared to scan the audience's faces until we were finished singing. It was just as well I hadn't noticed that lowlife, until the end of the performance. His presence would have distracted me.

"Strange he happened to be in this church tonight." I observed the other choir members and a few people from the audience on the street but didn't see him. "It couldn't be coincidence that he's here. The odds would be one million to one."

I remembered his confronting Martin in our hotel, a scene out of a movie about the Mob. "And why was he badgering Martin in London? What possible connection would those two have?"

Looking tired, Roxanne buttoned her jacket and slid her hands into her pockets. "Maybe Bonnie was right and the guy's a member of the paparazzi."

"Then where's his camera?"

"In his cell phone? And he could be carrying a hidden tape recorder."

Clare hurried past us toward the hotel like a woman on a mission. Big plans tonight, I wondered, or just hungry for dinner? Or was she avoiding Hal after her flawed performance?

"Clare is a head-turner," Roxanne said, following her at a leisurely speed. "The icon of beauty in the western world."

I fell in next to Roxanne. "True." I watched Clare's ankles wobble as she traversed the cobbled pavement. "She seems to cast a spell over every male she meets. But isn't our mystery man too old to be chasing her around? He must be fifty-something. Or does Clare seem young because I'm nearing middle-age?"

"Nah, they say sixty's the new middle-age."

"Thanks for the kind thought, but I can't picture my sixty-two-year-old mother as being middle-aged. She's a sweet *bobe*—a granny—who listens to Frank Sinatra, crochets teapot warmers, and goes to bed early. Which is fine with me, the way I like her. Stable. Reliable."

Drew wandered up behind us and placed a large hand on each of our shoulders. "That was a great concert. And our fearless leader seems happy." Meaning Hal.

"Yeah, we're officially international singers," Roxanne said, her green eyes coming alive. "Next thing we know, we'll be getting invitations to sing in Paris and Rome."

"I like the sound of that," he said. "But I doubt anyone famous will hear us on this trip."

My mind scrolled back to our performance and I was thankful I'd made it through the difficult spots without a hitch. But I knew better than to think I could let down my guard. We had four more concerts in the next four days. When Mom taught me to drive a car, she told me to never become complacent behind the wheel because I'd be twice as susceptible to having an accident. I sure didn't want a wreck in front of Hal, who struck me as a man who'd never forget mistakes. Tough to have for a husband and father. But he hadn't abandoned his wife and children, which earned him my respect.

Martin and Hal marched past us. "If I were you," Martin said, all business, "I'd start planning ahead."

"I suppose you're right." Hal lengthened his stride to keep up. "Dear, dear. What should I do?"

"Well, how many other sopranos do you have?"

"Only three. Let's see, there's Marci and Shirley and what's-her-name?"

Was he referring to little old me?

Nick was waiting just ahead. "Bravo," he said as the two men approached him. "*Bravisimo*! Beautiful music."

Hal slowed his pace to accept the praise, but Martin kept going—not even a nod.

Then Nick stepped toward me. "I was sitting in the back, but I think I could hear your voice," he said.

"I'm not sure that's possible." A blessing because it meant I hadn't sung out of turn or tripped over my own feet on the way in. "Maybe you heard Clare."

"One thing for sure, Jessica, you were the most beautiful to watch."

Was he for real? Unlikely, but his solicitousness was a lovely opposite of aloof Martin.

He moved closer, his arm grazing mine. "Are you hungry? I know a little restaurant nearby. May I take you out to dinner?"

Would supper with Nick in a public restaurant hint of impropriety? I asked myself as I watched the back of Hal's balding head. I elbowed Roxanne, who walked alongside of me. "What do you think?"

"Sure, go ahead, girlfriend. But don't stay out late. We have to get up early in the morning."

"Okay," I told Nick. "Let me get changed."

"But you look lovely as you are."

"I should save my only black dress for performances." And I needed time to decide how far I wanted this relationship to go. If it was a relationship. Was I taking a casual flirtation too seriously?

Back in the hotel room twenty minutes later, Clare emerged from the bathroom in her red lacy slip and high heels. It was hard not to stare.

"We had a full house," I said. "The audience seemed to enjoy itself."

"Big deal." She kicked off her shoes, one hitting the wall with a thud. "I wanted the news media to cover us."

"Hoping for your big break?"

"Yes, and I thought with Martin singing we'd get some type of coverage." She flopped down on her bed, her limbs stretching like a cat. "But leave it to Hal not to notify anyone ahead of time that we were traveling with a famous tenor."

My mind searched for a tactful way to ask about the man from the jet. "I noticed that gentleman you sat next to on the plane in the audience. Who's he?"

She flipped on her side and propped her head in one hand. "His name's Jerry, here on business. Some kind of insurance company dispute."

"And he drove all the way to Norwich to hear you sing?"

"We're not that far from London. Last year a man flew from Los Angeles to Seattle to take me out to dinner, and he let me order anything on the menu, even the Maine lobster. Another time a man drove down from Vancouver just to meet me at Starbucks for coffee. And he brought me flowers."

I believed men would chase after her. But as far as I could see, Jerry spelled trouble.

With only a few minutes to spruce myself up for dinner with Nick, I changed into slacks and a mauve-colored blouse that gave me a natural-looking blush that had faded years ago. Nothing I wouldn't do for any man I went out with. And what was wrong with Nick's finding me attractive?

"I don't mean to be nosy." I zipped up my slacks and fastening the button. "But what do you know about Jerry?"

"As much as you know about Nick, who slobbers over you like a Saint Bernard on a dish of ice cream."

I could feel heat rising up my throat. Had Nick and I been making spectacles of ourselves? Or did Clare resent not being the center of every male's attention? Maybe there was one man in the world who preferred short brunettes over leggy blondes with hourglass figures.

"I'm sure the tour company checked Nick's credentials and background when they hired him." I hoped so, anyway.

"Just because I don't know Jerry's social security number doesn't make him a serial killer who's out to kidnap me." She barked a cough, which seemed to take her by surprise, because she didn't cover her mouth. "If anything, he should be avoiding me. I'm getting sick. You heard me in the concert. My vocal cords are shot."

I had to agree that her voice had sounded forced, but to keep from coming off as critical I said, "I've never sung half as well on a good day." Which was true. Her worst was better than my best.

Her hand wrapped her neck, then her thumb and middle finger massaged her glands. "The inside of my throat feels like sandpaper. It hurts to swallow." She felt her forehead. "I'm coming down with something."

A wave of compassion washed through my heart. I considered how terrified I'd be singing her solo. As I glanced in the mirror to smooth my hair, I noticed her palpating her throat again.

"It seems like stress strikes the part of your body you need the most," I said. One Sunday morning a couple of months ago, my own throat refused to produce more than a frog's croak. I skipped church and spent the day on my couch shrouded under a blanket, and it paid off. The next day, I felt healthy enough to go to work.

"Maybe you should climb in bed early and give your vocal cords a break until tomorrow night. I can get dinner sent up here."

"I am hungry," she said. "But I have…an appointment."

With Jerry, I presumed.

"Tell you what, I'll stay in tonight and keep you company." I hated to give up my date with Nick, but it would benefit the whole choir if Clare's voice recouped. And what good could come from her seeing Jerry?

The phone jangled.

"That's for me." She popped up to grab it as if expecting a call from the million-dollar sweepstakes. Turning toward the wall, she whispered, "All right, but just for a little while." Then she hung up and wiggled out of her slip, left it a puddle on the floor.

"Who was that?" I asked.

"No one you know." She got busy changing into skinny jeans, a V-neck sweater that dipped way low, and her coat. Without a farewell she exited the room.

Ten minutes later, I hurried down to the hotel lobby. I spied Nick leaning against the counter chatting with the receptionist. Nick stood tall when he noticed me; an appreciative look spread across his face as he watched me walk toward him.

"Sorry I took so long," I said. "Clare was having a problem."

"Really? I saw her pass by a moment ago with a smile on her face."

"She's meeting someone. I hope she'll be all right." I was beginning to sound more and more like Mom, whom I regarded a fussbudget. Next thing I knew I'd be saying *"Mazel tov,"* to newlyweds, humming *"Hava Nagila,"* and talking to old ladies in the grocery store, which used to embarrass me no end.

"Let's not worry about Clare," he said. "Tonight—"

"Glad I found you" Hal launched over to Nick. "Will you join us for dinner here in the hotel?"

Nick shook his head. "I was planning—"

"But I have several questions about tomorrow that can't wait." Hal turned his head to include me. "Jessica, you'll be dining with us, won't you?" Proving he knew my name. "I'll be making announcements you won't want to miss."

As Hal steered Nick toward the dining room, I followed at a distance. I was tempted to remind Hal that tonight was listed as free time on the schedule, but I didn't want to jeopardize Nick's job or seem anxious to be alone with him.

"Ms. Nash?" I spun around to see Martin approaching me. He held his hands behind his back, as if worried about my biting him. After what had happened, I probably looked like a coiled rattlesnake.

"May I have a word with you?" He glanced at the carpet, then his gaze found mine. "About last night—the key business. I don't believe I thanked you properly."

The incident seemed to have happened weeks ago. "Forget about it," I said. "I have."

CHAPTER 12

THE NEXT MORNING, I rushed through breakfast, so I would have time to wander the medieval
streets of Norwich. Several blocks from the hotel, my
eyes traced an ancient stone windowsill. I peered into
a darkened bookshop.

Behind the aged, imperfect glass sat a white cat,
watching me. "Good morning, Kitty," I said.

"Good morning, Jessica." Nick had snuck up on me;
he must have seen me leaving the hotel.

"I wish things were open." I leaned toward the window
and saw a maze of tall bookshelves. "I could spend hours
in there." Not that I'd even started the book I'd brought
on the trip. My dog-eared copy of *Rebecca*, which I hadn't
read since college, had gotten as far as the bed stand last
night. But my eyes had drooped closed as soon as I'd
crawled between the sheets. I hadn't even heard Clare
return, sometime after eleven.

"At home I read every night," I said, noticing a pair of swallows flitting up in the eaves of the building across the street. "I'm a hopeless romantic."

The corners of his mouth curved up. "How delightful."

"I mean I like to read romance novels." A vein of love—lost or found—wove its way through all my favorite books.

He leaned closer. "I hope you do more than read about romance."

I wouldn't admit to anyone but Mom how long I'd been a spectator in the bleachers, watching others play the game of love.

We stepped to the next building, housing a flower shop. A sign in the window read, *Tell her you love her with roses.*

"A beautiful woman like you should never be alone," he said. "We'll change that tonight and have our dinner together."

Last night he and I had dined at opposite ends of a long table.

I felt myself blush, even though I figured he'd used the phrase many times before. "All right. Sorry about Hal. He's a hard man to say no to."

He took my elbow. "It is I who is sorry. But I must be available when duty calls."

We continued at a leisurely pace, passing a dress shop with a mannequin in the window clad in a sequined evening gown I'd love to wear while singing a solo at some posh gala. I shook my head. When would I give up that fantasy?

A crinkly-haired older woman walking two brown-and-white King Charles cavalier spaniels approached us. Nick and I hugged the white plaster building to give her room on the narrow sidewalk. Once she'd departed, Nick asked, "How is our Mr. Spear acting?"

"Compared to what?" When I'd seen Martin that morning, he'd been his usual un-charming self—pretentious and persnickety and private.

"Perhaps you could find out more about him?" Nick's voice went up at the end of his sentence, like a question.

"Why would you care?" I said. "He's at the bottom of my priority list."

"And where do I stand? Near the top, I hope." He was unabashedly straightforward, unlike many men back home. But what should I say? On this morning, I couldn't think of a man I found more attractive or engaging than Nick.

"Jessie?" Roxanne called, saving me from answering him. Trekking our way, she was panting like the kids in the schoolyard playing tag. "I'm glad I ran into you." Her cheeks glowed scarlet and her forehead glistened with perspiration. "I was walking off breakfast but got lost. I thought if I kept to my right, I'd end up at the hotel again, but that didn't work. I lost all sense of direction."

Nick raised his hand at a forty-five-degree angle to draw Roxanne's attention to the cathedral. "Use the spire as your guide. It's over three hundred feet high."

Roxanne glanced past his fingertips. "Oops, I didn't think to look up." She giggled and mopped her brow.

"Guess that's why you're leading us instead of the other way around."

I linked arms with her. "You seem exhausted. Are you all right?"

"Of course." She spoke into my ear. "You're not supposed to worry about me or tell anyone."

"I'll keep things to myself, but I can't guarantee I won't worry." Chill air swirled through my nostrils and into the back of my throat. As I expelled my breath, a thousand bottled-up anxieties concerning Cooper, my singing, my job, and my future, inundated my mind, making me feel helpless and out of control. I rarely admitted even to myself how small and weak I was.

The three of us rounded the last corner. I spotted Hal and Martin up ahead pacing in front of the hotel. Both men glared at us as we approached. Martin rolled back his jacket sleeve to peer at his stainless-steel-and-gold watch, then shot Nick a look of contempt.

"It's about time," Martin said, wagging a finger. "You should have unlocked the bus, so we could load our luggage."

Nick glanced at his own wristwatch. "It's still early." His eyes became dark slivers, but he smiled, his lips covering his teeth. "You should be inside enjoying another cup of coffee." He pulled a ring of keys out of his jacket pocket, jiggled them in the air for Martin to see, and unlocked the cargo door. He grabbed Martin's suitcase and pitched it in; it hit the back wall, then fell on its side. Then he picked up Hal's bag and carefully placed it in front of Martin's.

Hal strode toward the hotel. I jogged to catch up with him and said, "Could you make sure I have a new roommate tonight?" His frown told me now was not the time to be asking favors.

"We're keeping the status quo," he said. "If Clare's coming down with the flu I don't want her infecting the whole choir. Don't even ask me again."

I wanted to echo Mom's saying, "What am I—chopped liver?" but figured he didn't care what I thought; I was the newest member of the choir, low man on the totem pole.

I dashed back to my room to get my suitcase. Clare had already packed and was gone, although I found her slinky slip on the floor next to her bed. As I scooped it up, a small piece of paper twirled to the ground. I couldn't help but read the name "Jerry," followed by a string of numbers, the area code 212, from the USA. New York City? I folded the paper in half and stowed it and the slip in my suitcase, then headed out.

As I boarded the bus, I found Clare perched behind Nick again. She glanced up at me like I was a pesky gnat that should fly away before she swatted it. I decided to wait to mention her slip and the telephone number. Plenty of time later.

I wandered further back and settled next to Roxanne, who seemed to have recovered from her over-exertion. Within fifteen minutes, Nick was driving the bus along the coast, giving us dramatic views of the North Sea.

"We're coming to Blakeney, a fishing village noted for its flint stone houses and bird and wildlife preserve," he announced. He parked by the side of the road. "We'll stay here forty-five minutes. I suggest you wear your jackets."

I descended the steps. The wind blasted in gusts of damp chilliness, whipping my hair and billowing my jacket. I watched most of the group wander off to explore the village, but I stopped to gaze across the water at the marshy wetlands preserve. The wind and crashing waves sounded like distant bagpipes. As I breathed in the aroma of drying seaweed and moist sand, I recalled as a child going to Cannon Beach in Oregon every summer, before my parents split up. I'd stood on the flat, hard sand—watery foam washing between my toes—staring out to sea. The ocean seemed to expand forever. I'd decided it wasn't possible that the earth was round, the way my teacher said. It was flat, and I stood safely at the center of it. All that mattered was the salty smell and my father scooping me up and swinging me around in tears of laughter and joy. His arms had been strong, and I'd felt safe and loved—small but fearless.

Then Dad was gone, and summers were spent in town, with Mom saying the distant beach was too far to drive to by herself. Several years later, we returned to Cannon Beach with Mom's girlfriend, who had kids my age. I remembered my mother and her friend lounging on beach chairs on the dunes with fashion magazines and lemonade. I felt timid standing alone at the ocean's roar. I'd stared at the horizon and known the earth was a round ball held together by gravity, no matter what it looked like. Adult logic controlled my brain, squelching my curiosity and childhood dreams. Daddy lived with another woman, now his wife, and cradled a new child in his arms.

Two rogue tears leaked out my eyes and streaked down my cheeks. I closed my lids, letting the breeze dry my face. When I opened my eyes, Martin stood at my side. He looked like a silent-film actor, his lips moving but his words inaudible over the wind.

I cupped my ear. "What did you say?"

"Ms. Nash, I may ask for your assistance in the near future."

I peered up into his face, trying to catch his meaning. Why would he need me? To shine his shoes or fetch his paper?

"It may come to nothing," he said, "but should I need you to carry something for me, would you be available?"

"What do you mean? On the bus or through customs?"

He rubbed his jawbone. "I'd rather not say at this point."

His request sounded fishy. I remembered the hideous Pan Am crash over Lockerbie, Scotland. After that, authorities warned well-meaning travelers never to transport items without knowing the exact contents.

"How can I possibly answer your question unless you're more specific?" I was getting a stiff neck looking up at him. "What's this all about?"

His head jerked back, like I'd slapped him. "Never mind," he said. "This was a poor idea." He was acting like I'd done something wrong when in fact he could be some kind of terrorist. Maybe he'd pegged me as the easiest target in the choir. Which I resented. I liked to think I came across as level-headed.

I caught sight of a dozen terns, their black fluid shapes skimming the water's surface. As I watched them, my mind weighed Nick's appraisal of Martin. I could see Martin's guilt-ridden face splashed across the front of the *Enquire*. I didn't want to become his accomplice. I didn't want to be his anything. But I could play dumb and ask him leading questions. As a teacher I was skilled at extracting information from unwilling mouths.

But when I turned to him he was gone.

"It's too cold out here," Nick said, striding toward me from the other direction. He held his hands together and blew into them.

The sky lay overcast, but the water's surface began to sparkle as a ray of sunshine beamed down between the cumulus clouds.

"You've brought us good weather," he said.

"I thought women were bad luck at sea."

He laughed. "Some, perhaps. But I predict you'll bring me nothing but good fortune."

"THE QUEEN HAS one of her country homes nearby," Nick said over the speaker when we boarded again. He cranked the transmission into first. "We're going to have a look around in her absence." He pulled out onto the curving road, followed the rugged coast-line west, then veered south.

I sat in silent admiration as we neared Sandringham House, an imposing four-story structure with a sand-stone facade.

"Just think, people," Hal said. "The royal family comes here." He was the first to the door. "I don't suppose any of them will be around today?" he asked Nick.

"If they were, we wouldn't be allowed anywhere near, for security reasons," Nick said. "The queen will not be back until Christmas."

The choir set off to explore the grounds, bunching in clusters: Clare with her male entourage, Hal cornering Marci and Shirley to lecture them on Handel's early operas, and the easy-going altos—Gloria, Florence, who sang soprano before hitting sixty, and thirty-year-old Leticia—flocking after Nick. Martin and Drew chatted about politics in the Middle East.

Roxanne and I strolled past meticulously pruned yew and boxwood hedges. Paths meandered through plantings of fuchsia-colored rhododendrons and pink camellias.

"This is where I want to spend next Christmas," Roxanne told me. "Sure would be more fun than Christmas Day at my folks'." She let the others get ahead of us. "Why do my parents think everyone's going to magically get along once a year?"

I didn't have an answer for her. Would it be better to have my parents fighting around the tree or living on opposite sides of town, as they did? My mother and father might as well live on opposite ends of the country; they hadn't spoken for years, that I knew of.

"Too bad we don't all take the week before Christmas to talk things out," I said, thinking of the methods I used for conflict resolution in the classroom. "You know, have an armistice first."

"We don't talk in our house," Roxanne said. "With my folks it's the silent treatment or yelling. They have a routine. Mom buys the six-packs of Bud, then complains that Dad's a drunk. Dad says Mom's a slob but won't give her money for new clothes or take her out anywhere nice. Get the picture?"

"That doesn't sound fun." I gazed up to Sandringham House's gabled roof and turrets. I thought my Christmas mornings were too quiet. Cooper emptied his stocking and I stuck on Bing Crosby CDs and tried to create the feeling of more people as we waited for Mom to show up.

"At least they have each other," I said. "My mother insists she'll never remarry, but what's going to happen when she's too old to care for herself? She wants to die in her own bed, but if she's forced to move to assisted living, she'll have to sell the house to pay for it."

We followed the group into the car museum, once the stables. Stopping by Nick to admire the antique motorcars, I imagined the royal family on a picnic, a plaid blanket spread out on clipped grass.

"Maybe a duke will take me out for a spin in this one," Roxanne said, grinning into the polished chrome.

Drew, who recognized each model by name, stood at her elbow. "I didn't know you were interested in cars."

"Just the men who drive them." She stroked the Rolls Royce's shiny gunmetal gray surface. "Although this baby is so nice, I might take it without a man behind the wheel. No, I'd never figure out how to drive on the wrong side of the road." She turned to Nick. "How do you manage?"

"I was young when my family moved here. It's how I learned to drive." His smile expanded. "It is silly how the British insist on driving on the opposite side of the road as the rest of Europe."

"But when in Rome?" Drew said.

"Exactly." Nick's chest expanded, his volume increasing. "British cars are functional, but the Italians make the finest automobiles in the world. These clumsy boats aren't much fun to drive."

Martin swaggered around the end of the car and cleared his throat. "I beg to differ with you. My father owns one like this. I can assure you it's a fine machine and has never let him down."

Nick shrugged. "But they're not sleek like the Italians. They move like tractors."

"We in Great Britain don't need to prove we're men by driving too fast, careening around corners, and making fools of ourselves."

"Perhaps you don't know what real manhood is."

"I beg your pardon," Martin sputtered. He edged closer to Nick until the men stood nose to nose—except for Martin's towering height. There spanned a long moment when I wondered if a punch would be thrown. I'd never seen grown men act so ridiculously.

"Boys," Roxanne said, wedging herself between them like a referee in a boxing ring. "If you don't behave, I'll report you both to the principal."

The two stared into each other's eyes like plumed roosters ready for battle. Finally, Nick shoved his hands into his pockets and strolled away.

CHAPTER 13

I WAS AWAKENED FROM my catnap on the bus by Hal's elated words. "Look up there, people. That must be Nottingham Castle, as in the Sheriff of Nottingham."

Nick switched on the mike. "You're right, Hal, and there are many legends connected with it." He slowed the bus. "The fortress was built atop a hundred-and-thirty-three foot cliff. Caves and underground passages wind all through the rock."

Stretching to see out the window, I smiled as I thought about Robin Hood and Maid Marian. It was still hard to believe I was here in this land rich with legends and mystery.

Soon we were pulling up in front of our hotel.

"The concert's a five-minute drive away. Be back here in thirty minutes," Hal said. "Our driver's idea of 'plenty of time' and mine are not the same," he added as we went to the front desk to grab our keys.

I rolled my suitcase to the room and changed into my dress while Clare brushed her teeth in the bathroom. "It's time to go," I told her.

She spit in the sink. "One minute." She pulled out an arm-length thread of dental floss and continued cleaning her teeth.

I gathered my purse and jacket, then trotted down a flight of carpeted stairs to the lobby. Just inside the hotel's front door, Martin stood speaking to an older woman with neatly coifed silver hair wearing a Channel-style suit.

As I neared them, I heard Martin say, "Please, Mother. I'd do almost anything for you. But not that."

"Marty, this may be your last chance."

Martin's face took on a look of confusion. "What on earth are you talking about?"

His mother wrung her speckled hands. "It may be a long while before you're back again—" She stopped speaking when she saw me.

I smiled, and she half-smiled back with sad eyes.

I pushed open the glass door and stepped outside. It was hard to imagine Martin having such a lovely mother; he was one of the coldest people I'd ever encountered. Earlier, I had wondered if his parents were domineering or if he'd grown up without affection—at a military academy. I glanced back through the door to see Martin bending to embrace his mother. I tried to visualize him as a toddler taking his first step into her outstretched arms, the way Cooper had. Did Martin start out as sweet as Cooper? If so, when had he hardened into an iceman? I hoped my son never changed, and yet knew he was distancing himself from me; it was normal for preteen boys. But without a man in our house whom would he emulate?

I boarded the bus and sat with Roxanne. A moment later Martin, his face pale, lowered himself across the aisle, one row ahead of us. I watched him bow his head, resting his mouth and chin in his opened hand.

The bus sat idling ten more minutes as we waited for Clare's arrival. Hal stood outside tapping his fingers against the side of the bus like a snare drum. He scowled when she flitted on, though she didn't seem to notice. She eased down next to Martin and stretched one gazelle leg into the aisle.

As the bus rolled into traffic, she vocalized a musical line to Martin. It sounded like Bel Canto, a piece by Bellini.

"Sure, I know that," Martin said. "The closing duet from Act One of *La Sonnambula*."

"Would you sing it with me sometime?"

"Yes, we could give it a try."

"Sounds like Martin and Clare are planning a duet," Roxanne said in my ear.

Humph. Their voices would blend beautifully, but I had no desire to hear them harmonize. "In a few years we may see her at the Seattle Opera, center stage," I said in a hushed voice.

I remembered my first visit to the opera to hear Mozart's *Marriage of Figaro*. Perched in the balcony, my senses came alive when Countess Almaviva sang her aria, *Dove sono i bei momenti*? If my voice were like hers', would there be any greater joy? I'd thought. Birds warble symphonies; water trickling over a fountain plunks a melody; the wind rustles the treetops like hands clapping. And I wanted to create a beautiful sound, filling the audience with happiness.

As we drove across Nottingham Canal I recalled my recent conversation with my vocal coach. "A few days ago, I told Muriel I was done trying to get solo parts," I said to Roxanne. "Singing with the choir is all I can handle."

Roxanne's face radiated kindness. "Sing enough and you'll get over your stage fright. You have a pretty voice. Hey, I know a group doing *The Sound of Music* this summer. There are several women's parts in it."

"Thanks, but no thanks. I can't face another audition." I waggled my fingers for effect. "Fear surges through my arteries and my heart races out of control. Who needs it?"

"Stop being so hard on yourself." She elbowed me playfully. "Singing should be fun. Forget what other people think."

Roxanne was right; I needed to learn to be content. Why did I crave an audience?

An hour later I gazed out at the sixty or seventy people who'd come to hear us sing. I spotted Martin's mother in the second row looking as solemn as she had earlier. When Martin sang his solo, she leaned forward, then held her hands over her chest when he hit the stellar high A-flat. Afterward, she patted her eyes with a handkerchief.

However, Clare was not at her best. The piece started out low and easy. "I nothing lack if I am His, and He is mine forever." There was a change of emotion and key. "Perverse and foolish oft I'd strayed, but yet in love He sought me." Finally, the notes rose in pitch and dynamics. "Good Shepherd, may I sing thy praise forever and ever!"

Clare's ashen face strained as she followed Hal's baton. Hal's eyebrows almost touched in the center over beady eyes.

By the time the concert ended, I was glad to see him smiling again. He pushed the palms of his hands together and nodded to Martin, then the group, his gaze not stopping on anyone else. I knew Hal would catch up to Clare later that evening for one of his famous reprimands—words any singer would dread.

NICK STRODE THROUGH the hotel's front door and crossed the lobby. He whistled as he headed toward the stairs leading to the second and third floors.

"Nick," I said, reducing the distance between us. "We missed you at dinner." I'd saved him a spot at the hotel's restaurant.

"Sorry. There were things I needed to take care of for tomorrow's journey. Are you headed upstairs?"

"Yes. I can't wait to get to my room and put my feet up."

"Sounds like a perfect idea. After you, *signorina*."

Reaching the first-floor landing, I thought I heard somebody behind us. I paused to glance over my shoulder but saw no one. Was I expecting my mother, who wouldn't approve of my walking anywhere near my room with Nick?

"I'm down this hall," I said, moving in that direction. "See you tomorrow."

"I'm on the floor above you. But wait, please." He moved in on me. "Since the moment we met I've wanted to do this." Before I could blink, his hands slid around my waist and his lips met mine. The kiss was short, but tender.

He leaned back and pushed a stray hair away from my cheek. "Forgive me if I'm being too forward," he said.

I felt like draping my arms over his shoulders, resting my head against his chest, and hanging on. I'd been aching to be held. These last five years loneliness had eaten me alive, leaving only half a woman.

But prudence and good sense—and Mom's voice nattering in my ear—told me to remove myself from the situation.

"I find you irresistible," he said, stroking me under my chin. Then his arms encircled my waist and he kissed me again.

Something rattled sharply. My shoulders tightened. I pushed Nick away and turned to see Martin open his door only feet from us.

"I say!" He glared at Nick, then tossed me a look of disapproval.

Nick kept one hand on my waist, but I stepped away to let Martin pass by. I watched him march the length of the hall, then heard his footsteps tromping down the staircase.

I felt shy and couldn't bring myself to look Nick in the face. "We'd better say good night," I said.

His eyes revealed disappointment, but he said, "Of course, it's late. Pleasant dreams, my pretty one." He turned and climbed the next flight of stairs.

Strolling to my room, I felt glum at the prospect of being alone for the rest of the evening. I placed the key in the lock, then heard Clare inside gabbing on a phone. I hoped she was speaking to her mother or voice teacher and gleaning words of encouragement. Wishing to give her privacy, I dropped the key back in my purse.

I noticed an exit sign hanging over the door at the end of the hall. Opening the door, I discovered another staircase. I descended the steps to find myself in the darkened bar, an ancient room with eight tables—some occupied—and a stone fireplace standing higher than my shoulders. Flames from a fire fashioned of three-foot-long logs cast a golden hue across the room and a game of snooker was showing on the small TV set up above the bartender.

I sat at the table nearest the hearth to let the heat sooth my limbs, which now yearned for Nick. There was no question he was a desirable man. Was I falling for him? How loopy would that be? *Mashugana!* Mom would say.

Since Jeff's death I'd dated several men, but after a few weeks I'd fabricated excuses not to see them again. I'd thought Jonathon was nod-off boring and drove his Volkswagen bus like an old biddy. But wasn't I looking for someone stable? Steve seemed to work all the time, but in hindsight didn't I want an industrious man with a steady job? Watching flames lick the logs, I wondered if the fault was with me and not them.

"Please, Martin," a woman said plaintively. "If you'd reach out to him, I know he'd do the same."

I glanced over my shoulder and saw Martin and his mother in conversation at a nearby table.

"Why should I contact him?" Martin's voice sounded inflexible. "He should apologize to me first."

"Couldn't you possibly see it from his point of view?"

"There's no sense in discussing this further."

As I placed an order, I watched Martin's mother rise from the table and kiss her son's cheek. Then she left.

The waiter brought my mug of hot chocolate, topped with whipped cream and dark chocolate shavings. I took a sip, sending bitter-sweetness down my throat.

I looked over to find Martin staring past me into the rippling flames. "I assume that's your mother," I said, and he noticed me.

"Yes, my dear, naive mother." His face softened slightly. "She's trying to be helpful, but she's barking up the wrong tree, as they say."

"You mean you're not the one she should be talking to?"

He stood and moved next to me, then set his coffee cup on my table. "The person she should be speaking to is too bullheaded to listen."

More bullheaded than Martin?

A log popped, then hissed. I watched flames twist around the wood, releasing a curl of smoke. "The fire feels good, doesn't it?" I said.

He looked at me with narrowed eyes. "I thought I just saw you upstairs with your Italian Casanova."

I took another sip, licked the froth off my upper lip.

"I wouldn't get involved with him." He hoisted my unused spoon and clanked it on the side of his glass. "Nick's nothing but trouble."

"What makes you such an authority on human nature?" I asked.

"It's a long story and I shan't bore you with it."

I contained a smirk as I imagined what Roxanne had read about him in the tabloids. "From what I've heard, your story's anything but boring."

With his free hand, he raked his fingers through his thick hair. "You think I'm a thief and a washed-up tenor?"

Call me nuts, but I found myself feeling sorry for him. "I don't know what to think about your personal life," I said, "but your voice is fantastic."

"Thank you. I seem to be getting it back, but my life is still in shambles. If only there were a way to wash the slate clean and start anew."

"I've wished that a few times, myself."

"There might be a way to make my mother happy again." His voice took on an edge of harshness. "But no, the old man will never approve of anything I do. He can't imagine why I'd rather sing than follow in his footsteps. He won't admit that being the barrister to the Crown is also a form of entertainment."

His father was the queen's attorney? I tried not to let astonishment show on my poker-face, but heard my

voice rise in pitch. "By the Crown do you mean Buck-
ingham Palace?"

He shrugged one shoulder. "Yes."

"But you've sung for royalty and presidents. How
could your father not admire that?" I couldn't imagine
any parent not going to the ends of the earth to watch
his child perform. Who was I kidding? My own father
fit into that category once my folks split up.

"As far as he's concerned, there's only one way to live
one's life. His. He hates my singing, like I'm a sleazy
comedian telling distasteful jokes." He sank onto a chair
at my table. "Once Mother tricked him into attending
the opera in Paris where I was singing in *Don Pasquale*.
At intermission, Father complained of chest pains and
left, although he never went to see his physician."

His father sounded more obstinate than Martin. I
was beginning to understand where he inherited his
personality. But that wasn't a good enough excuse. I
hoped I wasn't anything like my father.

"For what it's worth, I think your father's wrong," I
said. "Once children reach adulthood they must chart
their own courses. And the world's a better place with
a beautiful voice like yours."

"Thanks. I appreciate your kindness." He raised his
glass to his lips. "I must admit Father was right when
he warned me not to get involved with Dorothea. I
shouldn't have been so foolish there." He sipped the
amber-colored liquid. "But when I almost went to jail
Father didn't raise a finger to help me."

Jail?

"I don't blame you for being angry, but couldn't you find a way to coexist with him for your mother's sake? If I couldn't invite my son home, I'd be heartbroken. I can't think of anything worse."

"I suppose you're right. But she can visit me in Seattle anytime she likes. My door is always open to her. And to Father, if he'd apologize."

"Maybe you could meet him halfway?"

He ignored my attempt at diplomacy. "Mother wants me to have dinner with them when I get back to London. That would be a fiasco."

"I think you should go, anyway."

As Martin finished his drink, I seized the moment to return to our previous conversation on the beach. "You asked me to carry something for you. Please tell me it's nothing illegal."

He gave his head the smallest shake. "I have committed no crime."

"Then does it have to do with your parents?" I waited for him to reveal he'd purchased a gift for his mother or something equally insignificant.

"Yes, and no." He paused, as if sorting through a tangle of possibilities.

I said, "It can't be all that bad." Or could it? What was I getting myself into?

His eyes canvassed the room, then he pulled his chair closer. "I thought if you were willing—"

The bartender muttered, "Bad shot," to a man about the snooker game on TV, and Martin froze.

"I'll handle it, myself," he said, springing to his feet.

CHAPTER 14

I CARTED MY SUITCASE through the lobby and out into the drizzly rain. The morning air felt like it often did in Seattle: moist and cool against my cheeks. As I neared the bus, Nick strode in my direction.

Getting dressed earlier, I'd decided our kiss would be a one-time occurrence. I'd never see Nick again after the end of the week, and I wasn't the kind of woman to rush into relationships.

But now that I saw Nick, my heart began skipping like a teenager suffering from her first crush.

He took my suitcase and stowed it into the side of the bus. "You've been on my mind, Jessica."

Before I could shape my reply, Roxanne pushed me forward. "Come on, girl, it's wet out here," she said.

The two of us climbed onto the bus and slid into seats several rows back.

I yawned as I pulled my arms out of my jacket and draped it over my shoulders.

"Up late?" Roxanne asked, surveying my expression.

"No, I turned in early. But Clare coughed all night." I wouldn't mention Nick's kiss or the unsettling conversation with Martin.

"You look more than sleepy. Are you sure that's all that's bothering you?"

"Well—I find myself in a quandary."

"Can I assume this has to do with a man?" Her eyebrows did a Groucho Marx wiggle, making me smile.

"Let's just say, I'm tired of being single."

"I know what you mean."

I felt warmth rising from the heating vent at my feet. Do all women have this insatiable need to be loved? I wondered as I sank into the cushion. Once Mom recovered from her divorce, she seemed fine without a husband. She'd dated a couple times, but the panic of being a single woman had subsided, and now she was content. "There's more to life than men," Mom said one Friday night when she didn't have a date. "If you're not happy with yourself, don't expect a man to fix it."

Hal climbed on the bus, followed by Martin, clad in his trench coat.

"Listen up, people," Hal said, clapping his hands together in rapid flutters. "I've got a real treat for us today. After we drive past Sherwood Forest—where Robin Hood lived—we'll visit Castle Bonview, usually only open to the public in June and July. Thanks to Martin, the owners, Lord and Lady Milton, will give us a private tour." He shook Martin's hand before letting him pass. "We're extremely lucky to have you with us."

As the bus bounced and grated along country roads, the rain subsided, leaving a low canopy of cement-colored clouds. We turned onto a lane and worked our way up a densely wooded hill, then passed through an opened gate. Ten-foot-high red rhododendrons lined the final leg of the drive.

We pulled in next to a Land Rover. I stepped off the bus and was met by two giant Irish Wolfhounds tall enough to eat off my kitchen table. The dogs languidly sniffed my upturned palm, then moved on to greet Marci and the others.

In the past, Cooper had begged me for a dog, but I didn't think I'd be home enough to care for it properly. Last year I finally agreed to purchase him a small rodent, thinking he'd choose a gerbil or guinea pig. But during his visit to the pet store he insisted on Pepper, a charcoal-gray-and-white rat that darted up his arm, then dove into his breast pocket. At first, I couldn't stand the look of Pepper—his bald tail, his whiskers twitching. Icky! But he grew on me because Cooper loved him. And Pepper turned out to be an intelligent and jovial little critter.

Martin strode to the small castle's front door to embrace a couple in their late sixties. "Marty, how wonderful to see you," the woman said. "It's been too long." Her silver hair was bobbed short and her plaid skirt hung below her calves.

Martin turned to the group as we approached. "I'd like to present Lord and Lady Milton."

Lord Milton stood almost as tall as Martin and sported wild eyebrows brushed out to the sides. "Do come in," he said, speaking past his unlit pipe. "Chilly out this morning."

Lady Milton, as lanky as her husband, extended an arm. "Make yourself at home." She stepped aside to let us enter. "Friends of Martin are always welcome."

"Thank you," Hal said, all a titter. "This is an honor."

In front of us stretched an entry room of cream-colored stone, with a ceiling so high I had to crane my neck to see the armor and antlers adorning the upper walls. Following Clare and several of the men, Roxanne, Drew, and I mounted stairs leading to rooms filled with antique furniture and tapestries.

Entering a sitting room, I noticed a plush velvet armchair positioned near a cavernous fireplace. Next to the chair stood an oval table with a framed photo of Lord Milton as a younger man atop a horse, foxhounds milling at its feet.

"I could be happy in a place like this," I said to Roxanne and Drew, the only other two in the room. "I'd come home from teaching every day and take my afternoon tea on a silver tea service, right here."

"I'll be your butler," said Drew. "You will need one of those, won't you?"

"Not likely." I grasped my hands together to keep from touching anything. "I can't afford one on a teacher's salary."

"At home I feel rich," Roxanne said. "Compared to most places in the world, the majority of us in the Northwest have it made." She heaved a sigh. "But here I feel like a pauper."

"You're right." My gaze took in a crystal vase over-flowing with fresh lilies, their honeyed scent filling my nostrils. "I've had to scrimp for my mortgage payment before, but I've never gone hungry."

Family portraits—oils framed in lavish gold leaf—covered the far wall. Roxanne inclined her round face to survey a painting of two young women in evening gowns, their white necks encircled with jewels. "They don't look like any of my relatives."

"They might be the Miltons' daughters," I said. "If so, Martin probably knows them." It dawned on me he'd grown up in this aristocratic wonderland. He could have married one of them.

"They sure are pretty," Roxanne said. "What a perfect life."

"Nah," Drew said. "They probably feel miserable sometimes, just like the rest of us."

"Well, I'd rather be miserable here than in my dumb little apartment."

I recalled my last visit to Roxanne's abode. I'd thought it was terrific—every square inch of wall space covered with framed snapshots, prints, and African fabric hangings.

"I love your place because it's so you," I said, curving my arm around her shoulder.

"Even the faux tiger-skin rug?"

"Absolutely. Hey, I should invite you over. I haven't redecorated our house since we moved in." My throat constricted as I thought of my king-sized bed, covered with the striped comforter Jeff picked out. The bed still stood several feet from the wall, so he could come and go easily when in fact I'd slept alone for years. I remembered the first few zombie weeks after Jeff's death; my legs went weak when I set foot in the bedroom. I'd slept on a mat in a sleeping bag at the side of Cooper's bed for several days, then moved to the couch. Finally, I convinced myself I needed to return to normalcy for our son's wellbeing. I crept into bed one night to find the sheets still smelled of Jeff. I'd lain awake wondering if I'd ever be happy again.

"I should redo my bedroom," I said. "A change might help me put the past behind. Make it feminine. Not that I can afford to buy all new stuff."

"I'll help you." Roxanne's eyes sparkled. "I can work wonders with a gallon of paint and a few designer sheets bought at a discount store."

"That would be great. I'll be your assistant, then cook you dinner."

"Ooh, I like that dinner part."

Descending the stairs minutes later, I noticed Martin had stayed by the front door to chat with our hosts. "This is a beautiful home," I said to Lord and Lady Milton. "Thank you for letting us come."

"No trouble at all," Lady Milton said, shaking my hand firmly. "It was a lovely chance to see Martin and entertain his friends." She turned to Martin. "Please give our regards to your dear parents."

He glanced at the door like one of my students waiting for the recess bell. Fingering the change in his pocket, he said nothing.

Lady Milton's hands moved to her hips as she studied Martin's face. "Haven't you gotten that mix-up straightened out yet?"

I wondered if the Miltons knew about his brush with the law. If they moved in the same social circles, they must. And they probably knew his father had rejected him.

"Please," Martin said, "let's not force everyone to listen to my problems." He gave Lady Milton a quick peck on the cheek. "We need to be on our way."

"You're right," Hal said. "But I hate to leave."

As Roxanne and I followed Martin out the door I could hear Hal thanking the Miltons. When we caught up with Martin, Roxanne said, "What other famous people do you know?"

He chuckled in response.

"How could you ever move away from this kind of life?" I asked.

His smile flattened. "It's the people I miss the most." He inhaled to the bottom of his diaphragm. "I've known the Miltons since I was a child. Their two girls were like sisters to me."

Roxanne gave him a little jab in the ribs and he added, "Both are quite happily married now."

"Do they have any cute brothers?"

He chuckled again. "No, sorry."

Minutes later on the bus, I plopped down next to Roxanne. "Roxie, you're too funny—the way you talk to everyone with such ease."

"Everyone?" Her eyes grew with amusement. "You mean Martin? He's just a man."

"Maybe so, but you're the only one who can make him crack the slightest smile."

Roxanne wrinkled her nose. "It's because I don't care. I'm only flirtatious with men I don't have a chance with. Get me in a serious conversation and I fall apart."

"I've never seen you without a clever comeback. You're always entertaining."

"I wish. I'm thirty-four, with no husband and no prospects."

"That can't be true. I'm sure plenty of men would jump at the chance to take you out."

Roxanne scanned up and down the aisle, then grimaced. "Name one."

Was she blind to Drew's attentions? Or did she know something about him that shouted, "Hands off!"

CHAPTER 15

THE BUS MOTORED into a parking lot enclosed on three sides by craggy stone walls and pulled up beside another tour bus. As the others disembarked, I noticed Roxanne still reading her travel guide.

I stretched to my feet and stood in the aisle with my elbow on the seatback. "Let's get moving." I sounded frighteningly like Hal.

"I think I'll stay here and take a siesta," Roxanne said. She and I had both eaten ploughman sandwiches at lunch, and I wouldn't have minded a nap myself.

"We can catch up on our sleep tonight," I insisted. "You told me you needed more exercise."

"Did I say that? What was I thinking?"

"Yes, now come on."

She shut the book. "I'm not really out of shape. I just never had any."

"Sure, you do. Our problem is we were born in the wrong century. One hundred years ago, no one would have given us guff about curvy hips or spongy thighs. We could have hidden everything under a floor-length skirt."

"With a bustle or a hoop." She grabbed hold of the seatback in front of her and pulled herself to her feet. "I might join a health club when we get home, but I'd have to lose some weight first. I don't want to be in the same room as those skinny women looking like this."

"Hey, aren't you the one who told me not to care what others thought?"

As I exited the bus I saw the fortress standing sentry atop a grassy knoll. Long ago deserted, Nick had explained earlier, it was bombarded by cannons, the walls scaled, the interior burned, then left to the elements.

"This way, everyone." Nick steered our crowd around the wall and along a zigzagging path. Minutes later, Roxanne and I peered up a staircase leading to the next two floors and the turret.

"I'm not going up there," Roxanne told me. "I suffer from claustrophobia—and laziness. Anyway, I need to find the restrooms."

As I placed my foot on the first step, Nick said, "Wait, I'll run up there with you."

"I'm not sure I'll be going over a snail's speed," I said.

"There's no hurry on a beautiful afternoon. Ladies first."

One hand on the railing, I climbed the well-worn stairs, all the time listening to Nick's footsteps padding behind me. As I mounted the final few steps, my eyes beheld the sky expanding like an endless ocean. Wispy clouds dabbing the blue reminded me of an Impressionist's brushstrokes on a canvas. Panting, I walked out onto the turret and peeked over the side. I'd always felt uneasy at heights, but the view distracted me. Below spread Kelly-green and molasses-brown squares and rectangles, divided by stone walls. The breeze swishing through my hair and lifting my bangs off my forehead smelled like freshly turned soil. My heart brimmed with gladness.

I watched a car enter a circular drive to a manor house that looked big enough to accommodate three families. "Wouldn't it be incredible to live there?"

Nick stood at my side. "Life can be very good in the United Kingdom if one is born into the right family," he said with a slice of sarcasm. "But in America every man is given an equal chance to better himself. No? And I hear your country has a different kind of beauty."

"Compared to this, the architecture's new in the Northwest, where I live. No sense of history."

"That may be true, and we Italians are particularly proud of our heritage. Rome, then Florence, was once the center of the civilized world. But I would love to go to a city where everything is new, like Los Angeles."

"You should. Then come to Seattle and I'll be your guide."

"I'd like that. To see you again. But I can't leave my job for more than a few days. Until winter, anyway. Our busy time of the year is coming up."

"I'll bet a man like you could land a good job in the States."

"That is my dream, but it's not easy." He smoothed his hair back, but the breeze plucked it up again. "To come for a short visit is one thing, but to work one must have a green card. My company runs a small office in Boston, but they don't need anyone else there. The company is growing, so maybe in a year or two."

I wanted to say my mother, who worked at an employment agency, could help him. She'd located a great job for a friend a few months back. Nick was educated, intelligent, and hardworking, just what businesses were begging for. But immigrating to the States was a legal matter.

"I asked my boss to keep me in mind, so who knows," he said. "I may come knocking on your door someday."

"I hope that happens. But I need to warn you, Boston's a long way from Seattle."

"It doesn't matter how long the journey, under no circumstances would I come to America and not visit you." He surveyed my face, his eyes embracing my features. "You're an incredible woman, my Jessica."

Warmth and longing mingled through my chest. I wanted to believe him but knew I should be wary. Did Nick chase after a woman on every tour? Was he hoping I was his means of escaping Great Britain? His ticket to prosperity?

"My father would appreciate your beauty," he said. "He is a master craftsman, who came to this country to help the British design furniture but was always treated like a mere carpenter. In our country my father was given great respect, but not here."

He paused to watch birds circling in wide arcs, riding the wind like flickering leaves. "In school I tried to rid myself of my Italian accent, but the other children could always hear it. I changed my name from Niccolò to Nick, but they still teased me."

"In Seattle people love foreign accents."

"You see, that's what I mean. I'm told in America the differences are more accepted."

"I think that's true, although children can be cruel anywhere." I'd experienced teasing as a child; the kids in my classroom could be brutal to each other. "Are your parents happy here?"

"My father is always content. He is a good man but lacks ambition. My mother returns to her hometown, Sienna, every year to visit her family."

"And you have siblings?"

"Two. My sister is married and lives in Liverpool, but my brother moved to *Napoli*—I mean Naples. He became a priest, of all things."

"He may help many people."

"Perhaps, but it seems like a depressing life. And without women? How could a man live?"

I heard Drew's bass laughter echoing up the stairwell, followed by Roxanne's groaning and Martin's voice. I stepped away from Nick, as if admiring the scenery well out of his reach.

"Come on, Roxie." The top of Drew's head burst into view. "You're almost there."

"How did I let myself get talked into this?" Roxanne sounded short of breath. She wandered out onto the turret. The breeze tousled her hair. Behind her, Martin trotted up the last steps.

"Good for you," I said to Roxanne as she slogged over to me. "You just burned up a quarter of the calories you ingested for lunch."

"Only a quarter?"

"Okay, one half."

"I'm glad the way back is easier." She glanced down at the bus. "Or I might have to spend the night up here."

A rogue gust of wind blasted out of the north, whistling in my ears. The thought of a transparent force tossing me helplessly over the wall made me shiver, and I inched toward the center of the platform.

Nick came to my side. "The weather in England is like a woman, always changing, never to be trusted."

"Sounds like you're quoting Verdi's '*La donna è mobile*,'" Roxanne said. "Personally, I trust women more than the wind—and most men."

Another gust flapped the corners of Nick's jacket. "I will tell you a secret," he said. "We men keep up a strong exterior only to protect our hearts from being broken by you women, the superior sex." He turned to include Martin. "Am I right, Mr. Spear?"

Martin stared down his nose at Nick. "You don't seem like the sort who'd let a woman get the upper hand," Martin said.

"No, he doesn't look like the lonely brokenhearted type, does he?" Roxanne said.

"Ah, men's hearts are broken, too, and they mend much slower than women's." Nick patted his chest.

"Unless a man is careful with his, he may find his heart is stolen, never to be replaced by another."

"That is, if he has a heart to begin with." Martin's voice bristled with hostility.

"And how about you?" Nick shrugged. "Behind that frigid exterior is there a heart of gold?"

The muscle running up the side of Martin's face flexed. "What I have or don't have is none of your concern."

Nick checked his watch and smiled at me. "I promised Hal everyone would be back to the bus in forty-five minutes." Then he saluted Martin and disappeared down the stairs.

As Roxanne and Drew took in the view, I approached Martin and said, "I've been thinking about you."

His eyebrows rose, but the rest of his symmetrical face remained motionless.

"And about your parents. I'd like to help, if I can." Even if Martin were a thief, it was evident his mother adored him just as I loved Cooper.

The wind whipped past us. He faced into it, squinting his eyes. "Let's pretend that conversation never happened."

I held my hair back with both hands to keep it out of my face. "It's too late for that."

CHAPTER 16

DRIVING THROUGH LANES lined with hedges almost as tall as the bus, Nick cut the speed so the choir could view a thatched roof up close. Minutes later, he slowed so we could take pictures of lambs frolicking in a pasture.

Hal called out, "We need to keep rolling or we won't make it to the hotel in time to explore York before dinner."

I was glad he was keeping us on the move. We had no concert tonight, but I wanted to look around the medieval village.

"I need to buy gifts for my wife and kids," he added. "I can't come home empty-handed."

The bus finally pulled up to the front of our hotel, a three-story brick building. I checked into my room and minutes later met Roxanne on the sidewalk. We ambled down the street to a cobbled lane blocked off from cars.

"It looks like we stepped back into the Middle Ages." I scanned the ancient timbered buildings and saw Hal dart into a souvenir shop.

Roxanne gravitated toward a store called York Fabrics and Gifts. As I followed her through the door, a bell tinkled overhead. A woman behind the counter welcomed us. The small space lay crammed with tables and shelves displaying bolts of plaid and paisley fabric, and racks of sweaters and other knitted clothing. The air smelled of warm wool and starched cotton, reminding me of childhood, when Mom used to sew my clothes. In middle school I'd felt like a dork in my homemade outfits, which seemed to advertise, "I'm poor!"

I'd never understood why Mom didn't demand child support from my dad, who could well afford to cough up a monthly pittance. Maybe she had but he'd refused to pay, in which case she should have pressed charges. Lock him in jail. I resented my father. I wondered if I'd ever come to a place of apathy, where I didn't care if I bumped into him on a crowded street or not—which I never did, although I searched a thousand faces hoping to recognize him. He'd never even met his grandson Cooper.

"I want to get something cute for each niece." Roxanne picked up a child's sweater. "My sister's two kids are darling. They call me Aunt Rockie."

"I wish Cooper had an aunt like you. You'll make the greatest mom, if it works out."

The buoyancy faded from Roxanne's voice. "I'm almost too old. I'll have to be content playing with other people's kids."

A tumble-haired boy chased by his sister scampered past us, both squealing with laughter. Then their mother scolded them to her side.

I thought of my son at home. What would my life be without him? An empty shell aching to be filled. I remembered after his birth wondering how it was possible to love one tiny person more than anything else in the whole world. But it wasn't enough; I also yearned for the other kind of love.

I wandered to a table heaped with neck scarves. Picking one up to admire its mossy-green color, my hands explored the nubbly texture. Next to me, Roxanne tried on a beret. Her curls wisped out to each side.

"Is this the real me?" she asked, then yanked it off, her face turning flat. "I've never told anyone this, but I've thought about adopting an orphan from a third-world country. I don't know if agencies let single women do that." Her voice grew faint. "But I'd rather feel my own child growing inside of me."

I gave her soft arm a pat. "I wish I could help."

Her doe-eyes blinked. "Guess I'm feeling shaky because my birthday's coming up in a few weeks. Thirty-five. Yikes. My clock is ticking."

"Many people still have kids at that age."

"Yeah, but it helps to be married."

THE AIR IN my hotel room smelled stuffy, like Mom's attic on a summer afternoon. I heard the radiator clicking under the window, hiking up the temperature. But at least Clare wasn't there to complain. In my absence, she'd appropriated the top of the bureau and the closet. Fine, I didn't feel like unpacking anyway.

I dropped my shopping bag containing a scarf for Mom to the floor, sat on the edge of the bed, and reached for the telephone. I calculated it was ten thirty AM. at home. Cooper might be off with my mother on an outing; Mom had promised to take him to the zoo, the aquarium, or somewhere exciting every day of spring vacation. He'd been looking forward to a week of nonstop Grandma Miriam for months, but I still felt a wave of guilt for not being there myself.

Dialing my home number, I longed to hug Cooper. I imagined his little-boy scent. Although lately the aroma of shampoo permeated his hair, and my nostrils told me he'd soon need deodorant. And he shrugged off my embraces and stood almost as tall as I.

On the fifth ring, when I was expecting to hear the answering machine click on, my mother said, "Hello," in a nasally voice.

"Mom, you sound like you're coming down with something."

"I just got up."

"You, sleeping in?" Mom was a morning person. She prided herself on rising with the sun.

"Cooper and I stayed up late watching a movie last night, then I didn't sleep well."

I detected a grate to her voice, like when her gall bladder was flaring up, but she didn't want me to worry. "Is Cooper around?"

"No, he's across the street at Joey's."

"Phooey." At this moment there was nothing I wanted more than to tell him I loved him. "How's he doing?"

"Fine, except—now don't get upset—we had a bit of a problem yesterday."

Pepper must have escaped from his cage. With a rat cavorting about the house, she wouldn't sleep a wink.

Her voice became hesitant. "After dinner I took Cooper to Rite Aid, near your house. I had a prescription to fill and told Cooper he could look around the store while we waited, but of course not to talk to strangers. I figured that was safe, don't you think?"

Now I was feeling edgy. "Yes, Mother. Cooper's been in that store one hundred times and he knows not to speak to strangers."

"*Oy,* I paid for my prescription. But as we left the store, a plain-clothes security guard stopped us and accused Cooper of shoplifting." Mom puffed into the receiver. "I said there must be some mistake, that I'd buy my grandson anything he wanted so there was no need for him to steal."

A hollow pause followed. Finally, she said, "When the guard wouldn't leave us alone, Cooper pulled a little car out of his pocket. I insisted he must have put it in there by mistake. But, no, the guard said he'd been watching him."

"Are you sure someone else didn't slip it into his pocket?" I said. "Or that he meant to ask you for the money and forgot?"

"I'm afraid not."

A sick feeling sludged through my stomach. As Mom spoke, I recalled finding several unfamiliar items in

Cooper's bedroom over the last few months: a baseball, a mechanical pencil, and a yo-yo. Cooper had claimed he'd found the ball and pencil while walking home from school, and a friend had given him the yo-yo. I considered myself almost clairvoyant at reading my students' faces, but was I blind to my own son's lies?

"Did he admit it?" I asked.

"Yes, and he started crying when the man said that although the store wouldn't press charges, Cooper couldn't come back for a whole year. Don't you think that's a bit harsh?"

"Not if he's guilty. It's essential for kids to understand there are consequences to their actions." What I spouted to my students' parents when their children were in trouble.

"But he's just a little boy. My *bubeleh*."

"Mom, I deal with kids all day." I couldn't believe we were talking about my own flesh and blood. "Cooper shouldn't be allowed to go anywhere today. He should be grounded."

"Honey, can't you punish him when you return and not ruin all our fun?"

"Maybe I should come home early. I'm not sure Hal would care." What was more important, this trip or my son?

"Don't be silly, Jessie. I'll handle things. I raised you, didn't I?"

"But I was a girl. I hardly ever got in trouble." Worried about my mother's fragile emotions after Dad left, I strove to be an exemplary daughter. For the most part. In truth, I'd shoplifted but never was caught.

Hanging up the phone, I felt drained, like damp laundry stuck in the spin cycle. Was Cooper's behavior my fault? I imagined him in his teens—only one year away—turning into a kleptomaniac and joining a gang. Young men without fathers were probably more likely to drink and use drugs to dull their pain. I had grown up without a dad, but I'd had Mom to cling to. Boys couldn't get by without men in their lives.

I grabbed the shopping bag and dumped the scarf in my lap. The yarn's mottled greens were the hues of the moors, the saleswoman had said. But under the dim overhead light it looked the color of dirt.

Maybe I should sign Cooper up for a Big Brother, I thought as I stood and wound the scarf around my neck too tightly. I glanced into the wall mirror and saw a woman with a drooping face and a sallow complexion.

CHAPTER 17

MY EYES CANVASSED the crowded pub. A dozen other choir members filled the three nearest tables. At the far end of the room stood a billiard table where a young woman stretched on tiptoes to position her cue stick. I heard a loud clack, followed by a ripple of applause from people sitting on stools at the L-shaped bar. The air bubbled with conversations, laughter, and music.

"It's a family type of place," Nick had assured Hal as we got up from the dinner table thirty minutes earlier.

"The choir must be at its best behavior at all times," Hal had warned, and didn't join us.

Listening to Drew and Roxanne chat across the table, I sat between Martin and Nick, the two men ignoring each other. But I was in no mood to keep a conversation going. As I sipped my soda through a straw, I rehashed my chat with Mom and wondered if a neighbor or friend had been in the store at the time. What would they think of me as a mother?

I flattened the straw between my teeth and stared at the maraschino cherry floating at the bottom of my glass. If Cooper couldn't go into Rite Aid for a year where would we shop? Anger and frustration replaced my guilt. How dare Cooper pull a stunt like this the moment I left town?

"She loves you, yeah, yeah, yeah," floated out of the sound system. Roxanne started singing the words and Drew joined in.

"I have an idea," Nick said to me. He got to his feet and strolled over to a dartboard on the nearby wall. Three blue and three yellow darts plumed from its surface. He plucked them out and sauntered back to me.

"Come, play with me," he said, setting the blue ones on the table.

I stood. "Okay, I'll give it a try." Any distraction sounded good. "But you'll have to teach me the rules."

He handed me a yellow dart, then pointed out a strip of white paint on the floor, about eight feet from the wall. "Here. Stand behind this line," he said.

I turned to face the dartboard: it was divided by a series of circles dissected into black-and-white wedges and marked at the rim by the numbers one through twenty. A pimento-red bull's-eye winked in the center. My thoughts skidded back to Cooper and the toy car. I'd never believed in spanking, but my son deserved a good swat on the backside.

Feeling the cool aluminum shaft in my right hand, I pulled it back behind my ear, then hurled the dart with all my might. It bounced against the wall, missing the target by six inches, and flopped to the floor like a bird flying into a glass door.

Roxanne giggled. I turned to see everyone at our three tables watching me.

"Maybe you should find someone else," I told Nick.

"No, you almost have it." He gave me another dart. "I'll help you."

As I held the dart between my thumb and forefinger, his hand slid around mine. Standing behind me, his cheek against mine, he guided my hand in slow motion toward the board. The song changed to a slow ballad. I felt Nick's body swaying slightly to the rhythm.

"Ready?" he asked. With a long motion, his hand propelled mine forward. At the last moment he let go, but the dart remained locked in my grasp.

"Oops," I said. "Did I mention I've never played before?"

"No matter." He stepped away. "Try again."

Fixing my eyes on the target, I held the dart near my temple, then tossed it. The dart wobbled through the air. It pierced the board near the outer rim, where it hung limply by the number one.

"Very good," he said. "This time relax and keep your weight evenly distributed."

I glanced down at my feet and placed my toes just within the line. Taking a deep breath, I tossed the dart and it landed an inch from the bull's eye in a wedge marked fourteen.

"*Brava*," Nick said.

Roxanne clapped her hands. "Jessie, you're a born natural."

I gave a curtsy in her direction. "That was sheer luck." I ignored my remaining dart. Better quit while I was ahead.

Nick strode over to the wall and retrieved my dart. Returning, he stood before the target and threw a dart, which came to rest just outside the bull's eye in a wedge marked eighteen. He threw the other two and they hit near the first.

"You're very good." I sank into my chair. "Roxie, Drew? Want a turn? I think I'm outclassed."

"No thanks," Roxanne said. "Marty, you play. You look too serious. We all need to loosen up now and then."

"All right, but it's been a while." Martin stood stiffly and picked up the darts from the table. From several feet behind the throw line, he aimed one missile. It sailed out of his hand and landed alongside Nick's dart, knocking it to the floor.

"Perhaps I should remove mine," Nick offered, his voice terse. He gathered his darts, all the while keeping an eye on Martin.

When Nick was out of the way, Martin moved to the throw line. He tossed another dart; it landed just outside the bull's eye in the wedge marked twenty.

Roxanne whooped. "Way to go, Marty."

"I see you've played before," Nick said, fanning his darts against his cheek.

"Not since I was a child." Martin threw the remaining dart and hit the bull's eye.

"Come on," I said. "Nobody's that good without years of practice."

"We had a dartboard when I was a boy," Martin said. "And I remember playing several times in college. But it always seemed rather tedious." He sat down and took a sip of his drink.

Nick wandered to the billiard table and spoke to a man chalking his cue.

"Which sport doesn't bore you?" I asked Martin.

"Cricket, rugby—that sort of thing. I'm a rather good marksman, but I don't have the stomach for hunting."

"Is that a fact?"

Martin reminded me of Josh from my classroom. During show and tell last month, when another boy announced his father was being shipped overseas, Josh insisted his father was a general in the navy. I knew Josh's father to be a salesman. And I figured Martin was stretching the truth, too. I was sick of boys and their juvenile antics.

"Why must men be so competitive?" I asked him.

"I'm not, I was simply stating the facts."

As he saw them? I speared my maraschino cherry with my straw and munched into the overly-sweetened orb.

"I'm ready to head back to the hotel." Roxanne's hand covered her yawning mouth.

"Good idea." Drew reached into his pocket for change and placed a tip on the table. "We've got a busy day tomorrow."

Nick returned with a handful of peanuts. "Leaving already?" He eased down into the chair on my other side. "It's still early." Under the table his foot nudged mine.

I could feel Martin's eyes probing me. He stood and shoved his chair against the table. "Yes, we should be going."

Nick spoke into my ear. "I think you have another admirer," he said, and tossed a nut into his mouth.

"Martin? Hardly. I don't think he approves of us."

"These Brits are a strange breed." Nick watched Roxanne, Drew, and several others follow Martin to the exit. "I've never figured them out, in spite of all my years here. So stilted, so formal. Life is more fun when it's spontaneous, no?"

The only image I could conger up was Cooper's impulsive act of shoplifting. Or had it been impulsive?

"I'll have to think on that one."

CHAPTER 18

"GO ON WITHOUT me," I told Nick the next day as the group ventured off to explore the walled city of Chester and find its famous clock tower.

I stood viewing the hotel's Tudor exterior of white-washed plaster set between blackened oak timbers. The doorman, clad in a top hat and long jacket, swung open the front door, and Hal dashed out.

He stopped short. "Not coming with us?" he asked me.

I shook my head. "I need some quiet time. I might check out the church we're singing in tonight."

"Good." He pointed to the opposite direction Nick was taking the choir. "It's only a block or so away."

As I wandered the two blocks, my mind wrestled with Cooper and our late-night telephone conversation. "Why did you take it?" I'd asked him, thinking about his bedroom floor, littered with so many toys it was dangerous to walk barefoot.

He words exhibited no remorse. "I wanted it."

"Have you stolen anything else?"

"No." His voice sounded defiant.

I'd felt pressure welling up in me like a beach ball held under water. "I don't believe you."

"You never believe anything I say."

I'd been stunned. "That's not true."

"Yes, it is. You're always on Mrs. Fletcher's side."

I recalled my last conference with Cooper's teacher. Cooper had claimed he didn't have any homework until he was four weeks behind.

"Mrs. Fletcher said you hadn't been turning in your work," I'd said. "Was she making it up?"

"I hate her. And I hate you, too."

The words punctured my gut, almost making me double over. Telling myself he didn't mean it, I'd tried not to let the hurt show in my voice. "We can talk about this better when I get home."

"I hope you never come back!" Then he hung up.

I spotted the massive church on the next corner. A minute later I crossed the threshold to find the air hanging damp and thick. The pews lay empty. My gaze was drawn to the stained-glass windows—shimmering cobalt blues and crimson reds.

Three more hours until our next concert, I thought, when the church would fill with people. I walked up the center aisle, sat down, and tipped my head back. My eyes followed the stone columns to where they met the rafters. The arched ceilings looked like granite waves surging to the heavens.

My lids felt heavy and I yawned. Trying to calm my mind last night, I'd stayed up too late reading in bed. *Rebecca* had intrigued me; I wondered if Manderlay had really existed. Mr. De Winter had asked a young woman he barely knew to be his bride. He hadn't loved her— he couldn't have. They'd only known each other for a few days, the same amount of time I'd known Nick. Yet that young woman left everything she'd known to be with De Winter.

I thought of Nick. When I went home it would probably be goodbye forever. And I might spend the rest of my life in solitude waiting for a perfect man who didn't exist.

Footsteps scuffled past me, echoing throughout the sanctuary. It was Martin, who found a seat several rows in front of me. He rubbed his face in his hands, then stared at a stained-glass window depicting the story of the Prodigal Son. As I got up and moved next to him he remained a statue.

"Aren't those magnificent windows?" I said. "And a beautiful story."

He wore a bleak expression as if he'd just witnessed a tragedy. "The Prodigal Son? It's a parable." His voice was rigid, detached. "Think about it. One son leaves home and commits sins his father despises. Yet when this son returns, his father welcomes him back as though he were the guest of honor."

"You don't believe that could happen?"

"No, it's an allegory to illustrate grace. Real fathers aren't like that."

"I'll bet there are plenty who are." Although I knew he was right; not all fathers loved their children. I had firsthand experience.

"Name one," he said, impatient.

"Hal? I've seen him interacting with his children. He's a wonderful dad." I'd also seen him lose his temper when they whined, but I wouldn't mention his short fuse.

"Don't get me wrong," Martin said. "I have great respect for Hal. But his kids are four, seven, and nine-years-old. Wait until they're teenagers or adults. We'll see how he does."

I felt like informing Martin children defy their parents well before they entered their teens. But that would mean discussing a painful subject with a man who'd give me no sympathy.

We sat quietly for several minutes. Finally, Martin stood and left, his head bent.

"A friend of yours?" a tiny woman down the row from me asked. I hadn't noticed her arrival. She wore layers of ragged clothes. Grizzled clumps of hair stuck out from under her rumpled felt hat.

"I sing with him," I said. "Our choir will be per-forming here tonight."

"I'm waiting for the music to start." The woman, schlepping a bulging plastic bag, drifted several seats closer. "I always come to the concerts. It's nice and warm in here. Who was that?"

"Martin Spear, the tenor."

The woman's birdlike eyes were glazed gray, no doubt dimming her eyesight. "I have a son." Her voice grew fuller. She looked to where Martin had stood. "Tall like him. Lives in America now."

"I have a son, too, but he's only twelve." Cooper would leave me one day. First off to college, then out on his own. There was no way to stop the sun from rising and setting.

The woman's face looked like a road map—jagged lines melding together. Had she started out like me? In Seattle she'd be called a bag lady, a street person. I'd read of women with doctorates pushing shopping carts full of trash, sleeping in alleys, under freeways. Smart, educated women. Were they mentally ill or just heartbroken?

I noticed the woman's hollow cheeks. "Have you had dinner?" I reached into my wallet and found a five-pound note.

The woman grinned back, revealing a missing tooth. "No, no, Dearie," she said when she saw the money. "I don't take charity."

"Please, get something to eat. It would make me happy." I placed the money in the woman's palm and folded my hand around her icy fingers. "Then come back and hear us sing."

Later that evening, standing in the choir loft, I scanned the heads of the hundred or so people who'd come to our concert. The old woman wasn't there. Perhaps she'd taken the money to the nearest pub and drunk it away. Maybe the old woman had no interest hearing us sing.

As the sanctuary hushed, Bonnie looked like a girl sitting before the huge organ. A moment later, Hal raised his baton, then sliced it through the air. The first note shot out of the pipes, followed by a flood of chords rocketing throughout the sanctuary like meteors flying across the stratosphere—a glorious sound no other instrument could attain.

I fastened my gaze on Hal, his eyes catching fire as the crescendo blossomed into a swell of brilliance. It felt good to be part of this music, transported to a place where nothing else mattered.

In what seemed like a flash, the concert was over. Hal's face glistened with perspiration as he nodded his approval to us, then turned to bow to the audience. Blood still danced through my veins. I could have continued singing for hours.

The choir left by the same door we'd used that afternoon. Outside, I saw the old lady, grinning at all who passed. When I reached her, I impulsively hugged the woman, feeling a gnarled bent frame.

Nick strode to my side. My need to be held by him was intense. In a man's arms—was that the only place I could feel whole?

"May I take you somewhere to eat?" His fingers curved around my hand. "Just the two of us?"

"Yes, I'd like that."

CHAPTER 19

STROLLING SEVERAL BLOCKS to the restaurant, Nick and I passed stores housed in medieval-looking structures. The evening sky had turned the color of slate and the chill air creeping up my jacket sleeves discouraged me from dawdling to window-shop.

"I hope you don't mind Italian food again," Nick said, indicating with his hand that I should turn onto a side street.

"Not at all. It's one of my favorites."

"And what is your favorite?"

"I love my mother's pot roast the best." I was glad Mom still prepared it every Sunday—one of the few traditions left. "Beef stewed with vegetables and potatoes. Lots of gravy."

"If you like it, I'm sure it's delicious."

"It reminds me of the good old days." Way, way back, happiness had reigned in our household. Sure, my folks had spats, but for the majority of the time they acted lovey-dovey. I remembered them dancing in the kitchen to the radio. I remembered the gold charm bracelet Dad gave Mom on her birthday. He promised to add a charm every year—which never happened because he vamoosed six months later. The rapidity of his complete evaporation still made my head swim.

"I like to think the best days are ahead," Nick said. "Who knows what the future may bring?"

"You're right. It wouldn't hurt me to be more optimistic." If I played the role of Pollyanna would my life take an abrupt one-eighty? By the end of the night would I be cloaked in self-confidence? Unlikely, but I decided to proceed expectedly.

"Here we are." Nick stopped at a glass door. Above it stretched a green cloth awning with the words La Dolce Vita inscribed in white letters. We crossed the threshold and stepped past a grouping of ficus trees in terra-cotta pots. Inhaling, I smelled the aroma of sweet garlic, warm olive oil, and boiling pasta. The soundtrack of Puccini's *La Bohème* lilted in the background.

"*Buona sera,*" the hostess said.

"*Una tavola per due, per favore.*" Nick sounded marvelous conversing in his native tongue.

The hostess led us to a corner table with a votive candle and left two menus.

Sitting with my back to the wall, I looked across the room with its two dozen tables. Framed watercolors of Rome and Florence hung on the walls; on the far side of the room, four people were sampling red wine.

Nick reached across the table; his fingers entwined with mine. "Tonight, let's pretend there are just the two of us," he said. "No one else."

I was struck by his eyes, how they focused on mine with the intensity of laser beams. Returning his stare, I tried to see behind them into the darkness where his true feelings lay hidden. What would the next step in our relationship look like? If things went further, would this be another addition to my long list of regrets? It wouldn't be the first time I'd fallen for someone who'd turned out to be not at all what I'd imagined. Yet, here was an exceptional man. This moment would soon vanish and disappear into history.

I heard voices and chairs moving at the table behind Nick. I tore my gaze away to see the hostess seating Martin and a woman about his age. Her blonde hair was styled away from her elegant face, emphasizing high cheekbones and Bambi eyes. She wore an understated Ferragamo-style suit, its short skirt exposing sculpted legs. At the base of her neck hung a pearl choker: spheres the size of marbles. Speaking in a hushed voice, Martin pulled his chair close to the woman's, and they fell into conversation.

"What's the matter, my pretty one?" Nick asked me.

"Nothing." I opened my menu and tried to ignore Martin's gaiety at something the woman said. He looked animated, happy, exuding a youthful quality.

"Tonight, you let me take care of everything," Nick said, as I tried to pronounce an Italian word. He took my menu and folded it. Signaling the waiter over, Nick ordered an antipasto plate followed by scaloppini.

"It won't be as good as my grandmother's," he said when the waiter was gone, "but I'm sure you'll like it."

Gnawing off the end of a breadstick and chomping into it, I could see Martin and the woman leaning toward each other and whispering intently.

Nick finally glanced over his shoulder, his gaze tracing the woman's legs. "Oh, him." His foot touched mine under the table. "Pay no attention."

My dinner tasted delicious, but whatever was happening at the next table seemed better. The chef came out to serve their dinner in person and was pleased when Martin pronounced it superb.

Nick noticed my vision resting on Martin's table again.

"It's annoying having them right next to us," I told Nick, with an attitude of indifference.

"Yes, it would be nice to be alone." He set down his fork and dabbed his lips with his napkin. "Perhaps later."

What did Nick expect of me? I sipped my water and accidentally swallowed an ice cube, chilling me down to my stomach.

Laughter erupted from the next table. Martin took the woman's hand and kissed it. "You're an angel," he said.

Like a swan, the woman's arms encircled his neck. "When have I ever been able to say no to you?" she asked. He whispered something in her ear, and she hugged him.

I couldn't help but stare. I lost my appetite. I picked at the rest of my dinner, followed by espresso and biscotti, and Nick paid the bill.

"I insist," he said and reached for my hand. "Let's get out of here. I know a place where we won't be disturbed."

As we passed Martin's table, he glanced up. "Ah, Ms. Nash with our Nick." He rose and introduced us to Pamela.

Her face flushed with pleasure. "Friends of Marty?" she said, her voice silky. "Then you must be the first to congratulate us. We're engaged." Her left hand rested on the table next to her glass of wine. A hefty pear-shaped diamond surrounded by smaller diamonds adorned her ring finger.

My face must have worn a look of incredulity because she fell into laughter. Beautiful, refined, and no doubt blue-blooded Pamela looked like one of the Milton's daughters grown up. A suitable mate for Martin. One his parents would appreciate.

"That's wonderful." Too much enthusiasm elevated my voice. "Congratulations." I heard a false ring.

"Thank you." She gushed with delight. "It's a dream come true."

Martin extracted his credit card from his billfold and gave it to the waiter. It was just like Martin to force his future bride to make the announcement. I hoped she knew what she was getting herself into. Oh well, it was none of my business.

Nick led me to the front door and pushed it open. Soggy air gusted in. Outside, sheets of rain slapped the street, invading the gutter.

He grimaced at the sky. "I'd suggest waiting for the weather to improve, but it could pour like this all night."

"We can walk. I'll be fine." We had no other choice, even if it meant ruining my only dress pumps.

I heard Martin's and Pamela's voices nearing. "Are you on foot?" Martin asked us.

Pamela said, "You'd better ride with us." She fastened her mohair coat. "I'm parked right out front."

When I saw her sleek Jaguar at the curb, I realized Pamela had picked Martin up our first day in London. Here I'd thought he was shattered over his broken marriage, when in truth he had a girlfriend waiting in the wings.

Nick and I climbed into the leather backseat. As we cruised up to the hotel, I said, "I really appreciate the ride. And I hope you two will be happy together."

In the rearview mirror, I could see Pamela's face beaming with satisfaction. "Thank you. I'd do anything for Marty."

Leaving Martin with Pamela, I stepped out of the car into an ankle-deep puddle, the icy water splashing over my shoe. I sloshed to the hotel with Nick behind me.

Hal met us inside the lobby. "I've been looking for you," he said to Nick. "The porter coming on duty a few minutes ago said the bus's door is open. Someone may have broken in."

"But why?" I said, thinking of the parking lot at the side of the hotel. "There's no luggage aboard."

"Who knows how criminals think?" Hal said.

"I've never had anything like this happen before," Nick said. "Have you checked to see if it's true?"

Hal looked out the hotel's front window. Rain still saturated the air. "It's pouring so hard. I didn't want to venture out there alone."

"Shouldn't we call the police?" I asked. "What if someone's on the bus?"

"No, they could take hours getting here." Nick zipped his jacket further and raised his collar. "If someone broke in, they're probably gone by now. I'll go look."

"I'd better join you," Hal said. Without glancing my way, they headed outside and disappeared around the side of the building.

Telling myself they'd be back in a moment, I stood just inside the door. Pamela's car was gone. I wondered what she and Martin were doing. Talking about chapels and ministers?

The rain beating down sounded like gravel pelting a metal roof. I shivered as I watched the drops splat against the ground. I wanted to cry. I felt vulnerable, alone.

Holding in the tears, I raced to my room.

CHAPTER 20

THE NEXT MORNING, I couldn't shake a nagging sense of worry as Roxanne and I strolled atop Chester's wall, elevated two stories, stretching around the perimeter of the city. I felt in need of protection. From what or whom I wasn't sure.

I gazed upon the River Dee and saw a man rowing a scull, his oars rhythmically carving the dark band of water. Cottony mist hovered just above him, like a cloak hiding turbulent undercurrents.

Earlier today, Hal had reported that someone indeed had entered the bus. "Lots of muddy footprints, but it appears nothing was damaged or taken," he said, sounding unconvinced. "Maybe a tramp wanted to get in from the cold, although the bus was empty when we arrived. I'm guessing our driver forgot to lock it properly."

But Nick assured me he'd secured and double-checked the bus. And his sunglasses and map bag were left untouched.

I heard a boy shout, then another, their voices garnering my attention. Moving to the other side of the walkway, I looked down on a two-lane street and spotted several lads about Cooper's age, dressed in navy-blue uniforms and wearing backpacks. Roughhousing, they were probably on their way to school.

"I wish I'd been able to get hold of my mother last night," I said to Roxanne. "No one was home when I called, meaning she and Cooper were out somewhere."

"What a nice grandma. You're lucky."

"I am, but sometimes she treats me as though I'm incompetent, like I don't know what's best for my own child."

"I thought you two got along."

"We do, except when it comes to Cooper."

A man in a suit hustled our way lugging a briefcase. I waited for him to pass before saying, "Please don't tell anyone, Roxie." I felt a wave of humiliation. "The other night Cooper was caught shoplifting."

Roxanne's smile showed compassion. "Lots of kids do dumb things like that."

"Sure, I've been one of them. But he and I have talked about stealing. He knows it's wrong and should be grounded, at least given timeout in his room—no TV, no friends. But instead Mom's probably treating him to dinner at the Space Needle."

"If you feel strongly about it, couldn't you tell her?"

"It's hard to lay down the law from the other side of the globe. I've butted heads with Mom over how many sweets are good for Cooper right before dinner. And she disregards his curfew on school nights. Somehow, she always wins the debates, leaving me the bad guy." I stared at the plump moss bulging between the reddish sandstone rocks at our feet. I relived the moment Cooper hung up on me, how shocked and hurt I'd been. I'd immediately redialed the number, only to find the line busy. The phone was off the hook. Had he intentionally removed it? I wanted to think someone had called the house at that moment, but my intuition said Cooper was out to punish me.

"Enough about me," I said. "How do you feel?"

"Like a million bucks, so don't worry."

"I'm glad." I searched her face and could find no trace of illness. Her vitality seemed to ebb and flow.

As we continued our walk, starlings cackled and whistled in the trees growing next to the wall. In places, feathery branches spread over us, forming avocado-green canopies.

"This is where we started." I came to a halt. "I recognize the staircase leading to the ground level."

Descending the uneven steps, I saw pedestrians milling before shop windows. When we reached the street, a man wearing running pants sprinted toward us, his feet pounding the cobbled street, until he was almost face-to-face with me. I let out a small gasp of surprise when I realized it was Martin.

"Good morning," he said, then sucked in a chestfull of air. His face was flushed with perspiration, his breathing irregular. Recalling his usual staid attire and demeanor, I gave him a once-over and noticed running shoes that looked like they'd covered many miles.

"I didn't know you jogged."

"I try to run three or four times a week," he said. "Weather permitting."

"I go to the mall two or three times a week," Roxanne said. "The weather's always good in there."

Martin smiled. "I'll bear that in mind the next time it's raining." Everything she said seemed to amuse him, while the opposite held true for me.

"I hear congratulations are in order," she said. "You're tying the knot. Why didn't you tell us you had a girlfriend?"

Martin glanced at me, the blabbermouth who'd obviously been gossiping about him. "I didn't know myself," he said.

"Someone new?" Roxanne asked.

"On the contrary." He unzipped his jacket, then zipped it up again. "I've known Pamela most of my life."

"There's got to be more to it than that," I blurted. "I mean, two people don't decide to get married out of the blue." Although Jeff and I had. No counseling. No discussion about values, finances, or children.

"They shouldn't." His brows rose creasing his forehead. "But a man gets tired of living by himself."

Roxanne giggled. "Mr. Spear, where have you been hiding this side of yourself?"

"Yes, well, it's really nothing very extraordinary. Pamela and I are forming a partnership."

"A lifelong commitment," Roxanne said.

"She's the one person I can count on."

British men certainly were inept at romance. Not that Martin was acting out of character. I couldn't imagine his professing undying love for Pamela or gushing on about her merits, especially to me. But I'd seen the ring—a honker of a diamond looking like it came from Tiffany's or Cartier. That exquisite gift expressed more than a pillowcase of fluffy words.

With Martin between Roxanne and me, we made our way toward the hotel.

"Have you two set a date?" I asked him, wondering if the choir would be invited.

"No, not yet."

"Will the wedding be here or in the States?" Roxanne said.

"I shall leave the details up to my future bride." He checked his plastic sports watch. "Please excuse me, I need to get back to the hotel to shower before we leave."

Without a show of effort, he trotted nimbly around the corner. Roxanne was right. Where had Martin been hiding this side of himself?

"What's Pamela like?" Roxanne asked as we waited on the curb for a car to pass.

"She's very attractive. Terribly chic." The phrase "good breeding shows" did a figure eight through my mind. "That's an understatement. Pamela is gorgeous."

Roxanne cut me a sideways glance. "Is that a problem?"

"No, not at all. I hope they're ecstatic together." I had no right to feel otherwise.

Ten minutes later, we strolled through the hotel's foyer, then rode the elevator to the third floor. Stepping into the corridor, I spied Martin still in his running attire at the far end of the hall, speaking to several men.

As Roxanne and I neared Martin's open door, I heard one of the men say, "Sorry for the inconvenience, sir."

I stepped closer and scoped Martin's room. It looked like a hurricane had rampaged through—drawers gaping open, clothes and papers flung everywhere. Except his stainless-steel-and-gold watch sat on the bed table. A thief would leave a Rolex?

"What happened?" I asked.

"The porter came by and found the door ajar." Martin seemed unruffled. "Apparently someone's mussed up my room."

Roxanne moved to my side. "This is worse than my sisters' and my room when we were teenagers."

One of the men wore a brass badge with the word *manager* engraved on it. Addressing Martin, he said, "After you've checked through your belongings, please let us know if anything's missing."

"There was nothing of value in the room." Martin motioned the man to leave. "I'm sure everything's still here. I don't need to file a complaint, do I?"

"I say, that's awfully kind of you, sir." The manager backstepped out the door.

The corners of Martin's lips quirked up. I tried to catch his eyes, but he looked away.

I surveyed the tipped chair and shirts and slacks lying helter-skelter. A teacher and a mother, I was a whiz at orchestrating chaos into order. "Do you need help straightening up?" I asked him.

"No thanks, Ms. Nash." Martin's hand moved to the doorknob—a sign he wanted us to leave. "Everything's quite under control."

CHAPTER 21

SITTING NEXT TO Roxanne on the bus an hour later, I snuggled into my jacket to keep warm. Only a trace of heat escaped from the vent at my feet.

Nick cranked the bus out onto the road and around a tight corner, forcing oncoming traffic to stop. For the first time on the trip, he leaned on the horn and grumbled at a motorist, reminding me of the driver we had our first day in London. I hadn't seen Nick at breakfast and he'd barely said good morning as I boarded the bus. Had I done something to offend him?

Traveling south over hills toward Bath on a road that ribboned through villages of thatch-roofed cottages, the bus slowed as it crossed a one-lane bridge. I noticed weeping willows dipping their branches into a stream. Three helmeted children riding piebald ponies ambled down a path at the water's edge.

Several miles further, the bus neared the village of Shottery and ground to a halt in a car park next to

Anne Hathaway's cottage. I had been looking forward to seeing where William Shakespeare's wife had lived. Glancing out the window, I could see the cottage's dark brown-and-cream facade, its diamond-paned windows, and its shaggy thatched roof. Wanting to speak to Nick first, I purposely sorted through my purse to find my ChapStick as the others got off the bus.

"Go ahead without me," I told Roxanne, twisting off the cap and dabbing the glossy gel on my lips. "I'll be a few minutes."

Roxanne grabbed her water bottle and headed for the door. When everyone else had departed, I moseyed outside. Smelling a hint of smoke, I noticed a gray thread curling up from one of the cottage's three chimneys. As I wandered toward the cottage, I saw Nick returning from the ticket booth near the entrance. I didn't believe for a moment he'd accidentally left the bus door open last night the way Hal suggested.

"Good morning," I said. "How are you?"

He came to a halt, his chin raised. "How would you expect me to be after last night?"

"What do you mean?" I hoped he and Hal weren't disputing Nick's competence.

"Couldn't you have waited five minutes for me to return?" He jiggled his keys. "Any little thing is more important than me."

"It's not that." I recalled the damp insoles of my shoes and how I'd draped my waterlogged jacket over the radiator in my room to dry it. "I was cold and tired and didn't know when you'd be back."

"After that nice dinner I assumed we'd spend more time together."

Had I neglected to express my gratitude properly? "It was a delicious meal, and I'd like to thank you by buying you lunch today."

"No," he said, "I don't want that. I want you." His hands reached for my waist, but he pulled back, and folded his arms across his chest. "Every moment we have together is precious. There's so little time left."

"I'm sorry."

"*Non importa*. You don't owe me an apology."

"If I've hurt your feelings, I do."

The cottage's door snapped open and Clare thrust her head out. Looking slim in her stretchy jeans and long-sleeved T-shirt, she paraded in our direction.

"You're done already?" I asked when she reached us.

"Yeah, it was boring."

"You didn't care for Anne Hathaway's home?" Nick asked her.

"No, and I don't know how that woman endured living there, with those crooked walls and tiny little staircase. People must have been much shorter back when it was built. I'd go bonkers." She rubbed her arms. "Is it always this cold in England? I haven't warmed up since I got here."

"I often feel the same way," Nick agreed with her. He pivoted toward the bus. "*Signorina* Clare, hop aboard. I'll turn the heat up to the highest setting, just for you."

"You're a sweetheart." She sent him a coquettish smile.

"*Il piacere è mio*. The pleasure is all mine."

"I'm going inside the cottage," I said, although Nick didn't seem to be listening. "How much time do I have?"

"Not much." He spoke over his shoulder. "Better hurry or Hal will be on my back again."

I padded through the garden, every inch crammed with perennials and sculpted hedges. Primroses flashed purple and yellow. I recognized thyme, rosemary, and lavender, and inhaled the honeyed aroma of blooming *Daphne adoro*. Thinking about Nick, I felt the urge to spin back to the bus and finish our conversation. But Clare was there, and soon the others would return. Tonight, after the choir's performance, I would speak to him in private.

As I neared the cottage's entrance, I heard chattering voices and saw Bonnie and Roxanne coming out of the building. Roxanne chugged a mouthful of water, then she hastened off to find the ladies room.

I crossed the threshold just as Hal was exiting. "Time to get back on the bus," he said, swooshing me with his hands.

"But, I—"

"No buts. We have a busy schedule ahead of us."

I scurried through the cottage at breakneck speed. Minutes later, I was seated with Roxanne. The road wound past farms and pastures, then through another village. In the tidy gardens, I admired fruit trees unfurling vibrant leaves. The first pink buds burst from roses climbing up the sides of stone cottages.

"I wish I could afford to rent a house, so I could try my hand at gardening." Roxanne pressed her face to the window.

I thought of my own backyard—a strip of crabgrass with a few unruly shrubs and a homely wooden fence listing between the supporting posts.

"I never have time to get out in the yard," I said. "I used to corral Jeff into clipping the grass with the push mower on weekends, but somehow Cooper finagles his way out of helping."

Roxanne turned to me. "When I was young, I earned money weeding for the neighbors. I hated yard work then, but now it sounds relaxing, even therapeutic. You've seen my potted plants."

I remembered the African violets and coleus flourishing on her kitchen windowsill and the spiky ferns in her bedroom. "In that case," I said, "come to my house for some free therapy. How are you at mending fences? Mine looks like it's ready for the morgue."

"Between the two of us, we could fix it."

"I still have Jeff's tools, but I don't know how to use them."

"I do. I was the son my father never had."

Except for choir practice, Roxanne and I spent little time together. When she wasn't tied up at work, I was busy being a mom. I pictured the corner room in my daylight basement, used for storage of boxes of things I didn't need that could be placed elsewhere or given away. The area was smallish but had its own bathroom. Close to the oil furnace, it remained snug in the winter, but cool in the summer.

"Would you consider moving in with me?" I asked her. "I have a spare bedroom with its own bathroom in my daylight basement." I wondered why I hadn't thought of it before.

Roxanne granted me a look of disbelief. "Are you serious?"

"Yes, absolutely. You could pay a little rent to help with the mortgage and keep up the yard."

"You don't want me living with you. You might get married again, and then you'd be stuck with a troll in the basement."

"You're not a troll," I said. "You're a princess. And the chance of my remarrying is slim to none."

Roxanne angled her head toward Nick. "What about him? How are you two getting along?"

BY AFTERNOON, I noticed the tall clouds parting, making way for a sunny day. When the bus stopped at gigantic Warwick Castle, Nick and Hal led the group, the two men chatting about the Hundred Years War and Richard III. Nick had returned to his usual gregarious self but hadn't waited for me. I followed at the end of the line, my face up, soaking in the warmth. Birds warbled in nearby trees, their arias mellowing my mood.

Martin and Clare strolled ahead of me. Beyond them I saw the magnificent medieval castle, its two towers standing tall like rooks in a giant game of chess. In the valley below, the River Avon flowed wide and lazy.

"Jerry's his name?" Martin said to Clare. "I'd like to meet this fellow. Why don't you ask him to join us for dinner?"

I couldn't hear what Clare said in return, but she was shaking her head.

"Listen to someone who's almost ruined his own voice and his career in the process," he continued. "If he were a worthy gentleman, he'd have your best interests in mind."

Nick stood on the other side of the moat in front of the entrance gate talking to one of the guards and passing out tickets to the choir members. His handsome face cast a stunning contrast to the stodgy old man in his drab uniform.

After Martin and Clare entered, Nick stepped toward me, meeting me partway across the wooden drawbridge.

"Have you forgiven me?" I asked.

"I didn't know you wanted forgiveness." He wore a wintry expression. "You don't seem sorry."

"I wish I'd waited." Was it possible I had this much effect on him? "I'm sorry."

"If I'm hurt, it's only because I care."

How long had I waited to hear a man say he gave a hoot about me? During my marriage I was lucky if Jeff thanked me for dinner. Before I said, "I do," he'd showered me with kisses, but after I announced my pregnancy, he never said he loved me again.

Was Nick cut from the same cloth? A fanfare of affection and compliments until I invested myself in a relationship with him?

CHAPTER 22

AFTER THE HOTEL receptionist in the city of Bath had distributed the keys to our rooms, Nick pulled me aside.

"I'll be gone for the night," he said. "Something has come up—at the main office." He glanced to the carpet. "I'm taking the train to London in twenty minutes."

"That seems a long way to go," I said.

"Not really." His gaze met mine. "Many people commute to London from this distance. Ordinarily I wouldn't leave, but I want to check on my cat. A neighbor in my apartment building is looking after her, but still, I worry."

"Understandable, if you need to make sure your kitty is okay."

"I'll be back before breakfast. I'd better run. *Ciao*."

As I entered my room, I considered the places I wanted to see in Bath. Nick had told us the Romans built England's first spa around a pool of bubbling

waters still considered medicinal. And I remembered
from college that Jane Austen had lived here in her
youth and wrote about the city.

I called Roxanne's room. "I'm going to lie down for
a while," she said in a sluggish voice.

Minutes later, I moseyed out of the hotel onto the
sidewalk. Two blocks away, I found the heart of Bath
bustling with tourists holding outstretched maps, local
shoppers, and women pushing strollers. On the corner
stood three musicians playing stringed instruments,
one on a violin and two on guitars. A hat sat at their
feet for tips. I dropped several coins in because they
were entertaining me, a job of sorts. Not shoplifting.

I noticed a sign pointing toward the Roman Baths
and found the Great Bath a block away, housed in a
Georgian-style building. I descended stairs to the edge
of the rectangular spring-fed pool surrounded by Ionic
columns. Smelling minerals and algae, I felt heat rising
off the water's surface as it had for two thousand years.
With no roof overhead, I could see the powder-blue sky
above and the crown of the Abbey Church next door.

On the way, I wandered through the famous Pump
Room, a formal dining and tea area where Jane Austen's
characters sipped the mineral waters, hoping to gain
strength and healing. I purchased a glass of water for
forty-five pence and sampled the bitter-tasting liquid,
then left the half-full glass on a nearby table.

Finally, back on the street and heading toward the
hotel, I spied a shop called The Sword and the Stone.
In its window stood dozens of metal figurines—dragons
and kings and soldiers. I guessed Cooper would prefer

a new video game and groan if I brought him something educational, but these silver-colored statues, many holding faceted crystals, might catch his fancy. I contemplated not taking anything home for him, as punishment. But I couldn't stay mad at him forever. Eventually I'd wrapped my arms around his shoulders, kiss his cheek, and tell him I forgave him. If he wanted forgiveness.

Inside the store, I picked up a statue of a woman in a long gown and was struck by its heavy weight.

"That's Lady Guinevere," said an older saleswoman with black-rim glasses and grizzled hair, standing behind the counter. "Next to her is Sir Lancelot."

"The consummate couple." I thought of how their love story still captured people's fancy after over one thousand years. "They had the perfect romance."

"What about King Arthur?" The woman raised an eyebrow.

"I can't remember how the tale went. Wasn't Lady Guinevere the reason Sir Lancelot performed his deeds of valor and fought in the tournaments?"

"But she was married to another." Her features hardened. "In most great love stories, there is tragedy. Someone is left crying."

"I don't agree." What a depressing attitude, not what I wanted to hear.

"Think about it," she said, coming around the counter. "Name one celebrated romance where everyone lived happily ever after."

My mind shuffled through stories of the world's greatest lovers—Romeo and Juliet, Tristan and Isolde,

Anthony and Cleopatra, my mother and father. "I guess. Still, that's a sad way to look at life."

I lifted a statuette of Merlin the Magician grasping a sparkling globe in his palm as if searching into its center for the truth. "Do you think they all really lived?"

"Maybe not Merlin, although I like to think so. But you can see where King Arthur and Lady G. are buried. It's a breathtaking spot. Their graves lie side by side, under the ruins of a cathedral. It's not far from here."

I forced a show of interest but had no intention of going there. I avoided cemeteries. I took Cooper to Jeff's graveside once a year. After each visit, Jeff's funeral—the whole surrealistic scene—replayed in my mind for days. The pastor officiating the service had no clue about Jeff's complexities and had described him as an adoring husband and doting father. His parents, who flew in from Massachusetts, barely exchanged two words with me—as if the car accident were somehow my fault. I'd tried to see the tragedy through a parent's eyes, but it hurt when my in-laws showed no interest in continuing our relationship. Except for a yearly birthday or Christmas present for Cooper, they were all but strangers.

The store's front door rattled open, and Roxanne moseyed in. "There you are, girlfriend. I about gave up finding you." She wore a crease on her cheek.

"Have a nice nap?" I asked, thinking she looked more fatigued than before.

"Yes, but I decided seeing Bath was more import-ant than getting beauty rest." Eyeing the figurines, she opened the lid of a metal goose-size egg and discovered a baby dragon. "How cute is that? Maybe I'll buy two. One for each niece."

I handed the saleswoman my credit card, and the Merlin statuette to be wrapped in tissue paper. Were the woman's pessimistic remarks about conflicted romance correct? I hoped not. Yet, operas like *Madame Butterfly* and *La Bohème* revolved around the theme of unrequited love. Few had happy endings. I remembered Jeff's and my ugly blowups. We'd hurled vicious words like daggers that could never be retracted.

CHAPTER 23

THAT EVENING, THE church was small. The
aged organ produced half the volume of the one
the night before. I was relieved for Clare, whose raspy
voice sounded like it was being transmitted over a
distant radio station.

"I'll be fine," Clare had snapped as she and I dressed
for the performance. Sopranos can be so competitive,
I'd thought, envisioning the alto section, getting along
like a school of angelfish. There was nothing I wanted
less than to sing Clare's solo.

Hal stood before us, donning a mask of exhaustion.
His eyelids drooped and his face wore a sickly cast,
like aging plaster. Maybe he'd caught Clare's cold or
run into another flu bug. He probably wished he were
home with his wife catering to him. The thought of Hal
sitting in bed with a cup of herbal tea was sweet, but the
director staring at us looked like an angry child ready
to throw a tantrum.

He raised his baton and sliced it through the air. Bonnie commenced playing the organ. The first anthem went smoothly, almost too smoothly.

I remembered Hal's warning us that once the choir knew a piece well, the music could become flat and boring. "Think about what the words mean each time you open your mouth," he'd instructed. "We're telling a story—not reciting random syllables."

Clare sounded pitiful, her voice brittle and her pitches sharp. Any jealousy or anger toward her dissolved into pity, then embarrassment. It was hard not to grimace, hard to make myself zero in on Hal, who looked as though he might murder his precious soloist. On the final chord, his lips pressed together like a clothespin.

"What were you thinking?" Hal bellowed at her after the concert ended and we were back in the rehearsal room. His Adam's apple protruded like a golf ball. "How could you embarrass us like that?" His face menaced only inches from Clare's, her eyes wide. "If you had no voice, why didn't you tell me?" They stood nose to nose for a moment, then he whirled to the others. "And it wasn't just Clare. People, what were you doing up there? That wasn't a concert; it was a travesty."

Words were trapped in his mouth. He shook his head as he tried to spit them out. Parading past each singer, he even glared at Martin, then stomped away.

"Don't be too hard on Hal," Roxanne said to me later at dinner. The whole choir, save Clare, had decided to stick together for moral support. "He'd be up there singing the solos himself if he could." She dribbled blue cheese dressing over her tossed salad. "He told me that years ago he wanted to study voice at Julliard but couldn't cut the mustard. It was a huge disappointment."

"Hal's too controlling." I tore off a hunk of bread. "He'd never submit to someone else directing him." I slathered butter on my bread and gnawed off a mouthful. True, he did have an excellent voice as he guided us through our lines in rehearsals. It was amazing how easily he learned everyone's parts. He read music as quickly as a newspaper. But did that give him the right to bawl us out like disobedient children?

"We did sound pretty bad," Drew said from my other side.

Martin, his face grim, sat across from us. "I wasn't pleased with my performance either," he said. "I'm glad my mother wasn't part of our audience."

"Still, I don't like being yelled at." I stabbed a lettuce leaf with my fork. I didn't know why I felt so miffed. Hal hadn't attacked me personally. "Poor Clare," I said. "I should have gone after her when she started crying."

"She doesn't want your pity," Martin said. "I tried to reason with her yesterday. A singer can end her career pushing the vocal cords like that."

"I wonder if she'll be able to sing tomorrow," Roxanne said. "She'd better take care of herself tonight."

"We're all tired," Martin said. "We should go to bed and pretend today never happened."

"No way." Roxanne's face brightened. "I'm not going to sleep with Hal's angry words blathering around in my brain. It's good to gain distance from these things before your head hits the pillow." Speaking past me to Drew, her eyes became merry. "You up for a party tonight?"

Drew's ruddy face brightened. "Just lead me to it."

Roxanne's infectious good humor spilled over onto most of the group. Even Martin agreed to tag along. Thirty minutes later, twelve of us were at a club with a live band grinding out oldies. Candles glowed on the wooden tables, and a mirrored globe hanging from the ceiling sent twirling lights across the darkened room.

Roxanne coaxed Martin out onto the parquet dance floor, and I danced with Drew. Martin belly laughed when Roxanne did the twist, then he joined in.

When the song ended, Roxanne took Drew's arm for support. "I've got to sit down," she said. "Let these two dance."

Martin turned to me. "You game, Ms. Nash?"

"Sure. Why not?" I hadn't danced in years. Not even in my living room with the curtains closed. I let the music carry me, swaying to the heavy bass beat, relaxed and flowing. Martin watched me with a faraway expression on his face, no doubt missing Pamela.

The band members set their instruments aside to take their break. As Martin and I headed back to our table, the jukebox played a slow piece.

Roxanne slumped in her chair, cradling her head in her hands. Drew patted her shoulder. "I'll get you more water." He motioned the waitress over.

I sat across from them. "Everything okay?"

Roxanne lifted her head, her face ghostlike under the lights.

"Roxie isn't feeling good." Drew said. "She has a killer headache."

Martin sank into the seat next to me. "Perhaps we should find a doctor," he said.

"No way." Roxanne rubbed one eye, smearing her mascara. "I'm just tired."

"But Roxie," I said. "Maybe it's more than fatigue."

Roxanne tossed me a fierce look. "I think I know what's going on in my own body."

"You might have a virus," Drew offered. "You said the dancing made you dizzy."

Roxanne's voice surged with anger. "That's the last time I tell you anything."

I pulled my chair closer to the table. "He's trying to help."

"I don't need help, and I can't afford to waste money on a doctor, let alone the pills they always want to shove down your throat."

The waitress brought a glass of water. Roxanne gulped it down, then trudged to the restroom.

I'd never seen Roxanne acting like Oscar the Grouch. Was it that time of the month? As I watched her weave her way across the room, I mulled over what it would be like living with her. Maybe a housemate was a bad idea after all. But the whole time I'd known Roxanne, I'd never seen her lose her temper, not even when drivers cut ahead of her in traffic.

"What do you think?" I asked Martin and Drew. "Does she look okay to you?"

Martin rubbed his chin. "She's not herself. That's obvious."

"Roxie told me she was having minor health problems, but nothing I should worry about," Drew said.

Martin nodded "Yes, she mentioned she'd been feeling tired."

"Maybe we should take her back to the hotel and tuck her into bed," I said, thinking we'd use a cab rather than walk. "We can't force her to see a doctor."

"I'll find a way." Martin got to his feet. "And I'll pay for the visit."

Drew also stood and pushed in his chair. "We'll split the bill."

An hour later, Roxanne and I sat in an exam room at the Royal United Hospital.

Roxanne had given up arguing. "I'm sorry I snarled at you." Her lifeless hands lay in her lap and her ankles crossed.

"That's okay. I can get cantankerous sometimes myself."

"And I'm sorry you got dragged into coming along. And poor Drew and Martin, stuck out in the waiting room."

I tried to stifle a yawn, but weariness invaded me. "None of us minds."

"I hate hospitals, don't you?" She glanced around the room, with its beige walls and linoleum floor. "This reminds me of when I had my appendix removed in the first grade. I was scared to death, spending the night by myself."

"That would be frightening." I breathed in the bitter smell of alcohol and cleaning solution. "Maybe hospitals didn't let parents stay the night back then."

"Nah. My mother was home gobbling tranquilizers to calm her nerves. And my father would have called me a sissy if I'd asked him to be there." She attempted a smile, but I could tell the memory pained her. "How about you?" she said. "Ever had surgery?"

"The only time I've spent in the hospital was giving birth to Cooper."

"One of the happiest days of your life?"

"Absolutely." I decided not to mention my torturous labor without Jeff, who'd showed up an hour after Cooper's birth with alcohol breath.

"Everything I went through was worth it when I held Cooper for the first time," I said. "It was the beginning of a love affair. Better than Fourth of July fireworks or an eclipse of the sun."

"You decided one kid was enough?"

"We wanted more—at least I did. But I couldn't get pregnant again. I asked Jeff if he'd secretly gotten a vasectomy, but he denied it. He implied there was something wrong with me, but my gynecologist said I looked normal."

"Sorry," Roxanne said. "I shouldn't have asked."

"That's okay. Truth is, Jeff and I didn't get along." It felt good to be honest. I never even told Mom how lonely married life was. "Jeff had a roving eye that rarely glanced in my direction. But I loved him anyway. Pretty pathetic."

The doorknob turned and the nurse, a striking East Indian woman, entered the room with the form Roxanne had filled out earlier affixed to a clipboard. The fine-boned nurse reached into the cabinet for a blood pressure cuff, landed on a swivel stool, and glided over to Roxanne, who offered her arm.

"How are you tonight?" the nurse asked, tightening the cuff around Roxanne's upper arm.

Roxanne stared across the room. "Fine," she said without conviction.

The nurse slipped her stethoscope under the cuff and listened. After jotting numbers down on the paper, she took Roxanne's pulse, then measured her blood pressure again.

"On any medications?" the nurse asked.

Roxanne shook her head.

"Do you smoke?"

"Only for three weeks in high school, until my mother found out." She chuckled. "You wouldn't want to tangle with her."

The nurse didn't respond. "The doctor will be in, in a moment." She left the room, shutting the door behind her.

"Which probably means an hour," Roxanne said.

People were speaking out in the hallway, then the door swung open and a woman looking close to retirement age strode in. "I'm Dr. McMillan." She glanced at me briefly, then extended a hand to Roxanne and shook hers. "Tell me about your symptoms."

"I was light-headed earlier." Roxanne massaged her temple. "And I had a headache, but I feel better now."

"Your blood pressure's elevated," Dr. McMillan said, no-nonsense. Light from the overhead fluorescent bulbs reflected off her tortoise shell glasses and filtered through her sparse frizzy hair. "Do you have a history of hypertension?"

"No, but it was high last week. My doc told me to have it monitored at the fire station. I love those cute firemen, but I was too busy between work and getting ready to come here. I figured I'd get started when I got home."

"And you've been tired, even before we left Seattle," I said, recalling Roxanne at our final rehearsal in the church basement.

"That's because I haven't been sleeping well. I get up to pee several times a night, then can't fall back asleep."

"You've been drinking lots of water?" Dr. McMillan folded her arms.

"Yes."

"Tell her what your doctor said," I urged.

"She thinks I have Type 2 diabetes—the good kind, what 90 percent of people with diabetes have."

"I didn't realize there was a good kind." Dr. McMillan pushed her glasses up onto the bridge of her nose. "Did your physician put you on medication?"

"Yes, but I didn't get a chance to fill the prescription."

"Did she advise you of the risks of leaving this condition untreated?"

"She gave me a pamphlet."

Dr. McMillan's voice rose with urgency. "Type 2 diabetes is extremely serious. Because many patients have no symptoms at all, a person can live with it for years. Left untreated, type 2 diabetes raises the risk of heart disease, stroke, and kidney failure. I'm surprised your physician didn't give you better instructions."

Roxanne managed a half-smile. "She told me to eat rabbit food. Vegetables and whole grains. And to exercise every day."

Dr. McMillan leaned back to assess Roxanne's full figure. "That sounds fine, although I think a daily thirty-minute walk will suffice in the beginning. And cut refined sugar and white flour out of your diet."

"I'll try."

"If I were you, I'd do more than try."

"We've been on the road all week. It's hard when you're eating your meals in restaurants. All that bread and butter, and dessert with every meal."

Dr. McMillan jotted something on the chart as she spoke. "You seem to be an intelligent young woman, but you're behaving as though you have no control over the matter."

Wanting to defend Roxanne, I felt myself lift off my chair. But arguing with Dr. McMillan wouldn't help Roxanne. In spite of the doctor's brusque manner, her lecture made sense.

"Did you know heart disease is the number one killer of women?" Dr. McMillan said. "You're more likely to die of heart-related disease than cancer. I should know, my own sister had a stroke two years ago. Thankfully, she's alive, but she lost the use of her right arm and leg. Think about that."

Roxanne gawked into the doctor's face. "I'm sorry about your sister."

"I'm not looking for sympathy. It's you I'm worried about. I'm going to give you some reading material." She reached into a drawer to retrieve several pamphlets.

Stretching my neck, I could read the titles *Type 2 Diabetes: The Silent Killer* and *Women and Heart Disease*.

Roxanne took the papers, perused the first one. "Thanks."

"I could keep you here longer to make sure you read them."

"No, that's okay," Roxanne said, hanging her head. "I promise, I'll look at them tonight."

"See that you do."

AFTER ESCORTING ROXANNE to her room, I returned to mine to find Clare still out. Was she with Jerry again? I hadn't seen him in the audience tonight. Attractive as Clare was, no man would track her from town to town like a bloodhound unless he was *meshugana*, as Mom would say.

I remembered the scrap of paper I'd found under Clare's slip and wish I hadn't returned it to her. I was tempted to dig through her suitcase to find it. But chances are it belonged to a boyfriend back home. I'd have egg on my face and give Clare another reason to loathe me.

I chose the twin bed in the corner with a Renoir print hanging above it. I changed into my nightgown, then scrambled under the covers. The sheets felt icy cold.

Shivering, I reached for the telephone sitting on the table between the two beds. I dialed my home number and listened to it drone until the answering machine began its message. I hung up and tried again without success.

Cooper loved going to his Grandma Miriam's house, I reminded myself. Maybe the two were settled at Mom's kitchen table, where I sat as a girl eating her homemade chocolate-swirl babka. I was thankful she'd kept the house. Each room sheltered endless childhood memories; when I visited, I was swathed with feelings of safety and stability.

I dialed her number and she answered on the second ring. "Hello?" she sang out with anticipation.

"Hi, it's me."

"Oh, hello, dear." Her voice returned to its usual timbre. "I wasn't expecting to hear from you again so soon."

"I know these calls are expensive, but I miss Cooper." I considered telling her about Roxanne's visit to the ER but decided to wait. No use getting Mom worried. "How's he doing?"

"Just fine. Now, don't give me any grief. He's spending the afternoon and night at Joey's."

"But Mom—"

"Listen, I needed a break."

Even I found a whole week of vacation tiring without lunch with a girlfriend or a stroll through the mall. "Okay, Mom, I understand."

Her doorbell chimed. I heard her, I assumed cordless phone in hand, open her front door.

"Hello, beautiful," a man with a deep voice said. "Almost ready?"

"I'll be with you in a minute," she said, sounding aflutter. "Make yourself at home."

"Who's that?" I demanded, winding the telephone cord around my finger.

Mom quieted her voice. "Someone I've been seeing."

"For how long?"

"Six months. No, make that nine."

"You've been going out with a man for more than half a year and never mentioned him?"

"Jessie, let me go in the bedroom." After a pause, Mom said, "I didn't want to say anything until I knew if it was serious, and I think it is."

"How serious?"

"I think Tim—that's his name, Tim O'Malley—may pop the question tonight."

I couldn't help being shocked, appalled. She was thinking of hitching up with someone I'd never even heard of? With a name like Tim O'Malley, he couldn't be Jewish. Not that it mattered. After all Mom stopped attending synagogue soon after Dad flew the coop. She claimed to prefer my church. But still.

"You mean he's going to ask you to marry him? After such a short time?"

"He's been hinting. Saying how lonely he's been since his wife passed away two years ago. Asking me how I'd feel about living in a fancy-schmancy lakefront condominium, which he just happens to own."

She'd be willing to sell her home and move in with a stranger because he was lonely? "Are you sure you know him well enough?" I said. "How old is he? What does he do for a living?"

Mom snickered. "You sound like me. Remember, in this relationship, I'm the mother."

"But I thought you liked being independent and didn't need a man."

"I don't need a man. I want one. Tim's very nice. You'll like him."

"I'm sure I will." Although I hadn't thought much of her last beau, the retired pharmacist. "Promise me you won't rush into anything."

"*Ketsele*, your father left me thirty years ago. I'd hardly call this a rebound romance."

I knew I should be elated for her. Weddings were joyous events. What kind of a horrible daughter would wish to deny her mother a chance for nuptial bliss? Mom was a vibrant woman of sixty-two, young enough to enjoy many more years of life.

"I'm sorry," I said. "I'm acting selfishly. I want you to be happy."

"Thanks. You and I could both use a dose of happiness. I need to run. I don't want to keep Tim waiting."

Hanging up the phone, I pictured Mom and this Tim person wrapped in each other's arms like teens making out. I tried to imagine what he was like and hoped he treated Mom like a queen. Was Tim a father, a grandfather? Would Cooper and I be forced to share Mom at Christmas and Thanksgiving with a huge extended family? Would our Sunday dinners come to an end? If they married, would she change her last name to his?

Not that there was any reason to hang onto my father's family name. I hadn't when I got married. But still...

I'd never fall asleep with these questions zinging through my brain. I dug into my suitcase for *Rebecca* and began reading. Manderley, the majestic stone manor, was not what the new Mrs. de Winter had expected when she hurriedly married her husband. Nor was her new life. She'd envisioned herself playing the part of the deceased Rebecca, her predecessor, performing all the specialties that pleased her new spouse. She'd tried to be a chameleon, as I had done.

I set the book on the nightstand. Did I know who I was anymore? Sure, I was a mother, but Cooper's stunt proved I hadn't done a good job. I was a daughter, but Mom was jetting off into a new life.

I shut off my light. Stretching out my legs, I lay in the stillness waiting for Clare's return.

CHAPTER 24

M Y ALARM CLOCK shrilled. My arm flew out to
silence it. A moment later, the phone clanged. I
turned over to see that Clare's bed had not been slept
in. I grabbed the phone off the bed table and heard her
muffled voice.

"You've got to do me a favor." Clare sounded far
away and under duress. "Pack my bag and make sure it
gets onboard, okay?"

"Are you all right?" I bolted up to a sitting position.
"Where are you? Do you need help?" Did 911 work in
Great Britain?

"I'm okay." Her hoarse voice showed none of its usual
cheekiness. "Don't tell Hal. I'll be there as quickly as
I can."

LATER, ON THE bus, Clare sobbed into my shoulder. "I found out Jerry's been following Martin, not

me." Her eyeliner was smeared into half-moons under her eyes. "He's a detective for an insurance company."

I pondered this snippet of information. An insurance company wouldn't go to the trouble of following Martin unless it had proof of his guilt. Jerry had been tailing him since Seattle, meaning he thought Martin had the necklace with him. Indignation welled up inside me as I remembered how Martin had attempted to involve me in his scheme. He'd asked me to transport stolen goods. If I were caught with it, I could be imprisoned in Great Britain.

"Jerry suggested I cozy up with Martin," Clare said. "To worm my way into his bedroom."

"That's disgusting. Does he think he's starring in a James Bond movie?"

She coughed into her palm and wiped her hand on her pants leg. "I feel so stupid. He told me he loved me, but this morning when he opened his wallet a photo of a woman came flying out."

"I'm sorry. That must hurt."

Her features melted like wax, giving her a clown's face. "I hate men, don't you?" She glanced around to see if anyone was listening, but the other choir members were engaged in conversation or busy looking out the window.

"I don't want anyone finding out what a chump I've been," she said. "You know how people talk." She was squeezing my hand so hard it hurt. "Can you keep this to yourself?"

"Clare, I'm not a gossip. Nor am I in the judgment game."

"Maybe God will punish me," she said. "If I can't sing anymore, I might as well commit suicide."

"You're going to be okay. I've been there before—at the bottom of the pit with only darkness above and no visible way to climb out. But look at me, I'm still here."

Clare's hand loosened its grip, then reached into her purse for a Kleenex.

A minute later, Hal wobbled down the aisle and tapped Clare on the shoulder. "Would you sit somewhere else so I can speak to Jessica?" he said.

Glowering, Clare got to her feet and moved to a seat several rows behind us.

Hal had done a sloppy job shaving, nicking his chin twice and leaving a rough patch on his jawline. "I'll need you to sing Clare's piece tonight," he advised me, rubbing his face.

He couldn't be serious. I studied his expression to see if he was joking, but he stared back with his usual intensity.

I answered immediately. "Thanks for the thought, but several others would do a better job." I tried to sound calm but heard myself whimpering like my neighbor's poodle when forgotten on the back porch.

"I don't agree." Hal drew closer and hushed his voice. "Shirley can't hit the high note and Marci doesn't have the classical training needed for this piece. It calls for technique. Your teacher Muriel Frank's brand."

He knew I studied with Muriel? What he didn't know was that, except for a few college girls, I was her most novice student. Hal had never listened to my voice without Clare embellishing it. If he'd heard me at my recent audition, I'd be the last person in the choir he'd ask. Why, even Roxanne faking the high notes would sound superior. I was in a quagmire. I didn't want to convince him I couldn't sing at all.

I sputtered a laugh. "I don't know the music." I pictured my brain going blank in front of the audience and my voice quivering like a ninety-five-year-old. No matter how poorly Clare sang last night, I'd sound a thousand times worse. I would humiliate the whole choir. Hal might kick me out and not let me sing on Sunday mornings anymore. And Nick would hear. Not to mention Martin.

Hal patted my hand like I was begging for a treat. "Don't worry," he said. "We'll go over the music before the performance."

CHAPTER 25

ONCE AT THE Victorian seaside town of Brighton, Roxanne and I wandered onto the giant pier standing high above the English Channel. The white buildings housing an amusement arcade were boarded up until warmer weather. Only two Union Jacks flying atop poles at either side of tall letters spelling Brighton Pier snapped in the wind.

I watched the breeze loosen and toss Roxanne's curls. Sunlight filtering through the fog turned her hair the color of a robin's breast.

"You look like you're feeling your old self," I said, noticing her rosy cheeks. "I hope you're not mad at us for making you see the doctor."

"Nah. More than anything, embarrassed. Sorry I acted like a jerk."

"You're forgiven." I slowed my pace to watch seagulls squabble over a dead fish bobbing in the churning waves below us.

"I'll find a way to pay Martin and Drew back when we get home," she said.

At the hospital, both men insisted they wanted nothing in return. I considered how I'd react in the same scenario and knew I'd want to repay the debt, especially to Martin. But I remembered how satisfying it felt to give the old woman in Chester money for supper.

"How about making them dinner?" I suggested.

"That's not enough. Not the way I cook."

"Yes, it is. Anyway, Martin seems well off, and Drew worked at Microsoft for fifteen years and hinted his stocks in the company have served him well. And he said he enjoyed helping a damsel in distress."

Laughter bubbled out of her mouth. "Me, a damsel?" She rested her elbows on the railing. "That doctor reminded me of the Wicked Witch in *The Wizard of Oz*. But she's right. I need to get with the program and shed this extra padding. I've decided I'm getting down to a size twelve by summer."

"I hope you're not planning to starve yourself."

"Nah, this is what I always say when I start a new diet. Jenny Craig, Weight Watchers—I've tried them all. I'm gung ho for the first three weeks, then I fall off the wagon and add ten extra pounds. How do you stay so thin?"

"I suffer, just like everyone else. At home I don't eat dessert, and I make myself ride my stationary bike and take neighborhood walks on weekends."

"You're disciplined."

"Not really, just practical. When my clothes get too tight, I've got nothing to wear. I can't afford a new wardrobe."

We started walking back toward shore to hook up with Nick, who had recommended a visit to the Royal Pavilion, a cream-puff version of the Taj Mahal built like an oriental palace.

The wind gusting against my back impelled my dragging feet. Ahead, I saw the long stretch of peachy-gold beach and hotels standing shoulder-to-shoulder beyond it on the other side of the road. As I listened to the seagulls' bleating cries I thought about my conversation with Hal. I had dreamed of soloing at church on a Sunday morning. But in this fantasy, I'd practiced the song for months. And the piece would be set in mid-range tessitura, so I wouldn't need my head voice for the elusive notes soaring into the ozone.

"You listen to yourself too much," Muriel had told me more than once. "Just sing. Give the music away."

Easy for her to say. Her voice filled the largest of halls like a monarch butterfly waltzing across the tips of daylilies—bright, agile, every syllable distinct, unlike my garbled squeaky notes. Just thinking how my voice sounded to others caused a swell of nausea to gurgle through my stomach.

"I won't have time to see the Royal Pavilion," I said as we neared the road. "I need to find Hal. He asked me to sing Clare's solo tonight."

"That's great, girlfriend! It's about time."

Roxanne was my close ally and not objective about my voice. There was no use arguing with her. When

Hal and I got together, I'd set things right. Maybe we could skip Clare's piece. The audience wouldn't care.

"I can hardly wait to hear you sing," Roxanne said as we parted.

"I wish I had your optimism."

She gave me a bear hug. "Too bad we can't do a trade. You give me a dose of your willpower, and I give you a shot of self-confidence."

WHILE THE OTHERS explored Brighton, Hal and I searched for a piano. Behind the hotel's restaurant, we found an upright in a lifeless room smelling of radiator dust.

Hal sat on the piano stool and arranged the sheet music. My pulse quickened and my mouth went dry. I should have brought water, but it was too late. As Hal played the bar before my entrance, my heart raced as though terrorists wielding assault rifles were about to mow us down.

Hal glanced over his shoulder, waiting for me to expel the first word, but I stood there like a goof. When I didn't sing, his fingers stopped tapping the keys.

"Hal." I didn't want to admit it, but he'd find out anyway. "When I get nervous, my brain goes blank. Even after I've studied the music until it should be second nature, I freeze and forget the words."

"But you'll have the score in front of you." He held his hands like an open book.

"I can't read the music and follow you at the same time." My words slurred themselves.

"I'll tell you a secret." Still sitting, he walked the piano stool closer. "I used to suffer from debilitating stage fright. I was fine in rehearsals, but performances made me physically ill. And it took days to recover."

"Good, then you understand."

"Not so fast." He motioned me over. "Let's try something." Standing, he placed his hands on my shoulders. "We know each other pretty well, don't we?"

I was gratified to see empathy in his eyes, but in reality, we barely knew each other. His show of kindness wouldn't see me through Clare's song.

"Let's try an experiment," he said. "What would happen if you sang to me and only me?"

"As you just witnessed, I can't."

"But we'll go over the piece until you relax."

"I guess if you were the only person in the room, I'd be okay. But there'll be a church full of people staring at me." The other choir members' disapproval worried me as much as the audience's.

"You could ignore them and pretend they're not there. Believe me, there's no use searching the audience's faces hoping for their approval. They won't give you what you're looking for."

He rolled the stool back to the piano, sat down, and played the first chord with grandiosity. Smiling at his rendition, he said, "You've heard Clare do this piece dozens of times. I'll bet you could sing it through without the music if you weren't under pressure. Give it a try."

As he played the four-bar introduction, I watched the notes dance by on the printed page but missed my cue.

He lifted his hands from the keys. "No problem, I'll start again." And he played through the introduction.

This time, I entered at the right spot and sang the first few words. "The king of love . . ." I winced as my notes warbled flat. Hal nodded at me to continue. With each line, my voice improved. I was loosening up, sounding more like I did during voice lessons in Muriel's living room, her cherrywood grand piano dominating the space, and her exotic Afghan hound lounging at her feet.

When I finished the piece, Hal repeated the introduction, and I sang through it two more times. "You'll do fine," he assured me and stood. "I'm running over to see the Royal Pavilion. Want to come?"

I'd be too distracted to enjoy myself until my performance was completed. "No, but thanks for your help."

"Not a problem." As he opened the door and we made our exit, I saw Nick across the lobby.

He ambled over to me and said, "I missed you last night. And you've been avoiding me all day. Are you angry at me for leaving?"

"No, just worried about tonight. I'm going to sing a solo." I'd left Hal feeling hopeful, but anxiety seeped in again. Who did I think I was? My whole life, Mom raved about my singing voice, but she was biased. Look how she was treating Cooper.

"I have just the thing to make you feel better," he whispered, bringing his lips inches from mine.

Part of me wanted to grab onto him, right here in public. But my chest ached for something intangible and far away. "I won't be any fun until after the concert," I said.

"Fine, I understand." He turned away abruptly and crossed the lobby.

"Nick," I called, but he kept going out the door and down the front steps. No use following him, I told myself. If I blew the concert and thoroughly humiliated myself, he might continue avoiding me.

I rode the elevator to my floor and entered my darkened room to find Clare lying in bed, her throat wrapped with a damp washcloth.

"You woke me up," she said with difficulty. "How long before I need to get dressed?"

"Stay in bed. No need to get up till morning."

She struggled to sit, then wilted against the headboard. "Hal doesn't think I can sing tonight. No doubt he's coaching Marci on the music as we speak."

I stood in the shadows, not knowing what to say. Clare had done this to herself, but at this moment I was too fragile to defend myself against an onslaught of her barbed words.

But if Mom were here, she'd tell me to swallow the medicine in one gulp and get the unpleasantness over with.

"It's not Marci," I said.

"Tell me he didn't ask Shirley. She's too old and has that wobbly vibrato." She snorted a sneeze. "That would be a joke and a half."

"Clare, Hal asked me to sing."

She flipped on the light above her bed. Her legs swung around and she sprang to her feet. "You're joking!" She swaggered forward, towering over me. Her laugh choked into a barking cough.

I imagined what my singing voice sounded like to Clare. My notes were tinny and shallow compared to hers. Like a weed before a mighty oak tree, I felt myself shrinking.

"Was this all your idea?" she said.

"No, but since you're sick, I went over the music with Hal."

"How dare you!" In a burst, she lunged toward me. Leaning back out of her reach, I lost my balance and landed on my rump with a painful thud. Her body quaking, she stood above me like a jackal closing in on its prey. I crawled to my feet, then darted toward the door.

"Get out!" she squawked. "You're ruining my voice on purpose."

I made my escape into the hall. I couldn't remember anyone, other than Jeff, speaking to me so harshly. And for what? I hadn't purposely tried to harm her. Hal had come to me asking for assistance, not the other way around. Clare was in no shape to sing. She'd be lucky if she didn't come down with laryngitis for the duration of the trip.

Well, I couldn't lurk out in the hall until performance time. Maybe if I distracted myself, I'd wake up the next morning and the singing ordeal would be behind me. I took the lift to the lobby and spotted Martin alone in the dining room. His table stood before a wide window overlooking the English Channel. The haze had lifted. Sunlight glinted off the water's choppy surface.

As I approached, he lowered his newspaper and flagged the waitress for another teacup. I sank into the chair across from him. Since I had Martin to myself, I'd ask him about the missing necklace. But I needed to be subtle or he'd pull his head in like a turtle.

"I've been curious," I said, framing my words with care. "How is it that a famous man like you was available to come sing with us?"

"I've been on sabbatical—not of my choosing." He passed me the milk. "In hindsight, I should have taken better care of myself, in more ways than one."

"That famous hindsight?"

"Indeed. If only one could erase everything and start anew. I was very foolish. It almost cost me my career. We singers . . ." He tipped his head to include me—a gratuitous compliment? "Our bodies are our instruments," he said. "I wasn't taking care of mine. I expected my vocal cords to keep giving and giving." His gaze drifted out the window where a gust of wind stirred up the water. "Perhaps I didn't care what happened. There was a time when I might have thrown in the towel."

"Stop singing?"

He aimed his vision on me and said, "Something unbearable happened. I could hardly function."

I could identify with feelings of despair. I felt so low after Jeff's death I didn't care whether I lived or died. Only my commitment to raise Cooper sustained me. And Mom. She'd never forgive me if I'd deserted her the way my father had.

"But when we give up," he said, "we end up hurting only ourselves, don't we?"

"Which makes me think of Clare. She's been pushing things to the limit."

"She's young and impetuous. But haven't you been impetuous too? It's difficult seeing a friend—if I may be so presumptuous to call you that—wading into quicksand. Young women can be blind to men's deceptions."

I returned the spotlight to Martin by saying, "Clare claims an insurance company hired Jerry to follow you."

I thought he'd look away or protest, but his gaze remained steady.

"You already knew?" I asked.

"I thought it probable. Several times last week someone with a private number phoned, then hung up. And one evening I came home to find my security system blaring."

"But I can't imagine an insurance company authorizing someone to break into your home."

"In any case, I'll wager whoever it was thinks I had the necklace with me all this time. But nothing could be further from the truth."

"I'm glad to hear that." Although there was a fifty-fifty chance he was lying. I had every reason to distrust him. "So you haven't seen the necklace since before it was stolen?"

"I wouldn't go that far. I had it for a short time." He must have seen my face blanch because he added, "No need for you to worry about my affairs. Hal mentioned you were singing in Clare's place tonight. You should be concentrating on that."

For ten minutes I'd forgotten I was about to tread into the jaws of my worst nightmare. "Did you have to remind me?"

CHAPTER 26

CLARE WAS RIGHT. I had no business performing her solo. But in less than an hour I'd have to. I'd asked Hal if omitting Clare's piece wasn't the best option, but he'd insisted we sing every item. "This is our final night. It's too late to change the programs."

With Clare hogging the bathroom—thankfully, so I wouldn't have to face her again—I changed into my dress. In preparation, I returned to the empty room with the piano to warm up my voice. Closing the door, I plunked middle C and started singing scales. My vowels pierced out like shards of glass and my pitches were sharp.

My temples pounded like runaway conga drums. Remembering Muriel's lessons, I stopped vocalizing and spent the next five minutes stretching, flopping over at the waist like Raggedy Ann and expanding my rib cage. A metallic taste coated my cotton-dry mouth.

The muscles in my throat constricted around my larynx and my heart beat erratically.

"La-la-la-la-la." I sang scales again and arpeggios, all the while listening to my crummy voice. My breathing was so shallow I started feeling dizzy. The feverish radiator seemed to be consuming all the air. I shouldn't have wasted time coming here. I tried to open the door, but my damp hand slipped on the knob. Was the room holding me captive?

Finally, out in the reception area, the clock over the desk informed me I needed to rush the four blocks to the church. I lumbered down the hotel's front steps. A woman carrying an open map asked me directions, but I told her I was a tourist myself and hurried on. Jogging along the sidewalk, I convinced myself I'd feel better once I got to the church. I pictured myself standing with the other choir members as Hal led us through warm-ups. I always sounded better with Hal at the helm. I'd be all right if I took his suggestion—sing to him, only to him.

Catching sight of the church, I brushed past slow-moving pedestrians to find the entrance. The first door I tried was locked. I sprinted to another and jerked it open, crashing it against my kneecap and sending a spasm of pain up my leg.

Hal met me at the rehearsal room door. "Jessica, I was beginning to worry. You missed warm-ups." He steered me to a corner. "Are you okay?"

I felt gripped in a straitjacket, my mouth barely able to form the words, "I don't know."

"Come on, you'll be fine." Then he drifted over to Bonnie, maybe to warn her I'd be singing.

All my failures spewed through my mind. But wasn't this exactly what I'd hoped for?

Muriel's words began humming in my ear. "A lucky break," she'd say if she were here. "You can do it."

I'd seen Muriel glide onto stage looking as composed as if she were in her own living room. A marvelous idea took root in the back of my mind. I'd pretend I was Muriel. I remembered her success performing the role of Rosalinde in Johann Strauss's *Die Fledermaus*. For one night, I'd behave like a diva basking in rave reviews. I was a good actress, wasn't I? I'd been bluffing my way through life like a pro. This notion eased the pinging in my ears. What would Muriel do to relax? She sang from her gut with a raised palate, but her neck and face remained relaxed, elastic.

Hal clapped his hands. "Attention, people."

I tried to smile, but my jaw was glued to my upper teeth. Unaware of the terror building in my chest, he flashed me a grin, then turned to the others.

"We share our last dinner together after the performance. Please, everyone, be at your best so we'll have something to celebrate."

In only three minutes I would proceed into the sanctuary and stand in Clare's place. I felt like I was waking up in the middle of a movie about someone else's life. I was about to face my moment of truth, my waterloo. I trembled inwardly at the frightening yet electrifying prospect.

"Clare," Hal said.

Clare strutted forward, her blonde mane flashing like a thoroughbred's. "The pharmacist gave me some throat spray that worked like a charm. I'm fine. Never felt better." Hal started to speak, but she interrupted him. "Listen, I came all this way to sing, and that's exactly what I intend to do."

I felt like I'd been smacked in the face. "I'm ready," I said meekly.

Clare's cackle was chilling. "Is that a fact?" Her glower shifted to Hal. "I've stuck it out with the choir all year because you promised me these concerts. And this is how you treat me?"

Hal glanced at his watch and chewed his lip. Martin and the other singers were lining up, trying not to stare. Hal motioned for them to start walking.

Clare shoved past, and I followed in her wake.

As Bonnie played the first introduction, all my attention was focused on controlling the tears pressing on the backs of my eyes. As the others started to sing, I stood in a daze, exhaustion covering me like a lead apron. Several measures later I opened my mouth, but the wrong words blubbered out. The piece flowed in simple four-four time, but I couldn't get the tempo right. My throat was squeezing my windpipe. I gasped for air and missed the next choral entrance.

Before I knew it, Bonnie was introducing Clare's solo. I turned to Clare just in case she bowed out at the last moment. Half of me wished she'd be struck down by lightening—torched like a matchstick—disintegrated. Or at least convulse into a sneezing fit. Hal would point to me and I'd give it my best.

"The king of love my shepherd is," flowed out of Clare's mouth as though she'd never been sick. Whatever she'd done to revive herself had worked. She sounded strong again, better than I ever would. I couldn't help wishing she'd emit one hacking cough, but she made it through the entire song effortlessly.

Hal didn't notice my mistakes because he'd managed to avoid looking at me the whole concert. When we finished our final piece, he bowed to the audience, then grabbed his music and vanished, his head bent. I heard Shirley congratulate Clare. Her voice had returned. Wasn't that wonderful?

All I wanted to do was hide. It was too painful to even talk to Roxanne. I nodded when she reminded me to meet for dinner. Then I hurried out of the church, almost bumping into Nick.

"What's wrong, my beautiful one?" he said.

My lower lip quivered stupidly. "I thought I was going to sing tonight."

"The choir didn't sing?"

"It did . . . we did." Feeling tears pricking the backs of my eyes again, I headed toward the hotel. I couldn't let the others see me weeping. I felt bad enough without a ration of well-meaning questions. And Clare? She'd delight in my tears.

He fell in next to me. "May I walk you back?"

"Yes, but I'll warn you I'm not good company." I was sapped of energy. If a bull came raging down the street, I might let it gore me.

"Let me be the judge of that" He took my hand, his fingers wrapping around mine. "I'll find a way to raise your spirits."

I almost pulled my hand out of his but decided I didn't care who saw us, least of all Hal. Our musical director had no backbone. He was a spineless weasel. But the truth was, if I were in his shoes, I wouldn't have offered me a solo in the first place.

I glanced over my shoulder and saw long-legged Martin and Clare behind us. As I quickened my pace, my toe snagged the uneven sidewalk. I floundered—falling forward. Nick's grip kept me upright, wrenching my shoulder. Pedestrians advancing from the opposite direction stared at me like I was a klutz. I heard Clare's laughter. Could anything else go wrong?

Less than a block from the hotel, Nick said, "Are you going to your room?"

I felt disjointed, off-kilter. I imagined triumphant Clare heading there to change into something smashing for the celebration feast.

"In twenty minutes," I said. "I'm going out on the pier for a bit of fresh air first."

"In the dark? I'd better come with you."

A mantle of fog had rolled in. The lamps above us glowed like white paper lanterns. The night air tasting of salt moistened my cheeks. Not that it mattered if my makeup smudged or my hair went limp. My singing career was over. Finished. Done. I would quit the choir when I got home and never be missed. I wouldn't have to follow Hal's baton again. I'd sleep in on Sunday mornings. What a relief.

Neither of us spoke as we strolled past the hotel, crossed the road, and stepped onto the pier. I could hear waves working against the pilings. The water looked like a black hole, yearning to suck me in. A dark figure moved at the far end of the pier like a phantom, making me glad for my male escort. What was someone doing out here in the dark?

"I'm sorry to see you so downhearted," Nick said.

"I don't know whether I'm disappointed or relieved."

"Maybe I can help." His hands encompassed my waist, pulling me firmly against him.

The two sides of my brain battled for supremacy. My feelings for Nick varied from animal-attraction to distrust to gratitude. I didn't resist his strength. His warmth felt like a down-filled blanket on a cold winter's night—comforting, what I needed. Or wanted, anyway. My arms slipped around him and I nestled into his embrace.

"I've waited for this moment." His lips lightly touched mine, then softened with passion.

I heard a man, then a woman's voice. I whipped my head around to see Roxanne and Drew. Roxanne said, "I thought that was you, Jessie. It's time for dinner."

"No, I can't face everyone."

Roxanne looked like she might cry out of sympathy. "Come have dinner. Friends need to stick together. I'll save you a place." She clasped me in a quick hug, then she and Drew departed to the hotel.

When I turned back to Nick, I noticed the figure I'd seen earlier coming our way. His shoulders and gait identified him as a male about Nick's height. In a moment, the man was halfway down the pier, striding right at us. As he stepped under the light, his mustached face came into view. Jerry? Here? I flinched, wanting to run. But I had no reason to fear him. Did I? Like stepping into a scene from a detective movie, I recalled Jerry's foot in Martin's door. Even if he worked for an insurance company, he was a ruffian.

On the alert, Nick straightened his spine as Jerry closed in on us. The air went quiet, except for the scuffing sound of Jerry's shoes on the wooden planks.

"Good evening," he finally said to us, and then I realized he was a security guard wearing a navy-blue uniform. I had to chuckle at my run-away imagination. Jerry had probably given up and returned to the States empty-handed—except for the fun he'd had at Clare's expense.

The temperature was dropping and an icy breeze bathed my legs. I longed to be in my Seattle living room wearing my flannel pj's and fuzzy slippers. I'd fix popcorn, surf the TV until I found a schmaltzy movie, and have a good cry. But now I needed to brave it through dinner.

"Let's go back," I said to Nick. "My nose is freezing and I guess I'm hungry." I pictured myself eating dinner tuck between Roxanne and Nick, at the farthest end of the room from Clare. I shouldn't be hiding out here in the cold. I'd done nothing wrong.

"Why must you Americans be in such a hurry?" He took my hand and lifted it to his lips. "In Italy, we don't eat until after nine o'clock."

"But our dinner's being served now, as planned."

"Then change your plans. You and I should spend this evening alone."

I found myself thinking of Jeff and recalled how easily he'd manipulated me. I went along with his get-rich-quick schemes and tolerated his late-night outings because I was afraid he'd leave me. And Mom, usually a plethora of advice, didn't comment, maybe because her own marriage had torpedoed and she didn't want to jinx mine.

"Nick, I'm still part of the choir and need to stick with them. You and I can go somewhere after."

"There's always an excuse to leave me." His mouth got pouty, reminding me of Marcello Mastroianni, Mom's favorite Italian actor.

"Don't you understand?" he said. "I want you." He pushed stray hairs away from my face with supple fingertips, then almost devoured me with a moist kiss.

When was the last time I necked with a man in public? Not since high school. But did I trust either one of us to be alone together?

"Please come to dinner with me," I said, but he shook his head.

"Food is the last thing on my mind." He draped an arm around my shoulder and headed us toward the hotel. As we left the pier and crossed the road, he retracted his arm. "I'm going to check on the bus," he said and took off down the street.

I mounted the hotel steps and entered the restaurant where Martin and I had spoken this afternoon. The aroma of stewing meats and browning crusts wove through the now dimly lit room. Most of the tables were filled. Waiters bustled about, carrying platters and uncorking bottles, and busboys poured water and refilled breadbaskets. A recorded saxophone crooned in the background, barely audible over spirited conversations and the clatter of plates.

I spotted Hal hunched at a corner table set. I wished I could hate him, but I didn't. If I was mad at anyone, I supposed it was at myself. Hal had acted on behalf of the choir. He'd saved the troop from embarrassment and kept his obligation to Clare.

Roxanne, sitting with a half a dozen other choir members at three rectangle tables pushed together, flagged me down and pointed at two vacant seats next to her.

As I landed on a chair and scooted in, she glanced behind me and asked, "No dinner companion?"

"We'll see each other later. Maybe."

Martin entered the restaurant and canvassed the room. Roxanne waved and motioned to the empty chair. He sat beside me and said, "I'm afraid our chat over tea wasn't helpful. I'm sorry if I made things worse for you. I never know what to say to allay another's fears." His hand moved to the back of my chair. "Growing up as I did, we simply weren't allowed to show our emotions. Stiff upper lip and all that."

"I thought I'd mastered that ability, but apparently not. I worried myself sick for nothing." I shook my head as I recalled the amount of energy spent, and all for naught. "At least I was saved from making a fool of myself."

"I'm sure you would have done fine. I should like to hear you sing someday."

I imagined him singing the role of the painter Mario Cavaradossi in Puccini's opera *Tosca*. "But you've performed with famous sopranos," I said. Like Dorothea Platt.

"If you sing half as well as you do everything else, I'm sure it would be more than adequate."

I was touched by his generosity, even if it was the flip side of reality. In the world of classical music, mediocre wasn't good enough. The pitch, duration, and clarity of every note had to be executed with perfection.

I watched his face grow serious. Following his stare, I saw Nick standing near the door speaking to the hostess. I started to get up, but Roxanne stopped me.

"He can see you," she said. "Let him come over here."

I tried to get Nick's attention, but he was flipping through a menu.

She passed me the breadbasket and deposited a pat of butter on my plate. "This is a party to celebrate our last night of singing. I want to see you enjoy yourself."

"Not much chance of that."

The waiter served us salads. I settled back into my chair but kept one eye on Nick, who was chatting with the hostess.

"If he's worth it, he'll wait," Roxanne said.

She was right. I would ignore Nick until I was done eating. The last thing I needed tonight was to play some childish game.

Martin sprinkled olive oil and vinegar over his greens. "What are your plans when we get home?" he asked me.

"I'm taking up a new hobby. Making useful items I can wear or give away at the end of my toils, like knitting or quilting. Less anxiety. If I make a mistake I can go back and fix it." With fork and knife, I halved a slice of cucumber. "I'm too old to sing. By the time I figure out how, my high notes will be gone."

He chuckled. "You're hardly over the hill. If Muriel Frank can still sing at seventy-five, you have many more years."

I was surprised he knew whom I studied with. Maybe Hal or Roxanne had told him. "You know her?" I asked.

"No, only of her. She was quite a performer in her day. Colorful offstage too. I'd love to meet her. Perhaps you can introduce us."

"Sure." I couldn't imagine the logistics. I doubted I'd ever see Martin again after we got home. As I bit into the cucumber, my eyes searched Nick out. The hostess, her head held at a jaunty angle, was giggling at something he'd said.

Martin turned to look at Nick, too. "Your friend seems to be having a pleasant evening."

"Steady, girl," Roxanne said in my other ear. "Wait this one out. He doesn't want a needy woman chasing after him." She reached for the wooden pepper mill. "I'm serious. Men are looking for independent women." She cranked the pepper mill over her salad, and a grayish-brown mist rained down upon her creamy dressing. "Maybe it's the challenge."

"You're right," I said, glancing back at Nick.

He was gone.

The waiter removed our salad plates and brought out the main course. My appetite had dwindled, but I managed to consume a chicken breast baked with mustard sauce and a few spikes of broccoli. Minutes later, the busboy circled the table, removing empty dinner plates while the waiter replaced them with dessert dishes.

I stared down at my fruit trifle, a yummy treat I'd sampled several times along our journey. Imagining the calories inflating my hips through osmosis, I beckoned the waiter to come back. "Thank you," I told him, "but I'm not going to eat this." The waistband on my slacks was tight enough already.

"Don't you want your dessert?" Drew asked.

Like a frog's tongue snaring a fly, Roxanne snapped up the dish before Drew could. "You'll have to fight me for it," she said, then froze and placed the trifle in front of him. "I almost forgot I gave up sweets."

"Then I'll skip dessert," Drew said. "That way you won't have to watch me eat mine."

"Does that mean you're going to start walking with me too?"

"Sure, I thought you'd never ask."

As Roxanne and Drew fell into conversation, Martin excused himself from the table. "I have a call to make," he said, and I imagined Pamela sitting by her telephone waiting to hear his voice.

A few minutes later, I headed for the exit. Out in the lobby, Nick was sitting on a leather couch reading a magazine. As I neared him, he jumped to his feet.

"Finished?" he asked. "I'm going to a café up the street. Would you like to come with me?"

"I'm stuffed, but I'll keep you company."

"Wonderful." His hands swiped over his back pockets. "I forgot my wallet in my room. Come with me."

I followed him upstairs. As he opened his door, I scanned the monochromatic room and saw a single bed cramped against the wall, a bed stand with a telephone, and a dresser. Only a low-wattage bulb burned in the wall lamp.

Nick dug through the pockets of another pair of slacks and found his wallet. Shoving it in his rear pocket, he turned to me and said, "I hate to see this week come to an end. I'm not ready to say goodbye."

He kissed me, his hands exploring my waist and hips. Then he stepped back and examined my face. "I can tell your mind is elsewhere. Is it because you will miss me? Or are you still thinking about the singing?" His voice took on an edge of impatience. "If singing with the choir makes you miserable, give it up. I'm a free man. I do exactly as I please."

"No one is completely free, is he?" Where did that remark come from? It sounded like something Mom would say.

He seemed to be controlling a smirk. "Ah, forgive me. I've started another argument when we should be enjoying each other's company." His hands skimmed around my shoulders, coming to rest on the small of my back. "This is not the time to be discussing philosophy."

He nuzzled my neck, but I wriggled out of his grasp. "We'd better go," I said.

"What's your hurry? We're both single adults of sound mind and body. How can this be wrong? You're impossible to resist. And why should I?"

"We hardly know each other."

"How can you say that after spending every day together for almost a week? I'd give up everything to be with you."

"That's impossible." My laugh came out shaky, a leaf caught in the wind. "You don't know me well enough to say what you'd do for me. And I wouldn't want you to give up everything."

"Do you love me or not?" he said.

Huh? His question dazed me.

"No, you don't." He frowned. "You've been toying with me from the start. I'm a big joke." He flew to the door and rammed it open so hard it shuddered on its hinges. "Then go."

And I did.

CHAPTER 27

THE NEXT MORNING before breakfast, I wandered outside to linger on the hotel's small front porch. I took in the horizon and noticed a cargo ship riding high on the Channel's pewter-colored water. As I listened to waves rolling against the shore on the other side of the road, I tried inhaling the smell of the ocean, but found my nasal passages clogged. Was Clare's flu bug harassing me?

Last night I'd dozed off only to awaken with a start, drenched in sweat. In my dream I'd relived my worst day of high school—the talent show, a catastrophe I'd banished from my conscious thoughts. Hurdled back through time, I felt the panic of standing off-stage waiting my turn. My heart was thrumming triple-time and my stomach thrashing like a codfish in a net. I'd been too nervous to eat breakfast that day and it was already past noon. I dreaded being the last one to perform in the annual event and knew my classmates would be restless for lunch.

I'd stared onto the stage. Five kids in a newly formed rock band belted out the Miracles' tune "Love Machine." The floor vibrated as the percussionist hammered on his drums and the bass guitarist banged his strings.

"I'm just a love machine," vocalist Maureen wailed, prancing around like a go-go dancer. "And I don't work for nobody but you."

Applause erupted as the lead guitarist writhed across the floor, then fell to his knees on the final chord.

Wanting more, the audience had cheered and stomped its feet.

The principal came out and spoke into the micro-phone. "Settle down. We have one more performer."

Several boys started booing. One of them was Curtis, a rowdy kid who spent more time in detention than anyone in the history of the large urban high school.

Mrs. Clutch, our prune-faced music teacher, who'd accompany me on piano, gave me a nudge from behind. "Let's get this over with," she said, and I passed her the songbook of show tunes.

I'd practiced my piece from *The Sound of Music* what seemed like a hundred times in my living room, but only once with Mrs. Clutch. I inched my way forward while the band members removed their instruments. The spotlight blurred my vision and white noise hissed in my ears. I felt the ground shifting and thought Earth-quake! then realized my legs were trembling.

The microphone at center stage was positioned ten inches too high. I shortened it, causing a piercing sound to screech throughout the auditorium. People plugged their ears. More hooting and booing followed.

When the crowd finally quieted, and Mrs. Clutch was seated at the piano, I signaled I was ready. She plunked an entrance. I tried to make sense of the unfamiliar notes and realized she was on the wrong page and playing a song I didn't know. My mind spun like a tire on ice. I looked back to her, but she was concentrating on the music. When I didn't start singing, she stopped.

During the vast desert of silence, I rushed over to her. "Page fifty-two," I said, and Mrs. Clutch flipped through the book to find the right song. As I repositioned myself, I could hear Curtis and his friends guffawing.

I waved to Mrs. Clutch and the melody began to unfold. "Raindrops on roses and whiskers on kittens," I sang, my voice booming back into my ears through the PA system. "Bright copper kettles ..."

"I'm your love machine!" Curtis hollered. The whole auditorium burst into a frenzy of laughter.

The principal raced out onstage and yelled into the microphone, "That's it. This assembly is over."

Thinking about that calamity still wrenched my insides. A life-changing event. I'd had a bunch of them, kite strings anchoring to me a past I couldn't shake.

Martin cruised up the sidewalk with a newspaper tucked under his elbow. "Good day," he said, looking chipper. "What are you doing outside without a jacket?"

"I was hoping the air would clear my head."

He climbed the half dozen steps. "Not feeling up to par?"

I sneezed, and he handed me his handkerchief, a fresh pressed one like my grandfather used to carry.

"I've had better days." I dabbed under my nose. "But I may have figured out why I get stage fright. At least I know the day it began."

"Jolly good. If you can pinpoint the onset, perhaps you'll overcome it."

"Do you know how to reverse time and stop fifteen hundred high school kids from laughing at my expense?"

"Ouch. That sounds miserable."

"A sixteen-year-old's worst nightmare."

"But you're a lovely young woman. I can't imagine anyone wishing to harm you."

I surveyed his expression, which revealed no hint of mockery. I asked, "Are you describing the obnoxious woman you were forced to sit with on the airplane ride over here?"

He stared at my shoes. "Was I rude?" His gaze rose to meet mine. "Yes, of course I was. I'm sorry, really, I am. I hadn't slept well and was in a rotten mood. But that's no excuse, is it?"

"Never mind." I slipped the handkerchief into my pocket. I'd need to launder it and find a way to get it back to him. "It seems like a lifetime ago. Water under the bridge."

"I meant it when I said you're still young. No need to give up singing because of minor stage fright."

"I wouldn't call it minor." I thought about Martin's calm presence before and during a performance. "You don't seem to suffer from it at all."

"Not true. There were times while waiting in the wings when I wondered if I'd be able to utter the first note, let alone complete an entire opera. Sweat beading on my forehead, my stomach tied in knots." He leaned against the wrought iron railing. "And now? I seriously don't know if I can pull it off anymore."

"I'm sure you will." I was grateful he hadn't mentioned my defeat last night. The whole situation may have slipped past him unnoticed.

He motioned me toward the door. "Let's get you inside. Have you had breakfast?"

"No, I was just heading for the dining room."

As we entered the restaurant, I noticed Hal sitting with Drew and two other men. Hal usually domineered conversations, but he was sipping coffee and listening to Drew.

I looked over the rest of the room and spotted Nick at a table against the far wall. He was spreading jam on a slice of toast, then he swallowed a mouthful with a gulp of orange juice. He looked well rested, his eyes alert and hair neatly brushed. I felt a tug in his direction, but saw Clare sashaying over to his table, balancing a plate from the buffet. She set her food next to Nick's and glided into a chair that was already pulled out.

"Care to join me?" Martin asked, offering me a spot at a nearby table.

As I landed, I felt a jab of pain on my rump where I'd fallen the day before. I thought about Clare's outburst. She had lashed out like a rabid Doberman pinscher, but getting dressed today, she was all smiles.

Martin sat beside me and waved to the waiter for coffee. A moment later, Roxanne arrived from the buffet with a plate burdened with melon balls, a mound of scrambled eggs, and a container of plain yogurt.

"Aren't you proud of me?" She sat across from us. "I'm eating healthy stuff." She analyzed my face. "What happened to you, girlfriend? Eat something. It'll make you feel better." She scooped scrambled eggs onto my plate.

I looked down at the yellow mass and felt my stomach lurch. "Thanks, but I'll stick to coffee."

"It's hard to believe we're going back to London already," Roxanne said. She opened her yogurt and swallowed a spoonful. "I wish we had another week."

I was surprised to hear Martin agree. "Yes, I'd enjoy that."

"I'm ready to snuggle into my own bed," I said. "And I miss Cooper." Even if he didn't miss me.

"Do you and Nick have plans for tonight?" Roxanne asked.

When I shook my head, she glanced around the room until she found him. Clare was holding a plump strawberry up to his mouth. Her eyes remained glued to his as he bit into it, then licked his lips.

"Yuck." Roxanne screwed up her mouth. "I can't stand watching that."

"Jessica will be too busy tonight to worry about that chap," Martin said. "I've decided to take Mother up on her request."

I looked at him without understanding.

"To see my parents," he said. "But only if you'll join me. I couldn't face them alone."

"How about Pamela?"

"I have my reasons for not asking her."

I would never understand British men. "But won't she care if you take another woman?"

"Not at all." He wore a deadpan face. "I've already made up my mind. You come with me, or I won't go. It's that simple."

With my eyes, I pleaded with Roxanne to take my place.

"Drew and I have plans for tonight," Roxanne shot back. "Whatever musical we can get tickets to."

"Then it's settled," Martin said to me. "Tonight, you will join me for dinner."

BACK IN MY room, I crammed my dirty laundry into a plastic bag and placed it in my suitcase. As I gathered my shoes, Clare flounced in humming "*La donna è mobile*," her shapely torso swaying to the three-four rhythm.

"I'm going to Italy next year." She hauled her suitcase onto her bed and opened it. "I can improve my Italian diction and see the most beautiful place on earth at the same time."

"Is that what Nick told you? I couldn't help seeing you sitting with him."

"I hope that isn't a problem." She snatched her nightgown off the end of her bed and dropped it into her suitcase. "We were just talking. Such a sweet, gentle man." She sighed dreamily. "He made me forget all that's happened."

I moved into the bathroom to retrieve my toiletries, then packed my cosmetic bag next to my gifts for Cooper and Mom.

"I wish I'd met someone as nice as Nick instead of— no, I won't mention his name again." As she bundled her soiled clothes into her suitcase, she hummed another bar of "*La donna è mobile.*"

"Too bad we're going back to London tonight," she said. "There'll be little chance for you to see Nick."

I glanced into the mirror over the dresser. My reflection reminded me of a scarecrow that had lost its stuffing. Leaning closer, I wondered if applying more makeup would camouflage the half circles under my eyes. My hair hung like overcooked fettuccine, but there wasn't time to fiddle with it.

"You look like you're getting sick," Clare said. "Oh well, the singing's over. It's been fun, but I'm quitting the choir as soon as we get home. My voice teacher says I should be preparing for the regional Metropolitan Opera regional auditions. I won't have time for church."

CHAPTER 28

WITH CLARE IN tow, Nick led our group across the drawbridge and into ivy-covered Hever Castle. Atop the petite, square three-story gatehouse, the Union Jack drifted like a minnow in a stream.

Roxanne and I lagged behind the other choir members. She slipped a hand under my arm and urged me forward. "Come on, girlfriend. You don't want to miss where Anne Boleyn lived as a child." She checked her guidebook. "Poor Anne. She married Henry VIII, only to lose her life when she couldn't produce a male heir. It's reported her ghost still walks the castle's halls. That people hear her climbing the stairs in the dead of night."

Roxanne and I strolled through the courtyard, into the castle's entry hall, a room adorned with carved wood panels and columns, Oriental carpets and brocade-covered furniture. Earlier in the day, we'd visited Stonehenge, then wandered magnificent Salisbury Cathedral.

I felt too tired to take another step, and stayed behind as Roxanne followed the others up the staircase, their voices fading. I stared at a portrait of a woman in a scarlet dress with lace encircling the neckline. It would be incredible to live like this—a slower, dignified pace of life. The world flew by in the city, but living here, each tick of the clock would be heard, each moment noticed.

I realized I'd spent too much time examining the portrait when I heard footsteps on the creaky floorboards overhead. The group was up on the next floor, and probably ready to head to the third, then exit the building for a tour of the elaborate gardens. I set off in the direction the choir had gone and noticed a winding, unlit staircase, perhaps originally used by servants. Glancing into the dark cavern, I inhaled cool damp air. A velvet cord hung across my path telling me the staircase was out of bounds for tourists. Maybe it was too steep to be scaled by older people. Or did it shelter Anne Boleyn's ghost? No, of course not, and I should run to the top and catch up with the others.

As my hand reached for the cord, a billow of shame flushed through my chest. I had to laugh at myself for being so intimidated by what others thought. When a child, I'd dutifully tread within the boundaries Mom had mapped out for me. I remembered my coloring books. I never dared scribble outside the lines. At my age, wasn't it about time I did something daring and free-spirited?

I unclipped the cord; it flopped to one side. Heavy blackness dominated the staircase. Blindly, I inched upward, my hands following the curve of the wall. How many others had climbed these crooked steps? Had Anne Boleyn shared an impassioned kiss with Henry VIII in this very staircase? I supposed the shopkeeper at The Sword and the Stone in Bath would use their ill-fated marriage as evidence that all great love affairs end in ruin, but the child in me refused to accept the impossibility of a storybook ending.

Suddenly I felt myself being slammed off my feet, my nose flattening. Had I walked into a closed door at the top of the stairs? I tumbled backward, my knees buckling underneath me. No way to stop myself!

Powerful arms caught me as if I were a feather.

Nick had followed me. My hero. His strength supported my weight. Our lips found each other. His kiss was soft and delicious, even better than I'd remembered. As we parted, I inhaled the fragrance of his spicy aftershave. My hands slipped around his shoulders to explore the wispy hairs at the back of his neck.

But wait. This hair was slightly longer than Nick's. The man cleared his throat.

"Martin?" My voice echoed up and down the staircase like a bat caught in an attic.

His hands still firmly on my waist, I couldn't step back. I felt rage, embarrassment. And pleasure?

He loosened his grasp. "Give me your hand," Martin said.

I hesitated, my mind reeling.

"Are you all right?" he asked.

My cheeks burning, I shook my head, but he couldn't possibly see me.

He found my hand and held it tightly. I cautiously took several steps down and the staircase walls began graying with light. At the bottom, Martin paused for a moment, his large hand still clasping mine. He finally loosened his grip and moved to a window.

"I see the others are outside," he said.

I expected him to apologize. He owed me an explanation. He was always nauseatingly proper, and I'd obviously thought he was another man. He was engaged to Pamela, but he'd kissed me. If I'd known who it was, I never would have kissed him back. Would I?

My hand at the base of my throat, I stood at his side for several moments trying to admire the Italianate garden, a series of rectangle terraces leading down to a small lake. But it was impossible to concentrate on landscape and ornamental plantings after what had just happened.

"Perhaps you should join the group." He glanced at me briefly, then headed to the entrance door and stepped back, allowing me to exit first. We crossed the moat and moved toward the garden path.

My mind struggled for equilibrium. I turned to speak to Martin but found myself alone. I spun around and saw his tall shape marching toward the bus.

As I walked to the pond, I noticed above me thick clouds blanketing the sky, save one azure patch. By the time I reached the water's edge, the blue had expanded as the clouds parted like alpine mountain peaks, allowing a shaft of sunlight to illuminate the water where stark-white swans floated on a sea of diamonds.

"My Jessica," I heard Nick say, and turned to see him striding toward me. "I have found you. Tonight, we will talk. Yes?"

THE NEXT FORTY-EIGHT hours would be a wind-down until we boarded the jet and flew home. As we drove back to London, I was grateful Martin had chosen to sit in the back of the bus, far away from me. My first impulse to avoid him on the trip had been a good one. That's exactly what I'd do from now on. Treat him like a loose cannon. I recalled reading Victor Hugo's *Ninety-Three*. In the gun deck of a battleship, a cannon broke free, demolishing the insides of the vessel. That was Martin—destroying from within.

Watching the colorless highway roll by, I turned my thoughts to the highlights of the tour. Which was my favorite stop? Bath, Cambridge, Norwich? If I weren't missing Cooper, I'd love to spend a week exploring London. I could remain there a month and still not see every neighborhood, church, or museum. If only there were a way to stay longer. I felt deflated, like a child who had not enough time to play with all her new toys after Christmas vacation.

The other choir members must have felt as somber as I because their usual chatter hovered just above a stage whisper.

CHAPTER 29

NICK PULLED UP to our London hotel and cut the engine. He stood with the microphone in hand. "Thank you for giving me the opportunity to serve you," he said. "I hope you enjoyed yourselves as much as I did, and that the next time your choir travels you will contact our agency again."

After Nick trotted outside to see about the luggage, Hal said, "Remember, people, to give our driver a tip. All in all, he's been most helpful."

"That's for sure." Roxanne let out a chuckle.

"I'm going to reward him handsomely," Clare said from a seat in front of us. "He really is overqualified for this job."

"I'm not sure I'd go that far," Martin said.

"You men are too hard on each other," Clare said. "Nick wants to move to the States, and I hope he does. Wouldn't it be fun to see him again?"

Nick waited at the bottom of the steps to thank each passenger. When I passed, I gave him a twenty-pound note. At first, he refused to accept my tip. When I insisted, he said, "Only because everyone is looking. I need to handle some paperwork and return the bus. I'll be back later, after seven o'clock."

As the hotel clerk distributed room keys, the young woman gave a written message to Martin, who perused it quickly, then hurried after me.

"It's from Mother," he said, and handed me the note. "She's confirming our dinner with her and Father. They eat early, so we'll need to leave within the hour."

I noticed Nick at the far end of the counter. Pen in hand, he was filling out a form and chatting with the clerk.

"You go, Martin." I returned the note to him without reading it. "But I can't. I made plans."

"But you promised. And after today, I thought—"

"You mean when we kissed?" My cheeks warmed as I recalled how much I'd enjoyed myself. "You must have known I thought you were Nick. And you're engaged to Pamela. Aren't you ashamed of yourself?"

His face stiffened, and his tone became biting, reminding me of the pit bull terrier sitting next to me on the plane ride over.

"Ms. Nash, please join me as planned. You can take up with that Nick fellow later if you must. I'm counting on your presence." He stood perfectly still, but I could sense a gnashing of emotions warring inside of him. I was ready to slap him or scream or do whatever it took to make him hear me. But when I looked into his pale face, I saw agony. I couldn't stand it if he cried.

THIRTY MINUTES LATER, I sat on the edge of my bed calling the front desk. "I'm part of the church choir tour from Seattle," I told the receptionist. "Do you know our guide, Nick?"

"Yes, madam," she said. "I believe he left the hotel several minutes ago."

Clare, combing her hair at the mirror, paused to listen.

"I should have gotten his telephone number," I said, hanging up. "There's nothing I can do about it. I've got to help Martin." I sorted through my suitcase to find my black dress. That poor thing had to make it through one last performance. When I got home, I was going to take myself shopping for a new and colorful outfit. To wear to Mom's wedding?

"You'd give up Nick for Martin?" Clare's head tilted. "They're both hunks, but I suppose Martin is the famous one. And he's probably rich, too."

I felt myself bristle. It was getting harder and harder to spend time with Clare. Before I could reply, knuckles rapped on our door.

"Just a minute," I said, thinking it was Roxanne. I stepped into my slip, tugged the dress over my head, then opened the door to see Nick.

He strolled in with his hands out but stopped when he noticed Clare. "Signorina Clare is with you? Two such lovely ladies in one room would stop any man's heart."

Clare's face bloomed with delight.

"I was just trying to reach you," I said.

"And here I am. Are you ready for our evening together? Finally, I will have you to myself with no interference." His gaze swept across me with approval. "You look ready. Let's go."

"But I thought you had to drive the bus to the garage."

"I made arrangements for someone else to take care of that."

Now what? I couldn't be in two places at once.

"I'm sorry, I can't go with you yet." I watched his smile disappear. "It's only five o'clock and I told Martin—"

"This Martin again!"

"It's not what you think." Nick seemed to grow six inches taller. I had to step back to look up into his eyes. "He's a friend in need," I said. "It won't take long to get him hooked up with his parents."

His brows pulled high and his jaw flexed. "You're meeting his parents? And I'm expected to wait around like a dog hoping for scraps?"

I touched his arm, but he jerked it out of my hand and left the room.

"I'll be back before seven," I called after him. If the past was the best predictor of the future, I would indeed see him.

The phone rang, and Clare said, "Jessica, it's for you."

I took the receiver from her and heard Martin ask me to meet him downstairs. Ten minutes later, he and I sat like two strangers as the taxi coasted up to the Brown's Hotel. I started to get out when the hotel's doorman approached the cab, but Martin stopped me.

"Wait." He slouched back in the seat. "This was a dreadful idea. I can't go through with it."

I could contain my frustration no longer. "After what I went through to get here, you've got to."

"I'm sorry I inconvenienced you. Really, I am. And I'm sure that Italian chap is waiting for you, so you two can be on your merry way in just a few minutes."

I found it preposterous that a man who dared perform an entire opera in front of thousands would tremble at the thought of seeing his own father, but Martin's face looked like Cooper's after he'd been chased home by a neighbor's German shepherd.

"Pretend you're waiting in the wings and the orchestra just played your entrance." I heard impatience twanging in my voice. "You're on."

The doorman opened my door and I stepped out. As Martin paid our driver, a chauffeur-driven Bentley rolled up behind us, and I recognized Martin's mother emerging. Martin came around to the curb and his mother kissed his cheek.

"Darling, I'm glad you came," she said. Then a question formed on her face as she noticed me. She must have been expecting Pamela. She extended an elegant hand. "Hello, I'm Elizabeth Spear."

"May I present Jessica Nash?" Martin said with formality.

Shaking Elizabeth's hand, I was tempted to add an explanation for my presence, then hop back into the cab and make my getaway. But I decided to wait until they were safely in the building.

The chauffeur helped an older gentleman exit the Bentley, and a moment later a silver-haired man walked over to us. Long legs, short steps, I thought, noticing his stilted gait.

"This is Martin's father, Martin Senior," Elizabeth said with hesitation. I was bewildered when Martin and he did not even exchange a nod of recognition. No connection at all, as far as I could tell. Like two men on an elevator waiting for their floor.

"How do you do?" his father muttered as he shook my hand. His fingers felt clammy and his grasp limp. Not what I expected from a man of his tall stature.

"Nice to meet you," I said, intrigued by the incongruities. The very existence of other people's fathers always fascinated me to some degree, but Martin Sr. was unlike anyone I'd met. And he hired a chauffeur? Trying not to stare, I looked him over. Martin's father was a handsome man, perhaps even more so than Martin. I saw the same straight nose and square jaw, rigid mouth and intelligent cool eyes. But the older man wore heavy vertical creases between his brows and a horizontal line chiseled across his forehead. Souvenirs from time spent in the courtroom or from personal disappointments?

As the doorman swept the hotel's door open for us, Elizabeth turned to me. "Shall we go in?" she asked.

The four of us crossed the threshold into the lobby of the hotel described as *refined* and *exclusive* in my travel guide. The first person I saw was a woman wearing an evening gown and fur wrap speaking with a man in a tuxedo. I glanced down at my jacket and ho-hum dress and felt out of place.

"I was only planning to stay for a minute," I told Elizabeth. "Until Martin got settled."

Martin positioned himself behind me, his hand on the small of my back. "I won't let you leave us yet," he said. Then, whispering in my ear, he added, "If it's too excruciating, I can use you as an excuse to leave. Please stay, I beg of you, just for a while."

We neared the restaurant entrance and the maître d' approached us. "Good evening, Lord and Lady Spear. It's a pleasure to see you again," he said.

As Elizabeth unbuttoned her coat and handed it to him, all eyes turned to the yellow diamond cross sparkling on her breast—a remarkable collection of about thirty stones the color and intensity of miniature suns. Nick's appraisal was correct. The necklace could very well sit among the Crown Jewels.

What a relief, I thought. I needn't worry about Martin being a thief anymore. I'd expended wasted energy fretting over nothing.

"I see you have it back," Martin said, without a show of surprise.

"Yes, Scotland Yard returned our Canary Cross this morning." Her voice cracked as it rose in pitch. "I was overcome with joy. And thankful this horrible ordeal is finally at an end." She polished the cross's glittering surface with her thumb. "They wouldn't divulge how it all happened. Just that it had been returned. Marty, you must tell me the whole story over dinner."

Martin's gaze darted to his father, then back to her. "That necklace almost cost me my freedom and I don't care to spend any more time discussing it."

"But darling—"

"Mother, you were one of the only people on earth who believed in my innocence. And I thank you for your confidence in me." He took her hand with tenderness. "But please, can we drop the subject?"

The maître d' led us into the posh dining room to a table laden with crystal and silver. As Elizabeth motioned for me to sit across from her, I noticed a single gold band on her ring finger. Her pale lavender silk dress was discreetly chic, and her perfume hinted of lilac. Mom, who could engage anyone in conversation—a trait that embarrassed me as a child, particularly at the grocery store—would have already had the dialogue moving. But what could I say? I sneaked a peek at Martin Sr.'s stony face as he perused the menu, all the while glancing sideways at his son. The man who'd represented the royal family, according to Martin, known throughout Europe for his fierce tenacity, seemed afraid to rest his eyes on his own son.

"Tell me about the choir tour," his mother finally said to me, as if she'd never heard us sing. I wondered if she'd snuck off without informing her husband.

I described several of our stops and how Martin's voice bolstered our tenor section, and she nodded in appreciation. Neither man said a word, but as I chatted with Elizabeth, I found her charming and intelligent, and grateful to be speaking to someone who knew her son.

"We've never been to Seattle," she said. "I hear the weather is like ours."

"Yes, we get our share of rain, but nothing torrential like other parts of the United States. And we have mild winters." Knowing that Martin's father disapproved of Martin's career, I was glad to get a conversation focused on something other than singing. "To the east of Seattle lies a range of snow-capped mountains, the Cascades, and to the west is Puget Sound, dotted with islands, with another mountain range as their backdrop, the Olympics."

"That sounds beautiful. Perhaps we'll visit someday."

Martin Sr. didn't acknowledge the statement, but she seemed pleased her husband hadn't protested.

"I'd be happy to show you around." I wondered if an English lady would enjoy shopping at Pike Place Market, with its fish vendors and fresh produce. Maybe she'd be happier sipping tea at the Queen Mary Tea Room, one of my favorite restaurants. "But I suppose Martin would want to do that," I added. It was unlikely he'd inform me if his parents came to town.

Martin and his father continued to stare at their menus in silence, both men pursing their mouths like a couple of elementary teachers stuck at the back of the auditorium when kids were misbehaving. Elizabeth excused herself to powder her nose and I joined her. If Martin and his father were alone, they'd be more likely to converse with each other.

"Thank you," Elizabeth said, as we stood before the mirror in the ladies' room minutes later. "I don't know how you talked my son into coming, but I'm eternally grateful." She paused, her reflected gaze meeting mine. "May I ask the nature of your relationship?"

"We're friends." Were we? If so, it was the oddest friendship I'd ever experienced.

Her liquid eyes searched mine. "I'm sure you're more than that if he invited you this evening."

"No, we met less than a week ago."

Elizabeth freshened her lipstick. "In any case, this evening means the world to me."

My gaze drifted to the necklace and I recalled Nick's statement that owning such a valuable piece of jewelry could change a man's destiny. It was unlikely Nick would ever possess anything of colossal value, I thought. He was more than a little interested in Martin, and he seemed to resent the upper crust—those born with advantage and money. Had Nick trashed Martin's hotel room in Chester searching for the necklace? No, my imagination was ballooning. Jerry would be the first suspect, or some vagrant who found his way up the fire escape and happened to find Martin's door unlocked.

When Elizabeth and I returned, the men were speaking in short sentences. No substance. Airless bubbles. Both started to rise when we sat down, then they fell quiet again.

A waiter approached the table. "What will Madame have this evening?" he asked Elizabeth.

Martin checked his watch. "Jessica and I had better skip dinner. I promised to get her back early. We should be on our way."

"Please, please, don't leave us yet." Elizabeth knotted her fingers together. "Stay at least through the main course. It's been so long since we've sat down at a meal together."

"I'd like to stay," I said. For Elizabeth's sake.

As we waited for our salads, Elizabeth opened her purse and pulled out a black velvet box. She unclasped her necklace, then held the cross with one hand as the weighty gold chain slithered down onto the table. She gazed at the cross for a moment, then slipped it into the box.

"Marty, your father and I want you to have this."

Martin put his hands up in protest. "What would I want with that accursed thing?"

"This cross has been in my family for three hundred years. I wore it the day your father and I were wed." She set the box on the table between them. "Someday, you shall marry. It will make a lovely present for your future bride."

I expected Martin to use this moment to announce his engagement to Pamela, but instead he arched his brows as he glanced at his father. "And what if you don't like my next choice any more than my first?"

His father shook his head. "That woman was nothing but a gold digger."

Indignation flared across Martin's face. He plucked his napkin from his lap and slapped the cloth onto the table. "I should have known you'd bring that mess up and rub my nose in it."

"Now, Marty," Elizabeth said. "You must admit that we made every effort to get along with Dorothea."

"Yes, you tried." He sniffed dryly, slipping the napkin back into his lap. "And she was vicious in return."

"That's behind us now. No more arguing." She nudged the box closer to Martin with her index finger. "As our eldest child, this is rightfully yours."

He looked to his father, who nodded once. "As you like," Martin said, depositing the box in a jacket pocket. "But after all I went through to get it back to you, this seems like lunacy."

"Dear, it was Scotland Yard who doubted you. Not your father nor I."

Martin frowned at his father, who stared back without a change of expression.

His mother spoke to me through the desert of silence. "Order whatever you like, dear."

For dinner, I ordered heirloom tomato salad with baked ricotta followed by minestrone soup, followed by oven-roasted lamb with a scrumptious sauce and scalloped potatoes. I savored every bite. Several times Nick's brooding face floated through the back of my mind, prodding me to finish my meal.

An hour later, after the plates had been removed, Martin set his napkin aside and stood. "We must be on our way. Jessica needs to return to the hotel." He took hold of the back of my chair to pull it out. "I've interfered with her evening quite enough."

I scanned the luxurious room. How wonderful to enter this world of refinement, which I would never see again.

"Marty, must you really leave so soon?" Elizabeth asked.

"Let the boy go." His father's voice was gruff, and he made a move to get to his feet. "We've detained him long enough." As Martin Sr. rose, a glazed expression solidified his features. He stared blankly and then began to tip forward.

Elizabeth sprang to her feet and grabbed his arm, but he looked ready to topple. Martin dashed around the table and took his other side.

"I'm fine." His father thudded down in his seat. "Stop making a fuss."

"Is he all right?" Martin asked Elizabeth.

She returned to her chair, not tugging it in. "Your father has been—"

"Elizabeth, enough!"

"Marty has every right to know." She spoke to Martin, while keeping watch on her husband. "Your father hasn't been well, to put it mildly. It's his heart, and he's not good about taking his medication."

Martin sat down, his elbows on the table. "Why wasn't I informed of this?"

"No use talking about it," his father said briskly.

"We're seeing the specialist again tomorrow morning," Elizabeth said. "He's warned Martin that without surgery very soon—"

"A waste of time and money on a man my age. I reduced my intake of cholesterol and salt. And I walk twenty minutes a day. That's all I'm willing to do."

"You must get better, dear. I'm not prepared to give you up yet." Elizabeth directed her words to Martin. "The cardiologist said your father should try to relax. To reduce stress and all that, which has been a challenge for him." She placed her pale hand on Martin's. "Won't you please stay a little longer? And you too, Jessica."

I like this woman, I thought, as I searched her translucent face. Our minds and hearts connected—perhaps because Elizabeth loved her son the way I loved Cooper, even when he acted horribly. She bent and swayed as her son and his father negotiated their footing. She was trying to hold her world together, the way I had many times.

"Jessica has a date waiting for her," Martin said, and Elizabeth's smile dimmed.

Martin and his father looked exhausted, and I felt drained. I'd assumed I'd be able to waltz out of the restaurant and away from his parents without feelings of regret. But when Elizabeth hugged me goodbye, I hugged her back, not wanting to let go.

"I hope we shall see you again," she said when we finally exited the restaurant.

"Me too." But I knew this was our final farewell.

While the doorman stood at Martin Sr.'s arm, ready to steady him, father and son shook hands like two business acquaintances finishing a fruitless negotiation.

Minutes later, Martin and I sat in a taxi watching the city lights spew by. As the cabbie zipped around a tight corner, I glanced over to see Martin had his face cupped in his hands.

"I'm glad that's over," he said. "I won't have to go through that awkwardness again for a while."

"What do you mean? It's a new beginning for you and your father. You can visit your parents tomorrow afternoon."

"We've talked enough."

"But your mother gave you the cross. It's a peace offering."

"The key word is *mother*. My father had nothing to do with it. He'd rather go to his grave than admit he was wrong."

"But what if he does pass away before you two reconcile?" I placed my hand on Martin's and felt warm smooth skin, not a block of ice after all.

"I do love my father," he said, "but every time we see each other, it's so difficult." He turned his hand over and grasped mine. "How is it that you can say exactly what's on your mind, while I'm trapped inside myself?"

"That's not exactly true. I haven't spoken to my father for years." I pictured my dad's fading hazel eyes and his graying brown hair—or maybe it was completely white by now. "There's unresolved conflict between us. I still feel like a kid every time I think about him." I let my knees fall against Martin's. "I get this fairy-tale idea sometimes that I'll go over to Mom's for dinner and Dad will be sitting at the table, just like when I was little. 'Come here, Jess,' he'll say. His long arms will catch me, and I'll be five years old again. Isn't that stupid?" My father was almost as old as Martin's and could die before I told him I loved him. In spite of my rage and crushed feelings, I still loved him—a strange affection that warped my every decision.

I envisioned myself going to Dad's lakefront house in Medina, only a twenty-minute drive from where I lived. My stepmother would answer the door, not bothering to hide her distaste of her husband's first child.

"I'm here to see my father," I would say, brushing past her. And then, "Daddy, can we talk?"

A suicidal idea, like stepping onto the firing range? If my father wanted to see me, he would have contacted me—or was he waiting for me to make the first move? As a teen, I hung up when he called. Speaking to him was too painful, a concrete reminder that I was different. Had Mom's influence over me colored my view of him too much?

"Forgive us our trespasses," I said, reciting what I'd repeated at church many times without giving the words a thought. "As we forgive those who trespass against us." Bitterness had been consuming me for too long.

"I don't know if I can," Martin said.

The cabbie braked and pounded his horn, but neither Martin nor I looked away.

"Hey, why didn't you tell your folks about Pamela?" I asked.

The image of Martin and her exchanging wedding vows in front of a garlanded church played itself out in my brain. I pictured the robed minister saying to the congregation, "If anyone here has an objection to this couple getting married, speak now or forever hold your peace." I imagined myself wanting to jump up and yell "I do" but being paralyzed, unable to move. Which would keep me from making a complete fool of myself. How could I contemplate ruining Martin's wedding?

I pushed the unwanted thoughts out of my mind and said, "Won't your mother be thrilled you're getting married?"

"She would like to see me remarry." Our hands loosened, parting.

"Then why didn't you say something?"

"I have my reasons." To do with his father, I assumed.

"Please, tell me the truth. Did Pamela bring the necklace to the authorities? You gave it to her that night at the restaurant, didn't you?"

"Yes, she's a sport. She insisted she'd do that for me." For the first time this evening, the corners of his mouth lifted into a smile. "She assured me no one would dare question her."

I wondered why that was, then remembered her refined countenance, how she radiated wealth and privilege. My opposite.

"Where had it been all that time?"

"In Cambridge, safely tucked away in a private vault."

I recalled Martin's chatting with the older man on the street, and Nick's keen interest in them. Martin might not have trusted me with the information earlier for fear I'd tell Nick, who might in turn . . .

"But how did it get there?" I said.

"When Dorothea accused me of stealing the necklace, I was in a panic and didn't know what to do." Crossing his arms, his fingers dug into his suit fabric. "Finally, I called my former law professor and told him I was in a jam, that I needed to store something while I was in the States. He didn't ask questions, just urged me to wrap whatever it was and drop it in the post. He'd keep it safe until I came for it."

"I'm glad there was someone to help you, since—"

"Since my own father wouldn't?" He bit into the words. "Yes, my old professor was the only person I could think of and he came through."

"Like a surrogate father?"

"You might say. Years ago, he was the man who gave me the courage to pursue my singing. 'If you don't give your vocal career a fighting chance, you may come to regret it later,' he told me. 'One can always go back to law school at age fifty, but to start singing so late would be almost impossible.'"

"I'm glad you had people you could rely on. First your professor, then Pamela." I felt the burden of regret slump my shoulders. "I wish I'd been there."

"You came to dinner with me tonight. Sitting down at that table was one of the hardest things I've ever done. I wouldn't have gone without you."

CHAPTER 30

A S THE CAB neared the hotel, Martin's speech turned formal again, his words punctuated with diction. "You've been most kind. Thank you for joining me."

"You're welcome, and thanks for the delicious meal. I enjoyed meeting your parents."

"I'm sure the feeling was mutual."

The cab came to an abrupt halt at the hotel's front door.

"Now, I suppose you'd better find Nick." Martin pulled out his billfold. "Please forgive my negative remarks about him. You're a grown woman who has not asked for my advice. I have no right to interfere."

While Martin paid the cab fare, I hopped out and entered the lobby. It stood empty, save for one young man behind the reception desk doing paperwork. I approached him to check for messages but found none, nor had he seen Nick for several hours. I read the wall clock and was surprised to see it was already eight o'clock. I shouldn't have let myself get distracted for so long but was pleased with the outcome of the dinner and satisfied the necklace caper was at an end, even if I thought Martin had acted improperly. If I'd been in Elizabeth's shoes, I would have instructed him to go to the authorities immediately. Not that my own son, Cooper, would have necessarily obeyed me.

The doors paused before opening. As I watched for them to part, I was seized by a sense of foreboding. Maybe the negative vibes rebounding between Martin and his father had affected me more than I realized. I stepped into the elevator. It labored up to my floor. Ahead, the corridor stretched—long and gloomy—but it looked safe enough. Walking to my room, I dug in the bottom of my purse for the key and opened the door.

The room was dark, but the hall light sent a sliver across Clare's bed. I saw something move and heard the mattress springs squeak.

As my pupils dilated, I made out Clare sitting on her bed with her back against the headboard, and a male figure perched on the end of the bed.

My mind thundered with revulsion. I reeled back into the hall and shut the door. Clare had hooked up with Jerry again knowing he was bad news? And she'd brought him to our room, where she knew I'd return, as if wanting me to walk in on them.

I felt a million miles from home. I leaned against the wall and tried to decide where I should go. But this was my room too. How dare Clare put me in this position?

I had every right to be here. I should stomp in there, flick on the light, and give them a piece of my mind.

The door handle turned and the door cracked enough for me to hear a man's muffled voice, then Clare's. The door opened wider. Nick, his hair mussed and his shirt wrinkled, crept out into the hall. When he saw me, his mouth gaped open like a kid caught cheating on a test.

I felt like slapping him across the face.

"It's not what you think." He raked his hands through his hair. "I came up here to wait for you." With rapid movements, he tucked in his shirt. "We were just talking."

"How stupid do you think I am?"

My thoughts careened back to the night Jeff admitted he'd been with another woman. "It didn't mean anything," he'd claimed. "I drank too much. A one-night fling."

I'd inhaled the raunchy smell of cheap perfume and alcohol. "You're worse than my father," I'd screamed. At least he hadn't cheated on Mom when she was pregnant.

"It's not my fault." Jeff had sent me a sad puppy-dog look. "You're always sick or tired, busy decorating the baby's room, or talking to your mother." He found my inflated belly repulsive. He'd kept me at arm's length for months. In the end, I accepted his apology and his promise to never stray again. What else could a woman eight months pregnant do?

"Ask Clare," Nick said. "Nothing happened. I was so hurt, so angry thinking about you out with another man. Martin Spear, of all people. He looks at me like I'm beneath him, and he is stealing my woman."

The words *my woman* reached out, luring me closer.

"*Mi dispiace*. I'm sorry." Nick's eyes went moist. All an act? "I'm falling in love with you, Jessica. I'm not used to this feeling of weakness. This jealousy."

A couple exited the elevator, laughing. Nick and I stared at each other until they passed.

"Please, we'll ask Clare. She'll tell you that I came up here to see you, only you."

I pitched the door open. Clare was skulking right inside, probably trying to hear us. She was wearing what she'd had on earlier but was barefoot and her lipstick smudged.

Nick ducked back into the room. "I asked Clare if I could wait for you." He checked his shirt around the waist, smoothed the front. "It was completely innocent."

"I see." I tossed out a laugh. "You two alone, on a bed?" Part of me wanted to believe it was possible.

"We only kissed," Clare said with a whimper, her face blotchy. "That's all, I promise."

"You two kissed?" My eyes hurled daggers through her chest. How I hated her. Not that Nick wasn't half of the equation. I flipped on the light and studied him like he was a portrait of a stranger hanging on the wall. I still found him a handsome man, but he looked smaller with the overhead light casting shadows down his face. Pale and weak.

Nick took my hand, massaged my fingers. "Please forgive me, Jessica."

I snatched my hand away and held it behind my back.

"Have you never done something stupid because you were hurt and angry?" he asked.

I had, of course. I'd done a myriad of dumb things and must forgive others as I hoped they'd forgive me. But would I ever trust Nick again? Unlikely. Forgiving others didn't mean I should let a bulldozer run me down a second time because the driver was sorry for hitting me the first.

The three of us stood like trees in a petrified forest. Finally, Clare said, "Maybe I'd better leave."

"Don't be ridiculous." I pointed out the door. "Nick. Get out."

He looked puzzled as he stepped into the hall. Then he turned to ask, "You will join me later?"

I was tempted to launch a few caustic verbal missiles his way, but I held in my animosity as I closed and bolted the door.

CHAPTER 31

"HAVE YOU CONSIDERED changing your tickets and staying in London another week?" I asked Martin over the breakfast table in the hotel restaurant the next day.

"No, I need to return to Seattle. I'm happy to report I have a role in Seattle Opera's upcoming production."

"Wonderful. Congratulations." I wondered why he'd kept it under his hat. "But what about your parents?"

"I called Mother this morning." He breathed deeply, his hand slipping under his jacket lapel and resting on his chest. "It's easier to speak on the phone. One is freer to express oneself." His eyes met mine tentatively, and it struck me he was a shy man behind his genteel exterior. He said, "I shall never be able to thank you enough for accompanying me last night."

"I'm glad I could help." I kneaded my napkin into a crumpled ball, then shook it flat again. "And I'm glad we've become friends."

He gave me a closer look. "You don't seem very happy
about it. Is the thought of a friendship with a rascal like
me depressing?"

"No, of course not. Although it adds complications."
The waiter topped off my coffee. A curl of steam rose
from my cup and evaporated into the air. "I didn't have
a very good evening after we parted last night."

"I see. That was my fault, wasn't it? I am sorry.
Really."

"Maybe it was a blessing in disguise. If I'd spent the
evening with Nick, I never would have found out." I
wasn't going to tell anyone what had transpired last
night. Clare's reputation was tenuous as it stood, and
I didn't want to be a purveyor of gossip. "The long and
the short of it is, you were right about Nick." I was surprised to hear my voice quiver, making me sound like
the bag lady from the church in Chester. Guess I was
more affected by Nick and Clare's rendezvous than I
thought.

I was gratified that Martin showed restraint by not
leaping into verbally burying Nick. Instead he took a
bite of croissant, then dabbed the corners of his mouth
with his napkin.

"People can be disappointing, can't they?" I said.

"I've found that if you put all your weight on them,
they can let you down."

I sipped my black coffee and felt the inside of my
mouth pucker from the bitter taste. "Maybe I expect
too much."

"Are we speaking of Nick? I've said some rather nasty things about him, which I shouldn't have. And I hope that hasn't influenced you."

I added cream to my coffee, but it still tasted harsh, as though the pot had spent too much time on the burner. "You didn't like him from the first moment you set eyes on him." Maybe what Nick said was true. Some Englishmen were prejudiced against Italians. "Why was that?"

"He reminds me of someone. Dorothea had—and still may have, for all I know—a fondness for a slimeball named Giovanni Bianco. I've only seen his stage photos, his face concealed with makeup, but he resembles Nick."

"I'm sorry."

"Yes, well, that's not your problem. Just because I can't hang on to a woman, I shouldn't be cynical. I had a part in our breakup. I'm not the easiest person to get along with."

I couldn't hold a straight face. "Who is?" Recalling my conversation with Nick the night before, I said, "Nick thought you and I had something going."

"Would that be so awful?"

"No, in many ways you're an incredible man." Making Pamela a fortunate woman. His satisfied expression faded when I added, "But you can see how a proud man like Nick might do something stupid if he was jealous enough."

He nodded. "Men act foolishly when they're jealous. Like me, for instance."

I couldn't fathom Martin losing control of his emotions. Dorothea's unfaithfulness had probably unleashed a hailstorm of bitterness. Or maybe he was referring to Pamela.

"Want to talk about it?" I asked.

"All right." His gaze flew up to a spot behind me. I felt a hand resting on my shoulder and turned my head to find Nick standing there.

Martin leapt to his feet, almost tipping over his chair. "I should be on my way."

I watched him depart, then I looked up at Nick. "Ciao," I said, attempting the one Italian word I knew.

"I'm so glad." His magnificent face came alive. "You don't hate me."

"No, I don't." No matter how angry and disappointed I was, I couldn't hate him.

"Then we can be together. I've been thinking about it all night. You and I should be married. Today, if you like."

Kneeling, he took both of my hands and pulled them to his chest. "Now don't laugh. I'm perfectly serious. I've never been so serious." He pressed my fingertips against his lips. "If we're married, I promise to make you happy. I know I can do that."

I'd dreamed of this moment, seen it in the movies, and read about it in novels—a man kneeling before me and professing undying love, unlike Jeff's blithe decision to marry me after he'd downed his fourth beer at a Mariners game.

I had to ask, "You'd be willing to leave everything—your job, your parents, and friends—just like that?"

"Why not? I've been waiting for the right woman. Waiting far too long. A man must eventually settle down. No?"

"But isn't this really about moving to the United States? Be honest, Nick. Please."

He hesitated, his eyes turning opaque. "Is complete honesty ever a good idea?"

"I think so."

"Yes, of course, we will be honest, you and I." He pulled out a chair at an angle and sat beside me. "I do want to reside in your country, and this is very attractive to me. But what's even more attractive is you, my Jessica. If you would rather live in Great Britain, then so be it. As long as we are together."

I sat back to think clearly. I had blundered my way into many hasty choices. On the other hand, had I protected myself too much over the last few years, such that I'd forever be single? My first impulse was to call Mom for advice, but she was preoccupied with Tim, a thought that still made me uneasy.

"This is an important decision, Nick." An understatement. "One we shouldn't decide so quickly."

"And why not? What is stopping us? You've forgiven me. I can see this in your eyes. And you care for me. This, too, I can see."

"I have a son—."

"I can hardly wait to meet him. He and I will get along famously if he's anything like you."

Last night's ugly scene ricocheted through my mind. Was my rage and resentment unfounded? Who was the real Nick?

"I'll need to think about it," I said, although I already knew my answer would be *no*. Only a wacky woman would run off with her suave Italian tour guide. Sensible people weighed the consequences of their actions with the greatest of care. They did all things in moderation.

In spite of my sound reasoning, my mind began pondering wedding bands, of all things. A plain one like Elizabeth's? And what kind of dress would I wear?

No, no, I couldn't contemplate the icing on the cake yet.

CHAPTER 32

I KNOCKED ON MARTIN'S door.
  "Who is it?" he asked with caution.
"Just me. Jessica."
Nick was busy in the lobby welcoming a choir group
from Winnipeg and would be tied up most of the day.
I'd told him I needed space to mull his proposal over,
although I was pretty sure I'd come to the same conclusion as my *no* reaction last night.
  Martin opened his door. "This is an unexpected
pleasure."
  I toddled in, sat on a wingback chair by the window,
and crossed my legs at the knee. Quite tidy for a man's
room, I thought. Everything in order. On the bed
table lay the velvet box his mother had given him. I
was tempted to ask him to let me play dress-up and try
the Canary Cross on but figured the next woman to
wear the necklace should be Pamela.
  "I didn't expect to see you again today," he said.

"Do you mind?"

"Of course not. I was just thinking how lonely a huge city can be when a man is by himself."

"Where's Pamela?"

"I just spoke to her. She's quite busy. Say, do you like Turner?" He was better at switching subjects than Cooper. Fine, I didn't want to talk about Pamela, who was probably in Paris selecting a haute couture wedding gown.

"Turner, did you say? I don't recognize the name."

"Joseph Mallord William Turner, the painter." He scooped up the box and stuck it in the breast pocket of his tweed jacket as casually as if it were a pack of gum. "Why not join me? Then you can see if you like his work, and perhaps make up your mind about other things."

Minutes later, our cab worked its way through traffic and along the banks of the River Thames.

Once inside the Clore Gallery, part of the Tate Museum, Martin explained, "Turner left the body of his work to the British nation on the condition that a site be donated and his paintings and drawings be kept together. This extension, opened in 1987, ful-filled that promise."

"You're as good a guide as Nick,"

His frown told me I'd offended him. "I'll try to take that as a compliment."

"It was." I examined the nearest oil painting and rec-ognized Venice at sunset. My eyes absorbed the colors of the flamboyant yellow-orange sky meeting the cobalt blue canal. Next to it hung a painting of a sky—tumultuous clouds of green and purple. We moved about the gallery at the same languid speed, floating in a state of tranquility.

A couple just ahead, a man and a woman in their late twenties, were speaking quietly, then they simultaneously turned and stared at Martin as if he were on display. I checked out their dress, making note of the woman's low-riding jeans and Nike shoes. American tourists, I decided, hoping their intrusion wouldn't ruin Martin's time here. They didn't strike me as opera lovers, meaning they might recognize his face from a newspaper article or TV segment about the missing necklace.

"These paintings are marvelous," I said, gathering Martin's attention. I was gratified to see the two gawkers moving toward the next room, leaving us alone. "When I get home, I might buy a Turner print to hang in my living room."

"I'm glad you like his work. One decision made. Now, what about the other?"

I remembered his hasty exit from the dining room this morning when Nick showed up. "You mean Nick?" I said too loudly, his name skidding off the wooden floor.

"I assume he won't give you up without a fight. Am I correct?"

I was surprised at Martin's accurate conclusion. Perhaps men were capable of interpreting each other's motives better than women. But could he be without prejudice when it came to Nick? No, the two men detested each other.

"He probably hopes to use me as a ticket to the States." Although I preferred to think he found me irresistible. When Martin didn't contradict me, I said, "I do think Nick likes me." I felt an embarrassed blush crawl up my neck. "But that's not enough, is it?"

"I can tell you from experience, it takes more than physical attraction and good times to hold a relationship together."

"I know that too."

"I must compliment Nick on his good taste in women." He moved closer, his face only feet from mine. "Don't sell yourself short, Ms. Nash. Most men would find you quite enchanting."

I noticed for the first time that his eyes were the darkest of blues, the same color Turner used to depict the brooding evening sky. And Martin's features were indeed those of the prince in my childhood book, just as I'd observed on the plane. I knew Martin's quirks as few of his fans ever would.

Without warning, a wellspring of emotions deep in my chest began to stir. What was happening? Had I developed a crush on him? I thought of Madame Butterfly. She fell in love with Lieutenant Pinkerton, who loved another woman—one of his own rank and station. The saleswoman at The Sword and the Stone in Bath was right about tragic endings. I didn't want to be part of a romantic triangle.

"I must confess," he said. "It's bothered me since breakfast—our conversation about honesty. I've kept things from you. I should have come clean long before this." He smoothed his chin. "I followed you at Hever

Castle, wanting to speak to you privately. I presumed you thought I was Nick. You're not the type of woman who kisses any man who happens to sneak up on her."

Not true. I'd proven I was.

"I acted very badly," he said. "I'm usually not impulsive—quite the contrary. I don't know what came over me."

His impulsivity was contagious? No, I had only myself to blame. "Maybe being so far from home, we both lost our bearings," I said. "I've felt disconnected from my life in Seattle since my first night here."

"Perhaps that's it." He turned to view a painting of undulating greenish-lavender clouds joining the sea—a misty horizon, removed from the world. "This last week has given me time to examine my life. I'm alone. Quite a scary place to be, really."

With Pamela as his wife, he wouldn't be lonely anymore, I wanted to argue, but didn't wish to interrupt his flow of thoughts.

His face rotated in my direction, but his focus drifted over my shoulder. "I realize—" He let out a breath. "False pride and vanity have ruled my life."

"I NEED TO grab a cab to Harrods," I said as we exited the gallery twenty minutes later. "I want to buy something special for Roxie."

"Fine, I'll come too." He held two fingers to his lips and blasted a whistle that would make any New Yorker proud. A cab swerved to the curb.

"I don't want to keep you." I still hoped he'd make peace with his parents. "Are you sure you have time?"

"Yes, I want to purchase a gift, also."

Wandering Harrods' first floor, Martin and I circled a glassed-in case resplendent with costume jewelry.

"Roxie's always doing nice things for others," I said. "I want to surprise her." I paid for her present and asked the saleswoman to wrap it. "Aren't you going to buy anything?" I asked Martin.

"I haven't seen the perfect gift yet."

If Pamela's pearl choker was any indication of her tastes, I imagined she was used to shopping at the swankiest of stores. Finding her a trinket would be a difficult feat.

"Would you like my help?" I asked, moving toward the fine jewelry case.

Later in the cab, I rubbed the back of my taut neck. My shoes felt too tight after hours of walking.; I looked forward to slipping them off and relaxing on my bed. I'd avoided thinking about Nick, but I couldn't do that forever. He'd be off work in the next hour and planned to meet me at the hotel. I'd hoped to discuss his marriage proposal—which my mind still couldn't assimilate—with Roxanne before I spoke with him again. But she and Drew were at the Victoria and Albert Museum. When she got back, she'd be bushed after tromping through the seven miles of galleries viewing decorative arts, from ceramics to Chinese watercolors. It sounded like creative Roxanne's cup of tea, but did she have the stamina?

The cab paused for a red light a few blocks from the hotel. I glanced at Martin, who held his purchase on his lap—a simple but unique gold brooch in the shape of a musical note.

"You look awfully serious." He studied my face. "Are you all right?"

"I was thinking about Roxie." I felt a shred of anxiety as I envisioned her condition worsening and her ending up in the ER again.

"She asked me to keep her in my prayers," he said.

At one time it would have been impossible to imagine Martin beseeching God for intervention on behalf of another. But his eyes showed genuine concern.

He spoke in monotone. "And are you also thinking about Nick?"

"Yes." My thoughts were too jumbled to describe. And when it came to Nick, Martin was the wrong person to seek advice from.

The taxi started rolling again. Martin glanced out the window and said nothing more. When we arrived at the hotel, he handed me my Harrods bag and again insisted on paying for the cab.

In the lobby, I spotted Nick sitting on a couch with Clare. His arm draped around her shoulder, she was snuggled up against him like a cat burrowing into a mountain of catnip. Seeing the woman whom I'd comforted as she declared she hated men latching her hooks into Nick stopped me cold. I felt like I'd walked into a glass door. Should I confront her, or should I make it easy on both of us and ask the receptionist if there was a way to get upstairs without passing them?

Clare noticed me, and her head jerked. She jiggled her knees against Nick's to get his attention, and he also looked my way.

Clutching Roxanne's present in hand, I walked over to them with as much dignity as I could muster. "Hello."

"So, you've come back." His voice flowed as warmly and confidently as ever. "How was your day?"

"Fine." My one-syllable answer sounded like Cooper when dodging questions.

"I saw you leave earlier with Martin. You two make a beautiful couple. *Simpatica*." I opened my mouth to speak, but he cut me off. "Seriously, I mean that. I've had all day to think, and I can see that you and I are not cut from the same vine."

"Martin and I are friends," I said. "He's engaged, and you were busy."

Nick shrugged one shoulder. "I welcomed our new guests to London, but once they'd boarded the bus for their tour of the city, I was free. So, I took Clare to lunch."

"The best Italian food I've ever eaten," she said with a gush.

"And I was impressed with your accent." He winked in Clare's direction and she cuddled closer. "With a few lessons, you'll do beautifully in Italy."

Clare practically twittered with delight. "I'll stay in Rome the first week—visit Saint Peters's and the Coliseum—then take the train to Florence. *Fierenze*, as you call it."

"Brava."

The thought of those two dining at the same table Nick and I had shared irked me. If he'd spent time with any other woman, I don't think I would have cared. But Clare had coughed in my face and whined every inch of the trip. She was the one who'd ripped away my chance of singing, and she'd accomplished it with glee.

She looked up at me with sheepish eyes that I assumed were feigned for my benefit. "I hope you don't mind, but Nick and I made plans for tonight." She dragged her hair over one shoulder and gave her head a flirtatious shake. "I mean, you weren't here."

"That's right." Nick's arm tightened around her shoulder.

If I'd been holding a glass of water, I might have dumped it on them. Childish behavior? Yes, but satisfying. "Nick," I said, "I was hoping we'd have a chance to talk."

"Talk? Always this talk and no action."

Clare stretched to her feet. "Maybe I should split until you two work this out."

"No, wait." As he stood, he sent Clare a forlorn expression. "You will desert me too?"

"I just thought—"

"That I would pass up the chance to spend the evening with a *bellisima signorina* like you? Absolutely not." He took a step toward the hotel's front door and Clare fell in next to him linking her arm through his.

CHAPTER 33

I PURCHASED A SANDWICH in the hotel's restaurant and carried the plate up to my room. Once there, I plumped my pillows against the headboard and eased down on the bed, grateful for the solitude.

Thirty minutes earlier, Roxanne had called, inviting me to accompany Drew and her for dinner and then a show, but I opted to stay in. "I feel fine," she'd assured me when I'd inquired about her health. "And I'll be with Drew. He promised to keep me safe and sound." I could tell from her fluttering voice that she was infatuated. How wonderful.

I found *Rebecca* on the bed table—the book fell open to the first page. The story started at the end. Manderley deserted and memories flooding the second Mrs. Max de Winter's mind of the drive past the blood-red rhododendrons to the gate. In her dream, she could pass right through the iron bars, and now I felt able to do the same, to reach back into my locked memory box and bravely observe my life as an impartial spectator.

I remembered the first time I'd read this tale of a woman's devotion to her new husband. I'd been a different person—eighteen years old and innocent, in some ways like the heroine in the story. In spite of my parents' divorce, I'd hoped anything was possible if two people loved each other enough. Later, I'd entered into marriage and parenthood with little practical knowledge. No role model at home. Images on television—*The Brady Bunch* and *The Partridge Family* had been Hollywood-style illusions. The idea that I could find my Prince Charming and depend on him was a fallacy. I'd thought if I did more and worked harder, Jeff would love me, and all would be well.

I'd been lugging the heaviness of Jeff's trash bin around with me too long. He hadn't intentionally abandoned me, and even if he had I needed to forgive him. Was it possible to forgive someone who hadn't repented or asked for forgiveness?

My parents came to the front of my mind. I remembered with clarity the morning my father wasn't at the breakfast table with his coffee and oatmeal. My mother, unable to look at me through swollen eyelids, told me Daddy wouldn't live with us anymore. "He still loves his little girl," she'd said with a faltering voice. But if that were true, why would he leave us? Mom cried for weeks, although she always tried to hide her sorrow. My ears straining for the familiar rumble of my father's sleek Porsche, I'd stood at the kitchen window waiting for his return wondering if somehow his leaving was my fault.

I needed to forgive my father too. But how?

And what about my singing? I considered how free I'd feel if I were not thinking about Hal or the others in the choir. Not vying for approval from the people in the audience, or even my mother. That's how to live one's life, I thought—centered.

A sense of peace washed over me as the heavy chain around my neck loosened its hold. I felt buoyant, like I was soaking in a pool of warm water where I would never sink.

I glanced back to the book again. Manderley had burned to the ground, but the de Winters' love lived on. It was sad to imagine that beautiful mansion gone forever, but I thought about a love that would overcome all obstacles, endure devastation, and come out on the other side stronger.

Would I ever find a man who loved me that much?

Someone out in the hall rap-rapped on my door. I set the book aside, stood to open it, and found Roxanne's face beaming at me.

"Get dressed, girlfriend," she said with gusto. "It's our last night in town and we need to celebrate."

"I'm staying right here tonight." I took her arm and gently pulled her into the room. "But I'm glad you came by." I grinned as I gave her a green box with a bow on the top. The saleswoman at Harrods had done a wonderful job wrapping my gift.

"You crazy lady." Roxanne giggled as she pulled off the ribbon, dug through layers of tissue paper, and found a rhinestone tiara. "I love it!" She placed the sparkling crown on her head, smiled into the mirror, and then hugged me.

"That is the real you," I said. "A princess."

She stood for a long minute. "I don't think anyone's ever just given me something for no reason."

"There is a reason. I love you, my dear friend. And when we get home, I want us to get healthy together— to find a nutritious eating routine and hold each other accountable. I'll buy a set of small weights and we can work out in my living room. And we can start walking together after work."

"You don't have to do all that."

"I want to, and I won't take no for an answer." We hugged each other again and I kissed her cheek.

"Now about tonight," Roxanne said. "Get yourself dressed in your black dress and meet me down in the lobby, pronto." She bulged her eyes for effect. "Do it! I won't take no for an answer."

CHAPTER 34

I N   T H E   L O B B Y ,   I found Hal pacing in a tight circle. Martin and about half of the choir members stood nearby, all clad in black—out of place here in our London hotel.

"Good, Roxanne located you." Hal's gaze finally rested on my face for the first time in two days. "We've been asked to give a small concert tonight." His voice trembled with excitement. He shook his head when I started to question him. "That's all I can say. It's a surprise and we have Martin to thank for it."

His hands in a prayerful position, Hal bowed in Martin's direction. "We'll only perform half our repertoire, but please give it your best, people." His head bobbed atop his neck like a marionette. "But don't be nervous. I'm not. No reason to be nervous. No, no."

We crammed into cabs and drove for five minutes to the stately Ritz Hotel. The doorman was expecting our arrival and led us to a sumptuous dining room that had been reserved for the evening. The choir crowded onto a stage in front of lavish surroundings. A circular Baroque painting framed in gold leaf floated above us on the ceiling. Tall mirrors reflected opulent chandeliers and wall murals. Women in sequined and satin gowns and men wearing tuxedos sat at round tables with floral centerpieces and taper candles.

The room hushed as Bonnie passed out the music, then she sat before a glossy grand piano. Hal nodded to her and she started the introduction to the first piece. The piano rippled like a river; the choir's words danced on its surface like water bugs. Singing with half the number of choir members in this spacious room felt relaxed and easy, like a rehearsal. I hadn't warmed up, but I could hear my voice soaring as if it could sail to any height.

We sang through another piece, then Bonnie played the introduction to Clare's solo. My head craned around searching for Clare, but she wasn't there. Now that I thought about it, I hadn't seen her in the hotel lobby. She must be with Nick.

I noticed Hal was aiming his concentrated stare at me as if I were the only one on stage. Why was he looking at me? Had I done something wrong? I could hear the introduction winding down. Hal began nodding at me. Did he want me to sing? There was no way I could, but there were only a few notes to go.

Before I could think, my mouth opened and out sailed, "The king of love my shepherd is, whose goodness faileth never."

I could hear my words, but they sounded far away, as if someone else were singing in a long tunnel. My head swam with Muriel's statement, "You listen to yourself too much," and Roxanne's saying, "Forget what other people think."

I glued my vision to Hal's baton instead of letting it wander to the audience. The crowd remained a blurred mass, but out of the corner of my eye I saw Roxanne grinning at me. She had the right idea. I shouldn't base my self-worth on what strangers or the other choir members thought of me.

In what seemed like an instant, my solo was completed. Without looking at a musical score once, I'd sung the whole piece by heart. My voice hadn't sounded the least like Clare's, which was substantial and round. Mine had been like sunlight shining through stained glass: pure and brilliant and colorful. My chest heaved with thankfulness as I watched Hal wink at me, then smile.

Martin, standing to my left, lightly squeezed my hand. "Well done," he whispered.

When I dared to look out at the audience, the room became a sea of clapping hands, everyone an individual who'd either approved or disapproved of my performance—and that was all right. I smiled at them and accepted their applause. I wished my mother could have heard me.

The rest of the concert felt like promenading through a castle filled with treasures. The whole group seemed energized, our sound tight and precise, yet moving.

After we'd taken our final bow, Roxanne threw her arms around me. "You've been holding out on us," she said. "You sounded fabulous."

The other choir members surrounded and congratulated me. Hal patted my shoulder. "That took guts and talent. You've got both."

"Where's Clare?" Drew said.

Hal fell quiet, but Bonnie answered. "She took off with Nick. I tried to say something to her, but she ignored me."

Hal directed us off stage. "People, we need to retain our stage manners until we're out in the lobby."

"I wonder who all these people are and what the big deal was," Roxanne said as we shuffled toward the exit.

"Maybe businessmen at a convention?" Drew offered.

She turned to appraise them. "In very expensive suits."

Martin spoke into my ear. "There's someone I need to say hello to." He seemed happy, yet determined I come with him. I felt his hand take mine as he guided me toward the center of the restaurant.

In the middle of the room stood a table, slightly larger than the others. As we approached, the men at the table instantly rose to their feet.

Martin lowered his head for a moment, then sent a smile to a silver-haired elderly woman wearing an emerald pendant the size of a half-dollar. "May I please present Jessica Nash?" he asked her.

"But, of course. Good to see you, Marty."

"Jessica, say hello to Princess Alexandra."

I was speechless as I shook the woman's bejeweled hand. Was I supposed to curtsy?

"Pleased to meet you," Princess Alexandra said. "What a delightful voice you have."

"Thank you, you're very kind." I wasn't accustomed to princesses bestowing praise upon me. I felt myself blush as I took in her words, which almost sounded like a foreign language.

As Martin introduced me to the others, I heard Lord and Lady before several of the names. "How do you do?" they all said.

"My nephew writes a column for the *London Times*," Princess Alexandra said to me. She addressed the young man on her right. "You were planning to include Martin's singing tonight. I assume you'll mention Ms. Nash's voice, too."

"Yes, I shall." He removed a small notebook from his breast pocket. "That's N-A-S-H, is it?"

"Yes." I had to remind myself this wasn't a dream.

"Martin." Princess Alexandra glanced up at him. "You must come and visit us again soon. I do hope you'll be returning to town more often."

He bowed slightly.

"I don't trust you." She reached out to grab his hand. "I shall hire you to perform for us in the fall. That way, I know I'll see you again." She turned her attention to me. "And bring this lovely soprano back with you. You two must sing my favorite Mozart duet from *The Marriage of Figaro*."

By the time Martin and I reached the front door, Roxie and Drew were climbing into a taxi. I started to yell to them, but Martin stopped me.

"There are plenty of cabs," he said. "And there's somewhere I want to take you. Do you mind?" Another cab sped up and Martin gave the driver our destination.

As we motored through traffic, I asked Martin, "Who was that woman?"

"A dear family friend I've known most of my life."

"I heard you call her Princess. Is she married to a nobleman?"

"Quite the contrary. She's the queen's cousin."

My jaw dropped. "Wow." I sounded like Cooper after the Blue Angels flew over our house last summer during Seafair. Then I chuckled at my small-town-girl reaction.

We drove over Westminster Bridge, then along the banks of the Thames River. The cab slowed down.

"Will this do, sir?" the cabbie asked in a cockney accent, making me think of *My Fair Lady*. I knew how Eliza Doolittle felt when she sang "I Could Have Danced All Night," but I'd change the word "danced" for "sung." This was my magical, perfect evening. Nothing could go wrong.

"Yes, this is fine," Martin said. "And please wait for us here." The cabbie nodded, then punched on his radio and unfolded a newspaper to the horse racing stats.

Martin reached past me to open the door. "After you," he said.

I stepped out and inhaled chill air smelling of wet pavement from an earlier downpour. A breeze fluttered against my face and legs, but my torso still radiated warmth from the excitement of the performance. Martin escorted me around a wall and up a flight of stairs to a deserted walkway. From there I could see the inky river below. Lights shimmered on the slow-moving water like flickering stars on a swatch of velvet. On the opposite bank stood the House of Parliament and Big Ben.

The night was glorious. I leaned against the railing and inhaled the damp air. I felt Martin close behind me, heard his sigh.

"No one should leave London without having a last look at the city," he said, "as an enticement to return."

"Leaving tomorrow." I breathed in a thousand years of history. "I wish we didn't have to go home yet. So much has happened in such a short time."

"Yes, it has for me too."

He briefly touched my shoulder. I turned and found him staring at me intently. He brought his hand to my cheek and stroked it with his fingertips. I felt myself drawing toward him, but he shook his head and took a step back.

"Jessica, if I kissed you, it would be taking advantage of this situation."

"And it would be wrong. You're getting married soon." I glanced down so he wouldn't see sadness in my eyes. "You are getting married, aren't you?"

"I hope to."

Suddenly his arms gathered me up, almost lifting me off my feet. He kissed me tenderly, like a man embracing his long-lost love after years at sea. I allowed myself to be swept up by his momentum.

As we parted, I felt a smack of shame. "We can't do that again," I said, thinking of my home-wrecking stepmother. "I refuse to be the other woman."

"Understandable."

From now on I would rely on the left side of my brain, where logic resides. This was not the real world. When Martin and I sang together in the choir, we shared small triumphs in an artificial situation orchestrated by Hal. Tomorrow when the tour dispersed, Martin and I would go our separate ways.

A streetlight blinked, then went out. Darkness surrounded us. A gust of icy air ruffled the hem of my dress. I rubbed my arms, trying to warm them.

He removed his jacket and hung it over my shoulders. "I need to take care of our new lead soprano. Mustn't let her catch cold."

I flashed him a contorted smirk. "That might be a slight exaggeration. Hal only chose me because Clare wasn't there." Maybe she'd hinted she was quitting the choir when we got home.

"Hal's too much of a perfectionist to accept second best," he said. "He would have skipped the piece entirely if he didn't have confidence in your vocal ability."

"Did you set the whole evening up?"

He suppressed a grin.

"Just so I could sing?"

"Guilty." He couldn't conceal his pleasure at pulling it off. "An excellent idea, if I say so myself."

I was touched by his generosity. No man had ever shown me such kindness. But I didn't feel worthy. "I'm not close to Clare's caliber."

"I disagree. Clare is a proficient performer, but she delivers the music as a vehicle to showcase her voice. She produces the correct sounds and pitches, but her words are without content. You, on the other hand, exhibit passion when you sing. Your voice is like a river that's gathered knowledge and understanding along its journey."

I visualized a logjammed railroad trestle spanning the Snohomish River after a spring flood. "A lot of dead branches would be more like it."

"We've all botched up a few times." He stroked a wisp of my hair that threatened to cover my eye. "There is a depth to your voice, a beautiful sound you can't hear. No singer can hear himself, even when his voice is recorded. That's a lesson I've had to learn."

A sharp *click* shattered the air. I spun around and saw Jerry pointing a small handgun at us. It looked like the .38 Special from Cooper's video game.

CHAPTER 35

"WHAT ARE YOU doing here?" I asked Jerry in a tinny voice. "Is this some perverted joke?"

Jerry edged closer, his hand shaking. A distant siren began to wail, and he stiffened. But the vehicle was on the other side of the river and moving away.

"He's a petty thug looking for a quick buck." Martin patted his breast pocket. "And he thought I might have something of value with me."

"The necklace belongs to me—to us, that is," Jerry said, his face swollen and his lips sloppy, like he'd belted down one too many.

"It does not," I said. "It belongs to Martin's family. Don't give it to him, Martin."

"Shut up." Spittle flew from Jerry's mouth. He glared at Martin with savage eyes. "Hand it over."

"This is utterly splendid." Martin's face remained as composed as it was five minutes ago. "I just solved the riddle. And I feel rather foolish for taking so long.

Jessica, meet Giovanni Bianco, an uninspired tenor who sings like a bleating goat."

Jerry bared his teeth. "Why you little— I ought to wipe that sneer off your face for good."

Martin didn't flinch. "I've never seen him in real life before," Martin said to me. "He's considerably older and shorter than I thought he'd be. And wearing a ridiculous mustache." He eyed Jerry like a fly in his soup. "Is it a stage prop, a phony like you?"

"It's real." Jerry's free hand wiped across his upper lip. "And so is this." He waved the gun with a wobbling hand.

Martin faced me, excluding Jerry from our conversation. "Don't you think it's reasonable that the bum who'd steal my wife would also steal my family's property?"

Nothing made sense. "Dorothea?" I said, and Martin nodded.

"She and I were in London." The veins in his neck thickened. "Her on a singing engagement, and me visiting friends and family. She'd seen Mother wearing the Canary Cross and asked to borrow it to flaunt at a cast party. To Dorothea, the necklace was simply a piece of expensive jewelry to show off. She craved being the center of attention—all eyes on her. Even though the necklace was insured, I was reluctant to let her take it. I should have heeded my instincts."

As Martin spoke, I could see Jerry's menacing shape out of the corner of my eye. The backs of my knees weakened, as if I were sinking into mud. I remembered reading Grimm's Fairy Tales. The stories inevitably led to the appearance of an evil entity. If only we could skip this chapter and escape.

"Over the next week," Martin said, "Dorothea used every excuse for not returning the necklace. I tried to reason with her, but she laughed in my face, then danced off to her closing night performance." His face tortured, he rubbed his ears. "I can still hear her taunting words in our hotel suite, calling me a mama's boy. When she left, I ran into the bedroom and searched through every drawer." His phrases spurted out, like he was barely keeping his head above water. "That was when I came across her diary, which described in sickening detail what they'd done together. My devoted wife hadn't bothered to hide it very well. Maybe she wanted me to read it. Then I dug through the room until I found the necklace concealed under a chair cushion."

Jerry's weight swayed back and forth. He steadied his gun with his other hand, signs he was growing restless, like a kid in front of the class who was about to have a meltdown. I wondered if he'd get impatient and kill Martin just to silence him.

"I spent that night at my private club." Martin's hands balled into fists, his knuckles white. "The next day, the police came to question me. According to them, Dorothea alleged that I'd physically assaulted her, of all preposterous accusations. That the night before, I'd stolen the necklace when I knew she'd be on stage, then taken off. I figured if I handed the necklace over to the police, they'd throw me in jail and give it to her. So I claimed ignorance."

A clumsy moth fluttered past us. The rest of London moved in slow motion. Horns beeped on the other side of the river, their outraged cries elongated like wayward sheep. I wanted to take Martin's hand, but I couldn't move. My muscles were frozen, my feet trapped in cement. This was a new kind of fear, making stage fright puny and manageable.

Martin pushed out his chin and narrowed his eyes at Jerry. "So the prima donna convinced you to come all this way to fetch it, has she? Like her cocker spaniel? Quite an undertaking, but aren't you afraid she's using you the way she exploited me? She is rather good at that."

Jerry's features twisted. "Cut the gab. And don't think I won't use this." He shifted his aim to my face and advanced closer. As I watched the gun barrel enlarge, my lungs trapped my breath in my chest.

So that's what a real gun looks like, I thought, not big enough to kill someone. But I could tell from Jerry's hideous expression it wasn't a toy. He had used Clare. He cared nothing for other people. I wanted to tell him what a monster he was, but my tongue went numb, like a dentist had injected it with Novocain. A coppery taste flooded my mouth. My pounding heart echoed in my ears. Surely Jerry could hear it.

"Say goodbye to your girlfriend." Jerry's hand shook, and the gun's cool muzzle grazed my face, feeling like a razor against my skin.

"No. Stop." Martin wrenched the box out of his pocket and brandished it. "Take it. But leave her alone."

Still pointing the gun at me, Jerry swiped out with his other hand to grab the box. He struggled to open the lid without dropping the gun. A section of gold chain appeared, then a sparkle of brilliance as a corner of the cross revealed itself.

Jerry fumbled and the necklace fell to the ground.

His pinprick eyes bulged. He stooped to retrieve it. The moment his gaze fell upon the necklace, Martin lunged forward. Jerry's arm swung up and the barrel met Martin in the stomach.

The silence crackled as the two men faced off.

"Let him go, Martin." I felt my throat close. "It's not worth it."

Martin's shoulders trembled with rage. He stood between me and Jerry, shielding me with his body.

Jerry, his gun arm still extended, plucked up the necklace with his other hand and crammed it in his pocket. He straightened his spine. "You're lucky I'm in a good mood," he said. Then, as if he were playing a new role and we were giving him a standing ovation, his face transformed. He flashed us a cordial grin.

"It's been a pleasure doing business with you." He turned to make his escape, his beefy legs setting him in motion. But he stopped short, sighting three men in dark uniforms waiting with guns drawn at the bottom of the steps.

Jerry swung around, turning his weapon back on Martin, and yelled, "Keep away or I'll shoot him. There's nothing that would make me happier."

The three men froze—powerless spectators. For a moment the world stopped, as though someone had pushed the pause button on my TV set.

In a rash move, Martin grabbed for the gun, but Jerry held onto it. The two scuffled, obscuring the revolver between them.

Then a crash louder than a Fourth of July bottle rocket splintered my eardrums.

"Martin!" I screamed.

He and Jerry stood holding each other like dancers caught in mid-step.

Finally, Jerry's hands drooped to his side and the gun scudded to the ground. He stepped away from Martin. A black streak trickled from Jerry's midsection. His mouth gaped open. In a burst, he scrambled to the railing, sprang over it, and hurled himself into the river.

The officers swarmed up the stairs and looked over the side. "I can't see him," one said, while another called for backup assistance from the river patrol.

"Are you all right?" I asked Martin. He nodded, his breath staggered. Then we both stood at the railing, staring into the river searching for Jerry's floating body, but the abyss had sucked him up.

"No one could survive that fall, could they?" I asked, ignoring the obvious. Jerry had received a bullet wound that would most likely kill him even if he were on dry land.

"The necklace," I said. "Gone."

The third officer removed his cap—a silver badge gracing the front. "Sorry we let that unpleasantness go on so long, Mr. Spear," he said to Martin. "We didn't dare step in with the young lady there."

"How do you know my name?" Martin's voice gathered anger.

The man, hooknosed and lanky, fiddled with the brim of his hat. "We've been tailing you."

"But why? I've been cleared. I'm innocent."

"Yes, sir. And we apologize for the intrusion. Your father—"

"What does he have to do with this?" Martin said with ferocity.

"He asked us—begged us, really—to keep an eye on you. He warned us this type of situation might occur."

"And you're sure it was my father?"

"Yes, my superior spoke to him in person."

Thirty minutes later, Martin and I got back in the cab. The driver, apparently oblivious to the presence of the two squad cars parked close by, turned down his radio and revved the engine. Martin gave him the hotel's address, and the driver made a U-turn, then sped across the bridge.

Exhaustion enveloped me. Although I was unscathed physically, I felt beaten up, every inch of my body bruised.

"I'm sorry," Martin said. "I should have stored the necklace in a hotel's safe. How could I have been so stupid to carry it with me?" He grasped both my hands. "You could have been killed. I'd never forgive myself."

Although the cab was warm, goose bumps erupted on my legs. "When I saw who it was, I was almost too mad to be scared." I shuddered uncontrollably and rubbed my forearms. "But then he pointed the gun at me."

"He was an animal." Martin spoke as if Jerry were a part of history, but I was unsure. I supposed the police would drag the river and find his bloated corpse. Then I would feel safe.

"I thought Jerry worked for an insurance company," I said.

"So did I." His voice sounded brittle. "Until tonight."

My imagination replayed the episode with a different finale, one where Martin's lifeless body lay at my feet.

"I'm so grateful you're all right," I said. "Even if it meant losing the necklace."

"Mother will be disappointed."

"Maybe when Jerry's body is recovered, the necklace will be returned to you." Or did the necklace slip from Jerry's pocket—lost forever at the bottom of the river?

"You did the right thing letting him have it," I said. "Your parents care far more about you than the necklace."

So did I.

"I only gave it to him because your life was in jeopardy." He clasped my hand like a man holding onto a life raft. "I would have gladly died before submitting to his demand. Yet I wish the police had apprehended him unscathed."

After the dart game with Nick, Martin had declared he didn't have the stomach for hunting. But tonight, he was forced to shoot a man. He'd had no choice.

"I can't get over the way the officers showed up," I said. "Your father was having us followed to protect you."

"Yes, that was a shock. It seems he really does care."

I remembered Martin's skeptical appraisal of the stained-glass windows in Chester and his callous words about fathers.

"Martin, I just realized something. You're the Prodigal Son."

CHAPTER 36

I COULDN'T FALL ASLEEP. No surprise there. And Clare was still out on the town.

Each time I closed my eyes, I saw the gun's muzzle aimed at me like a cyclops's eye. I relived the moment it touched my cheek and I felt a ripple of nausea.

In my mind, I watched Martin and Jerry wrestling for the gun, then saw Jerry's expression after the blast. A look of resolve? No, he must be dead. I never liked scary movies but had just lived through a scene from *The Untouchables*. If I'd been killed, Cooper would be without a parent. As an orphan, he'd be obliged to live with a grandma who was involved with a new beau. It was too gruesome to contemplate.

In an attempt to placate my out-of-control thoughts, I brought out *Rebecca* and forced my eyes to the page. It was past midnight when I read the final words. That beautiful estate, Manderley, burned to the ground. How many other gracious homes perished over the years? One spark and the flames engulfed all, leaving only charred remnants. One person abandons a family and it crumbles into devastation.

I thought about Cooper. It would take years for his wounds to heal, just as my heart still ached over my own father's desertion. As I lay in the darkness, I decided to talk about Jeff's death with Cooper when I got home. It would be a running dialogue for the rest of his life, something that would need to be explored again and again as he matured. It might be hard for my boy to trust others when his own father had left him, just as it was difficult for me.

I envisioned Cooper in Rite Aid stashing the toy car in his pocket and being caught. I hoped the security guard had scared a lifetime of sense into my son. I wondered if Cooper dreaded my return, like a man waiting for the judge and jury to file into the courtroom to pronounce judgment. He said he hoped I never came home, but I knew children sometimes said spiteful things because they were afraid or hurt inside.

My thoughts shifted. I saw Nick's face in my mind's eye. He was well-educated, intelligent, and downright handsome. If he ever visited Seattle, women's heads would turn in admiration. I had to admit, having him pursue me had boosted my ego. At home most men were passive. Women practically did the asking to get a date. I hated how roles were reversed and commitments taken lightly. I wanted to be in a relationship for the long haul, forever and ever. Maybe there were no guarantees, but I must build my future on solid ground. No more sand and silt.

I remembered meeting Martin on the jet. I'd been repelled, mistaking his distant air for arrogance. I hadn't recognized another injured person, his hopes crushed. A man afraid to let anyone close for fear of rejection. How good it felt to have him for an ally. And to have his lips... Had there ever been a sweeter kiss?

But I must not think this way. The kiss had been wrong. Sinful, Mom would say. It could never be repeated.

A jet thundering overhead reminded me of last night's applause after my solo. My heart expanded with gratitude. In the past, I'd fantasized about music flowing through me, and that's exactly how it felt.

My mind turned to Roxanne. The deepening of our friendship during the last week was another gift. I dared to imagine her diabetes worsening, damaging her eyes, her kidneys, her heart.

I tugged the covers up around my neck. Each day of life was precious, to be celebrated and appreciated. I would be Roxanne's support. Whatever she needed.

THE NEXT MORNING, the first thing I heard was Clare rustling under her covers.

"Are you awake?" she said, loud enough to rouse the soundest of sleepers.

I wasn't ready to face her yet. As I played possum, I contemplated how to tell her Jerry was an imposter. The story would probably hit the papers today. He'd be exposed as a greedy and vicious cur, and Martin would be exonerated. I hoped. Did Dorothea know the real

Jerry—I mean, Giovanni Bianco—or had he played a convincing adoring suitor, thus deceiving her? I wanted to believe Dorothea was an innocent victim, but Martin's descriptions of her hinted otherwise.

I squinted at the digital clock on my bed table to see the alarm would go off in a few minutes. We'd leave for the airport right after breakfast.

"You still speaking to me?" Clare asked.

I wanted to be left alone. I was done with drama. Done with intrigue.

"Well?" she said, apparently not used to being ignored.

I yawned. "I'm not mad at you. Okay?"

"Good. Most women don't like me. Mama says it's because I'm beautiful and everything comes easy for me. But you've always been nice."

I could think of many reasons women would wish to avoid Clare and very few incentives why they'd want to call her friend. And that thought made me pity her.

"If you don't have good women friends I strongly recommend you find some," I said, staring at the crack on the ceiling.

"What for? Besides my father, who's a traveling salesman and always on the road, Mama just has me. That's why I still live at home. She says she'd be too lonely without me and that no one will be as nice to me as she is. It was her idea that I become a singer." She stretched her arms over her head. "When I was a little girl, I dreamed of being a ballerina, but Mama said I'd be too tall. And she was right. In high school, I decided

I wanted to be a teacher. But she said that it didn't pay well enough, and it would waste my talents."

"You have a beautiful voice," I said. "Maybe you could be a music teacher."

"Mama wouldn't go for that. She wants me in the spotlight. And so do I." Clare propped herself on one elbow. "By the way, nothing happened between Nick and me last night. We went to a bar where everyone knew him, but he seemed distracted. I got to hang out with his friends, but he sat there like a lump. Guess Nick really likes you, and only you."

"Is that what he said?"

"More how he acted. Bummed out."

A ray of light peeked between the curtain and the wall. "Bummed out?" I asked. "Or like he'd lost a game?"

Clare got to her feet. The hem of her nightgown fell around her ankles. She flicked on the light and stood before the mirror. "I think it's you. Maybe he's not used to having a woman turn him down. Nick's a man you can't ignore, and I bet most women don't." She screwed up her mouth as she zeroed in on a blemish until she was only inches away from the glass. "He never made a move on me. Unless you count a peck on the cheek when he said goodnight."

The coward in me wanted to end the conversation there, but I gathered my courage and I said, "By the way, some of us got together and sang last night."

"Is that what Bonnie was babbling about?" She gave an exaggerated yawn, fanning her mouth. "I suppose you entertained some senior citizens?"

"Some of them were elderly." I hesitated. Would it be better to let Hal handle this? But he didn't like confrontation any more than I did. "I might as well tell you, there were some important people there."

Clare flipped her hair through her fingers, attempting to make the ends curl. "Trying to make me jealous, are we?"

"No, but I thought you should know I sang your piece. And after the concert I spoke to a reporter."

She wheeled around, almost tripping on her nightgown. "This is exactly what Mama warned me about, that other women would be envious and use me as a stepping-stone. It's a dog-eat-dog world, right?"

I rolled over and swamped my face in the pillow. I could hide until she started her shower, but I pulled myself up and looked her in the face.

"I'm going to give it to you straight," I said. "Crazy as it sounds, I think Martin and I were invited back in the fall to sing for some of the royal family."

A smirk widened her mouth. "Right. If you say so." She hiked her nightgown over her head and pitched it onto her bed, then stepped into her bathrobe and cinched the belt tight. "I'll be busy prepping for the Met auditions by then. I told you my teacher said I'm ready, didn't I?"

"Yes, you did." Thinking there might be little chance to speak to Clare alone after today, I added, "I hope you win first place and end up singing at the finest opera houses. And I also hope you meet the perfect man someday and have some wonderful children."

Her tongue jutted out of her down-turned mouth like a gargoyle. "Me, have kids? No way." Her hands outlined her silhouette. "I'd never let myself become so grotesquely fat I couldn't perform onstage. Now, that would be depressing."

I couldn't absorb the idea of remaining childless only to keep one's figure. I wanted to fill her in on the joys my son brought me—most of the time—but decided to let it slide. No use starting up another argument. Clare was young; she might change her mind when her hormonal clock chimed at age thirty. Anyway, I had another important topic to cover.

"There's more I need to tell you—about Jerry." I hated being the bearer of bad news.

At the sound of his name, her face brightened. Her arms wrapped around her ribcage. "Maybe I was too hard on him." She gave herself a hug. "I should let him know how to reach me in the States."

"Clare, there's no easy way to say this. Last night he was shot, and we think killed. He tried to rob Martin and me at gunpoint."

Forced laughter burbled from her mouth. "You expect me to believe that?"

"It's true. And Jerry's not his real name."

She pointed her index finger at me. "I get it, you're trying to drive me nuts."

CHAPTER 37

"ROXIE, YOU LOOK like the cat that ate the canary." I watched her from across the breakfast table. I hadn't told her about last night. After my conversation with Clare, I wasn't ready to bring Jerry's name up again until I was safely home. And why give Roxanne more to worry about?

She brought a piece of dry whole wheat toast to her lips and nibbled off a corner without answering.

"Come on, what is it?" I asked. "You look like you're going to burst."

She brought the toast back to her mouth, but her lips trembled with laughter. "All right, I'll tell you." She giggled, tapping her toes on the floor. "Drew and I have come to a decision." She dropped the toast back onto her plate, then patted under her eyes with her napkin. "We're going steady."

Her laughter was contagious. I began chuckling too. "That's great. I'm happy for you," I said, thankful to have my spirits lifted.

She dabbed her eyes again. "It seems funny to say at my age, but those are the only words that describe what we're doing." She reached for her water glass and gulped a mouthful. "So you're not the only woman with a new man in her life."

My smile collapsed. "You mean Nick? It's over between us. It's for the best, but I do want to talk with him on the bus, to say goodbye. Is that dumb?"

She threw her hands up. "I don't know. I'm having a hard enough time with my own life. But if you've decided Nick's not the one, maybe it isn't a good idea to speak to him again. Isn't that like tasting one more bite of dessert to see if it's really as good as you remember?" She reached for the dish of marmalade, then raspberry jam, and then shook her head. "Too many choices for women these days. Maybe it was easier back in our grandmothers' time."

"You're right," I said. "Nowadays, unless you have a finger in every pot, you're considered a failure. Women are expected to do it all and do it well."

A couple, the husband carrying a toddler and the wife leading a four-to-five-year-old boy by the hand, straggled past the table. Roxanne smiled at the little boy and he grinned in return.

"How I'd love to be one of those humdrum housewives," she said. "Like on the decades-old TV show *Leave It to Beaver*. But I'm a million miles from that."

"Maybe you and Drew will get serious."

"We decided we're going to move at tortoise speed. Here's my routine: follow my heart, without forgetting all that past experience has taught me."

"That sounds like good advice. Roxie, I still hope you'll move in with me."

"But what if it doesn't work out? What if one of us changes our mind? It might damage our friendship."

"Let's give it a six-month shot, until the end of summer."

"Okay, in a few days I'll come over to your house and check things out."

I felt like a girl planning a slumber party. "Goody, I can't wait."

"And after I get settled I'm looking for a new job. One with good health insurance. I've been living on a shoestring budget for too long."

Hal strode in the door and sat with Martin, Drew, and several others. Using his hands to emphasize his words, Hal was explaining something, but Martin wasn't paying attention. His glance drifted around the room and landed on me. I smiled and gave a small wave. His expression remained cool. He nodded hello as if he barely knew me. A moment later, he stood and walked out without passing our table.

The corners of my mouth sagged down. After all we'd been through together, the least he could do was swing by and say good morning. But I reminded myself he had more important problems on his mind. He'd probably killed Jerry, whose body had not yet been found. Even in self-defense, I couldn't imagine Martin's turmoil of feelings. I was such a softy. I doubt I could flush a sick goldfish down the toilet. And today Martin was leaving his homeland, his parents, and Pamela. Although I figured she would join him soon.

Hal got to his feet and came over to Roxanne's and my table. He tapped the face of his watch. "It's time to head for the airport. We must not miss our flight." He sounded like a radio announcer getting us stoked for the big game. "The bus should be here any minute. I spoke to Dave earlier and he promised he'd be here on time."

"Dave?" I felt a tightening in my scalp. "Who's he?"

"Our original driver," Roxanne said. "You know, the grumpy guy with laryngitis. I'm glad we didn't have him for the whole trip."

"But I assumed Nick would be here." I said to Roxanne as soon as Hal was gone. "Now how will I reach him?"

"He gave me his card with his cell number, but I don't have it anymore."

"I know what you're thinking," I said, standing. "I should get on that plane and pretend he never existed. He's not good for me. I don't even know if we share the same beliefs."

One thousand thoughts splatted through my mind like droplets spewing from a hose. I rubbed my temples. I thought about *Rebecca*, how the young woman in the story met her husband on holiday. Had I brought that book along for a purpose other than mere entertainment? Was there a message I was supposed to glean from reading it? If so, was Nick the man I should reach out to?

I was running out of time. I didn't know Nick's number and wasn't even sure how to spell his last name. I hurried to ask the front desk crew if they knew how to get in touch with him. A young woman handed me a copy of the tour company's brochure. I flipped it over and found the telephone number on the back. I asked to use the phone and let it ring until a message came on.

"We're open from nine a.m. to five p.m.," the recorded voice said.

I glanced at my watch and saw it was only eight. I gave the phone back to the girl, then rushed upstairs to pack.

Twenty minutes later, I took my suitcase out to the street and left it with Dave, who stood by the bus's open cargo area. He muttered how heavy my suitcase was as he pitched it in. I had to smile when I considered how opposite he was from Nick. I glanced up to the bus's windows and saw that most everyone was onboard. Hoping Nick would appear, I dawdled with Hal outside in the misty rain until the last person showed up. Then I whispered a farewell to London and followed Hal onto the bus.

An hour later, we lingered at Heathrow Airport, waiting in a security queue that made lines at Disneyland look short.

Standing next to me, Bonnie asked, "Where are you sitting?"

I examined my ticket. "27A."

"Good, we're next to each other. You and I can reminisce about our trip all the way home."

"Not ready to leave yet?"

Her carry-on lay at her feet propped between her legs. "Not even close. I didn't go inside the Tower of London or the National Gallery. And there were several musicals I would have liked to see."

"Sounds like you'll need to come back."

"I hope to. Maybe we can talk Hal into bringing the choir again."

Would I take another trip with the choir? Sure, if I could afford it.

With Drew inching along in front of me, I prodded my bag stuffed with presents with my foot. I remembered the morning I'd arrived. I'd felt dragged down by jet lag and lack of sleep, like I was lugging a ball and chain around my ankle. But I'd quickly adapted to London's time zone and felt energized. I recalled the bus tour on the first day, the monuments and parks I'd wanted to visit but hadn't. I hadn't even made it to the British Museum.

When would I return? I considered Princess Alexandra's invitation. Martin had seemed enthusiastic about it last night, but once he got back to Seattle and married Pamela he would forget about singing a duet with me. His vocal career would take off again; he'd be busy building a new life.

I scooted my bag forward another few inches. Anyway, I'd need to take Cooper on the next trip. And I might not be able to afford two tickets to London until he was out of college.

I noticed Martin, then Hal and Clare, nearing the head of the line. Martin had been avoiding me. I could think of nothing I'd done to incur this cold-shoulder treatment.

When Martin stepped through the metal detector, the alarm sounded. The TSA guard asked Martin to empty his pockets and place the contents in a rectangular plastic container on the belt to be examined under the X-ray scanner. Then the guard insisted Martin step to the side. He moved a wand the length of Martin's torso and patted him down with suspicion. Two other guards dug through Martin's carry-on, inspecting each item, then questioning him.

I wondered if Martin's name had appeared on a computerized list of persons of interest. Had Scotland Yard requested he not leave the country since Jerry's body hadn't been found? Had the authorities contacted Dorothea and had she repeated her accusations against Martin? Was the necklace still considered stolen property?

The guards looked doubtful, but finally allowed Martin to reclaim his jacket, shoes, and carry-on.

Then it was Clare's turn to have her purse and carry-on bag inspected. "I just bought that perfume," she said in a huff. "I will not throw it away." She was causing such a fracas that I wondered if she'd be detained and miss the flight. But finally, with Hal's coaxing, she checked her carry-on with the luggage and was allowed to proceed.

Only yards from the conveyer belt, I heard Nick's voice saying my name, and turned to see him striding in my direction.

"I wanted to say '*Arrivederci*,' in person," he declared.

I was pleased he'd come all the way to the airport, an arduous drive from London. But now what? If I stepped out of line would I lose my place?

"So this is really goodbye?" he said.

I nodded. "I'm afraid so."

"You are one woman I will never forget."

"Why is that?" I was pretty sure I knew the answer.

He moved closer, his face filling with emotion. "Because you are beautiful and your wonderful voice, your—"

"My resistance to you? Isn't that what this is all about?"

"It's part of your charm," he said, reaching for my hand. "A strong, independent woman is a rare find. We men like a challenge, this is true. But that's not all we like. Come with me right now. Stay another week at my place. I have a spare bedroom. I'll respect your privacy."

"I couldn't do that," I said. Several choir members behind me stepped around my carry-on. I moved it out of their way.

"Then get a room at the hotel," Nick said. "I can arrange an affordable rate through the agency. I have several days off next week. I'll show you more sights, take you to a musical or a play."

I felt like I was teetering on a fence. How lovely to receive this lavish attention, even if it was all wrong. I couldn't help toying with the idea of remaining a few more days. When was the last time I'd done something spontaneous? Even Mom, twenty-five years my senior, was ignoring caution and diving into a love affair.

"If you get bored with London, we can take the Chunnel to Paris," he said. "It's only a two-hour commute."

"Is that all?" I imagined myself riding the sleek train under the English Channel, then stepping out to hear people speaking French, the language I'd studied in college. How thrilling. What would I see first? The Eiffel Tower, Notre-Dame, the Arc de Triomphe?

"Come," Nick said. "Let's speak to the ticket agent. The airlines often overbook these flights, so you might get a free ticket for giving up your seat."

I'd heard of passengers getting bumped off their flights and being compensated with tickets. That would be a nice perk. I'd be able to take another trip all that much sooner.

My thoughts progressed to Cooper. He had yet to receive punishment for his shoplifting stunt. And he'd acted like a world-class brat on the phone. I hadn't figured out what I'd say when I saw him, but I couldn't act like nothing had happened. If I postponed returning, my surly and unrepentant son might start missing me so much he'd apologize and revert back into a nice little boy again. That made sense.

At this moment, Mom and Cooper were still asleep. I calculated Mom wouldn't pick me up at the airport for another twelve hours. There was plenty of time to call her and tell her not to come.

But then I imagined Cooper and her standing outside customs. I'd gather momentum when I spotted them. My son would lope toward me, then hug me with all his might—okay, maybe I'd do most of the hugging. But it didn't matter. My chest filled with a gladness no amount of sightseeing could replace. No matter how disappointed I was with Cooper, he was my sweetie, my precious one.

"It's time I got home." I watched Nick's smile wane. "My son is waiting for me."

"Your boy will be fine. How old is he? Too old to be needing his mother all the time like a baby, no? Stay with me and I promise you won't regret it."

"But school starts tomorrow. I have a room full of students depending on me." I couldn't take time off on a whim. "Plus, my mother has to get back to work. She's been a saint this week. I can't ask for more of her time."

I glanced back at the line and saw Roxanne and Drew snailing forward. Roxanne was right. I was acting like a woman on a diet tasting a sliver of chocolate cake. Next would come a larger wedge, then two scoops of ice cream.

"I can't," I told him.

"You Americans worry too much. You lack spontaneity." His words grew in intensity and volume. "If you stay with me, I promise you won't regret it. You'll be enjoying yourself so much you'll forget about everything else."

CHAPTER 38

I FELT A HAND lightly tap my shoulder, startling me. But when I turned, I saw no one in particular. A sea of people—a woman holding an infant, an older gentleman wearing a fedora, young men donning backpacks.

I rotated back to Nick. "I don't want to forget about everything," I said. "And I won't forget you either."

"Then I will join you as your husband."

I gave him a brief hug, then stepped back and shook my head.

He seemed unruffled as he presented me with his business card. Had my refusal meant nothing to him, or was he hiding his true feelings?

"You can call me at the office if you change your mind," he said.

I slipped the card into my purse. "All right, but I have the feeling you'll be too busy to think about me." I wondered if he'd already targeted a woman from this week's choir tour. But if he had, he would be at the hotel seeing her off this morning.

"I doubt I'll forget you that easily." His weight on one leg, he folded his arms across his chest, at ease even in this chaotic and fluctuating arena. "Man was created to be with a woman, no?"

"If it's the right woman. Now, goodbye. Thank you for lunch and dinner, and for being our tour guide extraordinaire."

"*Ciao.*" He winked. "Until we meet again." He turned away and disappeared into the crowd.

I worked my way back into the line behind Roxanne and Drew. Thirty minutes later, we were milling in the crowded lounge area. Children squirmed and nattered, two turbaned men spoke, and a mother fed her fussy baby a bottle of cream-colored liquid.

Keeping to himself, Martin stood gazing out the ceiling-to-floor window at the Boeing 777 we would soon board. A whale-gray wall of mist hung just above the jet's tail and gusts of wind whipped rain against the tarmac.

Hal stood chatting with a woman at the check-in counter at the gate. "Martin, please come over here," Hal said, loud enough for everyone to hear. "Your upgrade came through. Here's a business-class seat for you." Martin walked over to claim the ticket and thanked Hal.

"Oh, no," Hal said, his hand flying up to cover his forehead. "I just remembered I left my travel clock in my hotel room."

"Give them a call when you get home," Martin suggested. "They might send it." Then he turned his eyes to the window again.

A strawberry blonde with a southern drawl approached Martin and started raving about his role in Puccini's *La Bohème* in Houston three years ago. He must have mentioned his next performance would be in Seattle because she exclaimed, "Well, honey, Seattle is where my daughter lives." Her platinum-mink jacket hung over her arm. Her plunging V-neck sweater showcased her abundant curves. "I'll come hear you sing, then you come on over for supper at my daughter's in the Highlands. I'm president of the Dallas Opera Society. We're going to find a way to talk you into returning."

"Flight forty-nine, nonstop to Seattle," flooded the room. "We will begin boarding first and business classes now."

The woman fell in next to Martin as he shuffled toward the gate. Which made sense. There was nothing economy class about her.

When my section was called, I followed Roxanne and Drew onboard. I found my seat and sank in next to the window. Roxanne sat next to Drew again, two rows back.

"It was worth the twenty bucks I had to pay to get them to give me a seat next to you," he told Roxanne.

She shook with laughter. "You didn't."

"No. But I would have."

A portly woman wearing a dripping-wet overcoat and a floppy hat struggled to get through the aisle with her bags. She started to squeeze in next to me, then realized she was in the wrong seat.

"J is on the other side." The flight attendant pointed across the way at the empty spot next to Clare.

Perfect. I was glad Clare wouldn't be sitting next to another ne'er-do-well like Jerry. She'd stay out of trouble until we touched down in Seattle, where I hoped her parents would sweep her into a protective bubble. With any luck, Clare was out of my life for good.

Bonnie padded down the aisle to fill the seat next to me. I felt content listening to her describe her favorite highlights of the trip. As she spoke of Piccadilly Circus with its neon advertising billboards, I allowed my thoughts to zig and zag where they pleased.

I'd made the right decision about Nick. After Jeff died, I'd vowed I wouldn't get involved with another man unless he embodied the characteristics my father lacked—reliability, honesty, and the love of children, particularly my son. Nick, although sharp and entertaining, didn't seem to possess the maturity needed to maintain a lasting relationship. And I wasn't so needy that I'd settle for second best. If that meant living forever single, so be it.

As I watched an attendant move toward the nose of the jet, I wondered how Martin was faring in business class with his admirer. I figured the attendants were fussing over him and seeing to his every need. That was his station in life and the privileges he was brought up to enjoy—dining at the Brown's Hotel, visiting friends in castles, and rubbing elbows with royalty at the Ritz.

Yet he'd treated Hal with the same respect he would bestow upon a conductor at the Metropolitan Opera, he enjoyed Roxanne's jokes, and he was what Mom called a *mensch*—a good person—features I'd require of a future mate.

The hatch door closed, then a flight attendant bustled by, checking seatbelts, raising trays and seatbacks. Bonnie stopped talking as we taxied onto the runway. Metal began vibrating. The engines thundered like Niagara Falls. Different from our departure from Seattle, I found myself relaxing in the knowledge that security at the airport was stringent, and now the pilot and ground control were monitoring the aircraft. My heart was lubb-dupping along at a steady rhythm instead of doing cartwheels. My palms weren't sweaty nor was I prattling on as I often did when nervous. Had facing stage fright coupled with Jerry's loaded gun rid me of my anxieties? That would be the best souvenir I could bring home. If it stuck.

The seatback propelled me forward like a hand scooping a baseball through the air. The roaring of the turbines flooded my ears. Outside, the airport whizzed by, then dropped out of sight. The jet muscled through clouds as thick as Mom's matzo ball soup. Raindrops streamed horizontally across the windows. Then sunlight burst through as we soared into the blue cosmos. The jet finally leveled off and the engines quieted. For the next few hours, as I ate lunch, then watched a movie without wearing the headset, I thought about my life, past and future.

Soon I might have a stepdad. My initial reaction to Mom's news had been negative. I'd acted childishly. I wondered if I was subconsciously keeping the vacancy of her husband open in case my father wandered home. No chance that would happen. I needed to embrace whatever decision Mom made. She wasn't the type of woman to slide from man to man, let alone hop into marriage without careful consideration. Now that I thought about it, Tim could serve as a role model for Cooper and even be a friend to me.

Another thing I'd do when I got home was fill Muriel in about my singing victory. I knew she'd be ecstatic, and I'd graciously accept her praise instead of trying to diminish it, as I often did. And I'd ask Hal to keep me in mind for future performances. I'd start practicing several pieces he might like, just in case. I might even sing at Mom's wedding. If I could keep from crying— tears of joy.

As my mind percolated about the areas of my life needing adjustment, I reflected on my career. If teaching third graders wasn't my lifelong dream, it was my responsibility to improve my attitude or make a change. The idea of educating high school students appealed to me. Or was that loony? I could take the needed classes, then teach English literature—foster the love of reading while enjoying my favorite novels. And instructing older students would prepare me for rearing my challenging son. I needed to keep several strides ahead of him.

After the movie concluded, I opened the window shade. Heading west, we'd kept pace with the sun and the sky still sparkled with midday light. Below us, jagged white mountain peaks stretched to the North Pole. At thirty-five thousand feet, I felt weightless yet grounded. So many things didn't make sense at first glance. The earth was a giant orb rotating in space. Serenity was accepting what I could not see, yet knew was true.

CHAPTER 39

BONNIE GOT UP and left to use the restroom. A few minutes later, Martin ambled down the aisle. I assumed he was on his way to speak to Hal, who sat several rows behind me. I wondered if Martin would pass without acknowledging me as he had all morning. But he lowered himself into Bonnie's seat.

"Hello." He sent me a half smile.

"Hello, yourself. What's up?"

"Bonnie and I agreed to trade seats."

"How did you know she and I were sitting together?"

"She mentioned it in the airport." Gazing out the window, he seemed uneasy. "I hope you don't mind."

"No, although I can't think why you'd want to leave the luxury of business class. I've heard the food's gourmet quality and the seats tilt way back like easy chairs and you can even lie down."

"Yes, it's rather more comfortable, but I wanted to speak to you before we landed."

Unsure where the conversation was headed, I stared at him and waited.

He finally said, "If I may be so presumptuous to inquire, what did you and Nick decide?"

"He and I are going our separate ways." The further I got from London, the happier I was the relationship had come to an end.

"I decided it was best if I kept my distance and stayed out of the picture." He looked me square in the face. "I wanted you to make up your own mind without my influence."

"I'm not sure it was completely without your influence. I respect your opinion even if you acted less than magnanimously toward Nick."

An attendant was working her way toward us, handing out cups of water. When she reached our row, I realized she was the woman who'd fawned over Martin on the Seattle-to-London flight. Martin and I lowered our tray tables, and she handed me a plastic cup while casting a hopeful smile upon him.

"Why, hello, Mr. Spear. How was your stay in Great Britain?"

"Not at all what I expected." He took a cup from her. "Full of surprises."

"I hope all good," she said.

"I'm not sure yet."

When she'd moved to the next row I said, "Now it's my turn to be nosy, Martin. What's going on with Pamela? Will she be following you?"

"Not if her husband has anything to say about it."

I couldn't believe my ears. Martin was the last man I'd suspect of adultery. "You're having an affair with a married woman?"

"No, I'd never do that."

"Well, are you or are you not involved with Pamela?"

"Strictly as a friend, I swear."

"But you two are engaged."

"Those were Pamela's words. I said we were partners and meant partners in crime. Not that the necklace was really stolen at all."

I recalled Pamela's saying, "I'd do anything for Martin." She'd acted like he was the last piece of Godiva chocolate left in the hemisphere.

"But why would she say such a thing?" My words tripped over each other.

"For my benefit. She was trying to boost my battered ego. When I saw you and Nick in the restaurant that night, I confided in her how attractive I found you and how jealous I was."

Was this British humor? He had to be pulling my leg. "That's how you act when you're jealous?" I steadied my cup as we jounced through a pocket of lumpy air. "You couldn't keep far enough away from me the first half of the trip. You treated me like I had chicken pox."

"I'd been avoiding women, particularly beautiful ones."

It was difficult maintaining my cool demeanor after he'd just called me beautiful. But I contained a grin and sipped my water as I waited for him to continue.

"When Pamela announced our engagement, I was too stunned to contradict her," he said. "The next day,

I was too embarrassed to admit it was a hoax for fear you'd think I was ridiculous."

"Martin, I have every right to be angry." But I wasn't. If anything, I was relieved.

"I agree and I'm sorry. I should have squelched that silliness immediately and told you the truth. But you were spending every moment with Nick, and I felt so miserably alone." He directed an uncertain grimace in my direction. "Will you forgive me?"

I looked into his clear eyes. Such a hard facade, I thought, but I could see a gentle soul inside. Tender and caring.

"Yes, I forgive you, Martin. But please, no more charades."

He raised his right hand. "I promise."

A thread of jealousy wove its way through my heart. "I can see why any man would be attracted to Pamela. She's beautiful and sophisticated."

"And a terrible tease. I've known her and her husband since we were children. Our parents are close friends, and so are we."

"One can never have too many friends."

"I agree."

"But what about the brooch you bought Pamela? A thank-you gift?"

He reached into his pocket and brought out the small Harrods box. I understood why the metal detector had gone off at the airport when he passed through it.

He lifted the lid to expose the gold eighth note. "When I bought it," he said, "I had you in mind." He took the pin from the box and clasped it onto the front of my cardigan sweater. And for once I let someone other than Mom or Cooper give me a present without pangs of guilt or feelings of inadequacy.

A burst of Roxanne's giggling embellished with Drew's bass laughter erupted from behind us. I glanced over the seatback to see the tops of their heads tilting close together.

"Love is in the air," I said to Martin.

"Indeed, it is." He gave me a genuine smile. "I shall miss seeing you every day. Would it be all right if I called on you?"

"Sure, I'd like that. But because we're friends, that doesn't mean you're stuck singing with me, like Princess Alexandra wanted."

"I don't look at performing a duet with you as an obligation. It's a pleasure I look forward to."

His words brought a burst of joy, more gratifying than the applause following my solo.

"All right," I said. Then I took a moment to consider his musical expertise compared to mine. Martin could sight-read well enough to sing a new piece of music without practicing it first.

"I'd better go over the music with Muriel," I said. About a zillion times.

"Perhaps I could join you and get a chance to meet her."

"Okay." I'd plunge into the deep end of the pool with my eyes wide open. Why not? "When will you be available for our first rehearsal?"

He took my hand and lifted my fingertips to his lips. "How about tomorrow evening?"

RECIPE:

English Cream Scones

It's hard for me to imagine England without thinking of tea and scones served with butter and jam. Here is one recipe:

2 cups flour (You may use gluten-free flour)

2 teaspoon baking powder

1/2 teaspoon salt

1 tablespoon sugar

4 teaspoon butter (diced)

2 eggs, well beaten

1/2 cup cream

Add dried currants or raisins if you wish

Preheat oven to 425 F.

Lightly butter a cookie sheet

Mix the flour, baking powder, sugar, and salt in a mixing bowl. Work in the batter with your fingers or a pastry blender until the mixture resembles coarse meal. Add the eggs and cream and stir until blended. Turn onto a lightly floured board and knead for about a minute. (Warning: over-working the dough will make the scones tough.) Pat or roll the dough about three-quarter inch thick and cut into circles or wedges. A drinking glass will work if you don't own a round cookie cutter. If you desire a shiny surface, brush with eggs or cream or. Place on a cookie sheet and bake for about 15 minutes or until golden brown.

Enjoy them with butter, jam, marmalade, or clotted cream, also known as Cornwall or Devonshire cream. It's loved for the creamy texture, similar to butter, rather than a particular sweetness or flavor.

You can find clotted cream in some American stores, but you can also make your own. It takes a lot of cream and time to make a small amount of clotted cream, and it's a long process. Make the day before you bake your scones.

Pour a pint of heavy organic cream (not whipping cream) into a 9 x 9 glass baking dish and let it sit uncovered in a 180 F oven for 12 hours. (Yes, you read that right.) The yellow stuff on top is the clotted cream. As I said, it's always a good idea to make clotted cream the day before you want to make scones, so you don't waste any cream. After separating the clotted cream from the liquid cream and chill the clotted cream overnight. Spoon it into a jar and use the milky leftovers in a batch of scones

ACKNOWLEDGEMENTS

I AM GRATEFUL FOR my critique group, all of them published authors and terrific cheerleaders: Roberta Kehle, Marty Nystrom, Thornton Ford, Kathleen Kohler, and Judy Bodmer. I can't thank Mary Jackson enough for her support.

A round of applause to my publishing consultant Beth Jusino and copy editor Kathy Burge. Many thanks to Margaret and Don Coppock. Thank you to my vocal coach, the extraordinary soprano Marianne Weltmann.

Thanks to my parents for traveling to Great Britain often and turning me into an Anglophile. My husband Noel and I even chose to spend our honeymoon in London, and after my mother's death, my father and I enjoyed several coach tours through Great Britain, as did my husband and I with our two sons.

ABOUT THE AUTHOR

Bestselling author Kate Lloyd is a passionate observer of human relationships. A native of Baltimore, she now lives in Seattle, WA. She's the author of half a dozen novels, including the bestselling Leaving Lancaster series.

Over the years, Kate worked a variety of jobs, including car salesman and restaurateur. For relaxation and fun, Kate enjoys walking with her camera in hand, beachcombing, and singing. Kate studied voice, sang in choirs and musical theatre productions, and has traveled throughout Great Britain many times.

Find out more about Kate Lloyd:
Website: www.katelloyd.com
Blog: http://katelloyd.com/blog/
Facebook: www.facebook.com/katelloydbooks
Instagram: katelloydauthor
Twitter: @KateLloydAuthor
Pinterest: @KateLloydAuthor

Kate loves hearing from readers!